Mark Griffin began his v  ive

years of gold medal awards al.
In 1996 he moved to Lo his
attention to acting, script v

After returning to England, Mark continued in this profession and was shortlisted in the top five out of 3500 entrants in a national crime thriller writing competition sponsored by Random House Publishing and the *Daily Mail* for his debut, *When Darkness Calls.*

When Darkness Calls was the first novel in the Holly Wakefield series and it was longlisted for the CWA New Blood Dagger Award. *When Evil Wakes* is the fourth Holly Wakefield thriller.

Praise for Mark Griffin:

'A thrilling new talent, destined to become a big name in British crime writing' Peter James

'Mightily impressive . . . deviously plotted' *Daily Mail*

'Creepy, twisted and gripping' *Sun*

'Dark, compelling and expertly paced . . . one of the best police procedurals I've read for a long time' M. W. Craven

'Meticulously plotted and devious in its execution . . . utterly compelling' Lesley Kara

'As many twists and turns as a rollercoaster! It's the kind of writing which grabs you and won't let you go' Amy Lloyd

By Mark Griffin

THE HOLLY WAKEFIELD THRILLERS

When Darkness Calls
When Angels Sleep
When Silence Kills
When Evil Wakes

WHEN EVIL WAKES

MARK GRIFFIN

PIATKUS

PIATKUS

First published in Great Britain in 2022 by Piatkus
This paperback edition published in 2023 by Piatkus

1 3 5 7 9 10 8 6 4 2

All characters and events in this publication, other than those clearly in the public domain, are fictitious and any resemblance to real persons, living or dead, is purely coincidental.

A CIP catalogue record for this book
is available from the British Library.

ISBN 978-0-349-42899-4

Typeset in Baskerville by M Rules
Printed and bound in Great Britain by
Clays Ltd, Elcograf S.p.A.

Papers used by Piatkus are from well-managed forests
and other responsible sources.

Piatkus
An imprint of
Little, Brown Book Group
Carmelite House
50 Victoria Embankment
London EC4Y 0DZ

An Hachette UK Company
www.hachette.co.uk

www.littlebrown.co.uk

In memory of my father
who I knew deep down was very proud of me.

And to my mother
who always insisted I take a book with me wherever I went
so I would never be alone.
Thank you for everything, Mum,
you always manage to smile, no matter what
and when you smile, we all smile.

One

It was August and seemed too early for rain, but it drummed on Constable Samuel Jefferson's car roof and splashed boot-high off the road.

He had the engine on and kept the windscreen wipers going so he could see the house. The living room lights were on and the curtains were drawn. There had been no activity from any of the other houses on the street, just the occasional pigeon as it flapped from tree to tree.

The rain wasn't going to let up, so he wrapped himself in his anorak, got out of the car and ran for it. Along the path and past the wooden *for sale* sign staked into the lawn, trying to keep the notepad under his arm dry, but by the time he got to the front door he was wet. Jefferson was in his sixties with an angular face. He was lean, with veins that stood out on his big hands and jaw muscles that bunched every time he swallowed. His hair was short and silver and it shone in the porch light.

He rapped on the door and rang the bell in quick succession. Straightened his uniform and dried off the notepad on his trousers. He heard footsteps on the wooden floor inside then a voice:

'Just a minute.'

The chain was pulled back and the door opened.

The man who met him was fifty-three years old and five foot eight with a side-parting and round glasses. He was wearing a white woollen sweater that was tight over his thin arms and belly.

'John Newsome?' PC Jefferson said.

'Yes? How can I help?'

'Actually, sir, it's your wife I need to talk to, Mrs Sandra Newsome. I'm with the Metropolitan Police.' He flashed his ID.

The man nodded, a sudden look of apprehension on his face. He retreated slightly then came back.

'Can I ask what this is about?'

'Actually I do need to talk to Mrs Newsome first, although you can be present at all times.'

'Right, well you'd better come in then.'

He entered and shut the door behind him.

'Can I take your coat?'

'Thank you,' and PC Jefferson shucked it off and Mr Newsome hung it on the coat stand. The stairs to the second floor were on the left, the kitchen straight ahead and the glass double doors to the right opened onto the living room where John directed him.

'Darling?' John said.

Sandra Newsome rose from the sofa at their entrance. She wore a white blouse, blue skirt and blue cardigan. She had pale hands and smoothed the hair back from her face.

'Hello,' she said quietly.

'Darling, this police officer – sorry I didn't get your name?'

'Jefferson, Constable Jefferson.'

'Right. Constable Jefferson needs to talk to you about something.'

'Yes, I'm sorry to disturb you on a Sunday evening – this won't take long.' He studied his notes. 'Mrs Newsome, you work for Domum and Casa estate agency as a sales negotiator?'

'Yes, are you interested in a property?'

'Actually no,' he smiled back. 'I don't know quite how to say this, so I'll dive straight in. I regret to inform you that a body has been found in one of the houses you have listed.'

She blinked, looked at her husband then back to the constable.

'A body?' she whispered.

'I'm afraid so.'

'As in – you don't mean a cat or a dog, do you? You mean a . . .'

'Yes. A human body.'

'Oh my God.' Her voice came out as a shriek and her hand went to her throat. She fingered the orange coral necklace around her neck nervously. 'I don't believe it. That's ridiculous, which one?'

'It's a local property and I'm sorry but I can't divulge the address—'

'Thurston Avenue? Bennington Place?'

'It's an ongoing investigation, so I'm not at liberty to tell you—'

'Was it a suicide?'

'I'm afraid it would appear the victim—'

'The victim?'

'It would appear the victim had met with a violent death.'

A brittle silence.

‘Bloody hell,’ John said. ‘I wasn’t expecting this.’

‘It was one of your empty properties, so I don’t think it will be any of your clients or anyone you know, but I can inform you the body was found three hours ago when a neighbour called the police because the front door had been left open.’

‘The front door? Oh God, I mean, I have keys to all my listings.’

‘That’s the thing. There were no signs of a forced entry, so it looks as though the perpetrator used a key.’

‘That’s not possible – all the keys are kept inside a lockbox outside each property.’

‘So perhaps they knew the lockbox combination?’

‘I don’t see how. I set the codes myself.’

‘And you never give a set of keys to anybody or make copies?’

‘No, never.’

Her nostrils flared at the thought and she smoothed her skirt with her hands.

‘Maybe you should sit down, darling?’ John said. ‘Let me put the kettle on and we’ll all have a cup of coffee. Would you like a cup of coffee, Constable Jefferson?’

‘That would be nice, thank you. Just milk, no sugar.’

John nodded eagerly and headed for the kitchen.

Constable Jefferson sat on the edge of the chair. He turned a page in his notepad and watched Mrs Newsome. Her lips were pressed so tightly together they were white, then she suddenly said:

‘Wait – have you spoken to Jason?’

‘Jason?’

‘Jason Oppenhein, he’s the owner of Domum and Casa. I should call him.’

‘We’ve already done that, that’s how we got your address.’

'Of course it is. Sorry, I'm not thinking. How did – I mean – a murder in our neighbourhood. And you can't tell me which house it is?'

'It will be in all the newspapers tomorrow, I'm sure,' Constable Jefferson said. A quick thought: 'You'll be here tomorrow morning, won't you?'

'Yes.'

'Well perhaps myself or one of the other officers on the case could come by and pick you up and take you to the property to make a statement to the SIO.'

'What's an SIO?'

'Senior Investigating Officer. It will be DI William Bishop, from the Met Serious Crime squad. He's very good.' A check of his notes, 'And he might bring a young woman with him – Holly Wakefield. She's a forensic psychologist.'

'A what?'

'She helps catch killers who are . . .' he hesitated, ' . . . particularly violent.'

'Oh God, is there much blood?'

'Again, I can't discuss—'

'I'll need to get professional cleaners in. I've got twenty-two empty listings, but it can't be Bedford Terrace, I was there just over an hour ago.'

'No, it's not Bedford Terrace,' Constable Jefferson said.

She looked at him conspiratorially.

'Is it Mellington Mews?'

'I can't, I'm not supposed to . . .' He took a breath, squeezed his eyes shut and when he opened them he said:

'I could get into trouble for this.'

'I won't tell a soul, I promise.'

'One of your listings is 107 Bishops Drive, is that correct?'

'Yes, but that's . . .' she hesitated, 'that's here. This is 107 Bishops Drive.'

Constable Jefferson checked his notes.

'It says here – body discovered at 107 Bishops Drive.'

And she suddenly laughed like uncorked champagne.

'Well that's wrong!' she said. 'That's wrong!' And then with a hint of a smile: 'There's an empty house for sale on Bishops Crescent? Is that what you mean?'

'Bishops Crescent?'

'Yes, it's two streets away. That must be it, and it's not even one of my listings! John! John, come quick!' and she couldn't stop laughing.

'What is it?' John said as he entered with three cups of coffee on a tray and a plate of chocolate biscuits.

'They've got the wrong address, it's Bishops Crescent, not here!'

'Not here? What address?'

'I'm so sorry,' Constable Jefferson said and stood up. 'Bishops Drive is where you live – I must have copied it down wrong at the station. I'm such a fool. I need to radio back to dispatch and tell them I made a mistake, then they'll have to send a different officer to the other address. I'm so sorry to have troubled you. I'll get my coat.' He made a move to go when—

'No, no,' Sandra said. 'You're here now, you can have your coffee at least.'

'Yes, you must, and it's still raining,' her husband added, and turned his attention to the coffee table, which was packed high with magazines and a vase of roses, deciding whether to chance a landing or clear the table first.

'Well, that's very kind. At least let me help,' Constable

Jefferson said. He reached out for the tray but lost his grip and the cups fell and coffee spilled everywhere.

'Buggeration!' John swore.

Sandra was up on her feet and cleared away the magazines.

'Get some kitchen tissue,' her husband said to her.

The constable watched Mrs Newsome go and said:

'I'm so sorry.'

'It's fine.' John dropped onto his knees and started pooling the coffee using his white woollen arms like a soggy dam.

'It's gone everywhere . . .'

'Can I help? Can I—'

'No, it's fine. Just relax.'

Constable Jefferson nodded and knelt by John's side. He whispered softly:

'I promise I won't touch your daughter upstairs,' he said.

John turned, eyes wide—

'What did you say?'

Under his shirt and jacket, Constable Jefferson had a thick metal cuff around his right wrist and when he angled his hand back, a long, thin knife shot out and struck John in the neck like a matador. The blade was pulled free and retracted into the spring-loaded cuff with a metallic click and the constable lowered the torso gently onto the coffee table just as Mrs Newsome reappeared with a roll of kitchen tissue.

'This is such a strange night . . .'

'John's had an accident,' the constable said.

'What happened?'

'He just sort of collapsed.'

She looked down at the blood spilling from her husband's neck but couldn't comprehend, and then the man grabbed her by the throat, turned her around and the blade flashed from his wrist again and he stabbed her incredibly hard in the back. The thin blade missed her spine, punctured her heart, passed through her ribs and tore apart the front of her blouse. Constable Jefferson let the body drop to the floor.

He stared at what he had done for the briefest moment, then retracted the knife into the cuff and very carefully put on a pair of transparent latex gloves.

His hard mouth softened into a smile as he dipped a finger in the frothing mix of coffee and blood and wrote a message on the wall.

Two

'What is evil?'

Holly Wakefield asked the question as she sat on the end of her desk in King's College London. Fifty-plus students watched her from all levels of the tiered seating in the main lecture hall. One of the students raised a hand.

'Yes, Ben?'

'Something that is inherent in all of us?'

'In all of us? Really?'

There was a ripple of laughter.

'Maybe not all of us,' she smiled, 'but most definitely in some. The word you used, *inherent*, implies it exists as a permanent characteristic, which is another interesting thought. Or can evil be created, can it be fashioned?'

She turned and wrote on the whiteboard as she spoke:

'The definition of evil is "profoundly immoral and wicked" or "the opposite and the absence of good". A rather medieval interpretation perhaps, because when we think of evil we don't generally conjure up images of a moral compass, do we – we think instead of creatures or beings. We like to give evil a substance. Something we can see, or feel or touch. Dark spirits and witches in the night. The bogeyman. The creature under the bed that waits for the lights to go out before it appears and scares the living shit out of us.' A beat as she strode to the centre of the stage. 'That is the stylised evil of comic books, films and our imagination, but what does real evil look like in the twenty-first century?'

'Massive corporations screwing us over and stealing our pensions.'

'Thank you, Matthew, yes, and here's an interesting point. How many of your parents are CEOs of companies?'

Hands raised until there were about a dozen.

'Approximately one in five CEOs can be clinically classified as a psychopath. That's twenty per cent of all CEOs in the world, which is the same percentage of psychopaths that are in the prison population. So, statistically speaking, two of you in this room have a psychopathic mother or father – I'm not going to ask who, but I don't recommend bringing this up at dinner tonight. Now let me quickly clarify – not all psychopaths kill, in the same way not all sociopaths kill, but twenty per cent of those who help run this country will have clinical traits with characteristics such as – don't bother with hands up – just shout them out,' Holly said as she uncapped a Sharpie.

'No empathy,' Ben said.

'Yes, the inability to empathise with your fellow human beings,' she said, writing on the whiteboard behind her.

'Pathological lying,' from someone in the front row.

'Yes,' she turned and wrote again.

'Insincerity.'

'Yes.'

'Cocky – arrogant.'

'Yes – we like to call it a *grandiose sense of self-worth*.'

'Manipulative.'

'You guys are on fire today.'

'No emotions?'

'Yes – a disparate range of feelings, if any.'

Her pen hovered, waiting for the next item.

'Come on,' she said.

'A lack of remorse.'

The voice threw her. It was sandpaper rough, cigarettes and whisky. She turned away from the board and smiled curiously.

Detective Inspector Bishop.

They were supposed to meet for lunch but he was an hour early. He made his way down a few of the auditorium steps and sat at the back. Gestured for her to continue.

'Yes,' she said. 'A lack of remorse. Thank you, Detective Inspector Bishop.'

A few of the students turned briefly to look at the newcomer as she wrote *lack of remorse* on the board and then resumed the class.

'Whether they're screwing people out of a pension or stabbing someone twenty times in the chest, the psychopath rule is – *I don't care*.' She re-capped her pen. 'Like I said, very few CEOs will actually go out and kill someone, so let's look at the individuals who will, and reasses my original question: what is evil? Or rather, what does evil look like – that which is housed within a human soul? How do you spot a psychopath?' She pointed to a girl three rows up with dark hair: 'Clara, if you saw a mass murderer walking down the street, would you know straight away?'

'Probably not.'

'Simon – what about a serial rapist sitting at a bar?'

'No.'

'Erica – a serial killer offering to carry your shopping when you get out of the lift in your block of flats?'

'I hope I would sense something, but—'

'You probably wouldn't,' Holly said. 'The simple answer to the question "how do you spot a psychopath?" is, you don't. Because psychopaths at this level of duplicity are very good at blending in and becoming one with the crowd. We must never forget that evil is intelligent, it's smart, and a lot of times it's invisible until it's too late.'

The bell rang and the students began to move. Holly shouted after them:

'Christian theologists argue that natural evil is the result of original sin. I want two thousand words on this for next Monday, please!'

The footsteps faded and her eyes locked on Bishop's as he walked down the steps towards her. Six feet two inches tall, dark hair flecked with grey. He was wearing a charcoal suit and white shirt with a black tie. He looked good.

'It's nice to see you in your natural environment,' he smiled. 'So these are the shrinks of the future?'

'Some shrinks, some lawyers,' she said as she put away her books. 'I thought we said one o'clock?'

'We did, my apologies.'

'I still have another lecture. Do you want to come and watch?'

'Can you cancel it?'

She froze. There was an urgency in his dark-blue eyes.

'Seriously?' she said.

He nodded.

'I need you to cancel it, Holly.'

Three

Bishop drove out of central London and headed east on the motorway.

After half an hour they broke into the Hertfordshire countryside of cornfields and hedges. The air was muggy, the afternoon sun hidden by thick grey clouds.

'It's a double murder, a husband and wife,' Bishop said. 'The victims are John and Sandra Newsome. He was a computer tech guy who sold crypto-currencies and she was an estate agent. They were both stabbed, he in the neck, she between the ribs and into the heart.'

'Who's the coroner?'

'Angela Swan.'

Holly nodded. She had worked with Angela on her last three cases.

'Angela's doing the autopsy tonight,' Bishop said. 'We'll get the report tomorrow morning. She thinks the killer used a thin blade, like a stiletto knife.'

'That's unusual. A stiletto blade is easy to conceal and very efficient. Where were they killed?'

'Downstairs in their living room. No signs of forced entry – it appears they let the killer in.'

She nodded as if she had expected as much.

'Any witnesses?'

'None. It's a quiet street in an affluent neighbourhood, and it was raining heavily last night so nobody was out walking dogs or heard a car, and the closest CCTV is three miles from the house.'

'Have you seen the crime scene?'

'I got there two hours ago, made a preliminary report,' he paused, 'and drove straight to you.'

Holly took a second and shot him a look.

'Why?'

He said nothing but blinked rapidly several times.

'Bishop?'

'This one is different to the others I've taken you to in the last few months. This one is . . .'

'Is what?'

'Truth be told, I don't know what it is. And I don't know what it means.'

Holly thought for a few moments and then it clicked.

'My God, you think it's him, don't you?' she said. 'The Animal?'

He kept his eyes on the road.

'Jesus Christ, Bishop – The Animal? Sebastian Carstairs? The man who killed my parents when I was nine years old?'

'And sixteen other people,' he said flatly. 'And the man was sent to Broadmoor prison for life, and the man who's supposed to be dead.'

Holly's head was spinning.

Three months ago The Animal had been pronounced dead

from stage four cancer. Holly had even gone to his cremation. She had firmly believed the chapter of her life that began when she came home from school and saw The Animal standing over the dead bodies of her parents was closed for good. But as part of his last parole application he'd been required to write to the families of each of his victims, and Holly had found a secret code in the letter he wrote to her suggesting he was still alive. Moreover, in the letter he had called her *Jessica* – her real name before she had been put into witness relocation and granted a new identity. She'd tried to alert the authorities, but they insisted the letter was nothing more than a spiteful hoax. So far as they were concerned, The Animal was dead and buried. But deep down Holly feared the worst.

'If he is somehow still alive . . .'

'Hold on a second,' Bishop said. 'We can't prove anything at this stage.'

'No, of course not, but . . . we can profile this crime scene and analyse the kill. A stiletto knife, you said?'

'Possibly.'

'The Animal used multiple types of weapons during his killing spree: kitchen knives, hammers, acid, rope. But a stiletto knife – he could be adapting.'

'In what way?'

'He'll be sixty years old now. He won't have the strength he once had.'

She took a breath. Bishop was right, she mustn't get ahead of herself. She hadn't even seen the crime scene yet. 'It could be another false trail,' she said.

'Mr and Mrs Newsome had three daughters. The two eldest are twins and were having a sleepover about half a mile away. The youngest was asleep upstairs. She's six years old.'

'He didn't kill her?'

'No, but he watched her. We found bloody footprints in her doorway, size twelves.'

'That's his shoe size and we know The Animal doesn't kill children, which is another psychological tic, but it *could* be someone else. Why did you come and get me today?'

He turned to her, almost apologetic:

'You need to see what's written on the wall.'

Four

Six police cars had blocked off the tree-lined street and reporters and curious neighbours were being held back by crime scene tape.

Bishop parked fifty metres away and they both got out and walked. He showed his warrant card to one of the duty officers as Holly took in the locale: a greenbelt village of wealthy single-family houses all with gravel driveways and separated from each other by thick, high hedges. She stopped when she spotted a narrow tree-lined footpath by the side of one of the properties that seemed to lead to a dense forest.

'Beyond the treeline are open fields,' Bishop said. 'About a hundred acres with no vehicle access. The nearest train station is seven miles away and the buses don't come within a mile, so it's safe to say he would have driven. Unfortunately, if his car left any traces they would have been washed away by the rain last night.'

The house was a new build: two storeys high with an added loft conversion and a beautiful front garden.

‘What are the neighbours saying?’

‘They’re understandably nervous, though they don’t yet know what happened. When they see the newspapers I imagine a few of them might add some additional security or pack up and leave. We’ve done preliminary background checks on Mr and Mrs Newsome, but nothing stands out. Lots of friends, no enemies, no debts or marital affairs that we know of.’

He handed her a pair of booties and gloves.

‘You ready?’

She nodded and followed him inside.

The hallway was white pine with white walls and carpeted stairs to the left; the kitchen lay ahead and the living room was to the right past open glass doors. Holly went and stood by them. Her jaw clenched when she saw the sticky riot of blood in the room – the sofa, coffee table and the cream carpet underneath were drenched.

‘When did they take the bodies?’ Holly asked.

‘About an hour ago. Angela thinks the husband was killed first. One stab wound to the neck, and he was left kneeling on the floor with his torso resting on the coffee table. His wife was lying face down on the carpet to his right.’

‘Were the bodies staged? Positioned deliberately?’

‘Impact marks in the carpet and blood spatter confirm they were found where they fell. There were three coffee cups upturned on the carpet. It looks as if they made the killer a drink and brought out some biscuits, but then at some point an argument happened or a struggle and the tray of drinks was knocked over. The daughter entered the room through these doors. You can see her footprints in the blood – there and there.’

He pointed and Holly saw the bloody impressions from her little feet.

'We need to go through the kitchen so we don't tread on the carpet,' he said.

She followed him along the white pine corridor and past a door that opened into the country-style kitchen with black countertops and a black oven. It was clean and tidy. A carton of milk had been left on the counter along with a jar of instant coffee, a teaspoon and an open packet of chocolate biscuits.

Bishop led her through a second door into the living room. The back of the sofa and the coffee table were directly in front of them. There was a gas fireplace opposite, a television on a stand, two more chairs and family photos on the shelves. To the left was an archway that led to the dining room. She could smell the heady mix of coffee and cold blood.

'This way.' Bishop led her through the archway.

The dining room was bigger than she had thought, the table long and made of a light wood with matching chairs. A sideboard and decanter sat below a wide mirror and glass sliders to the left led out to a large back garden. A SOCO was taking photos of a partially hidden alcove and when he noticed them he stepped aside and moved quietly away.

Bishop motioned to the alcove.

Holly had no idea what to expect, but what she saw made her breath catch in her throat. Scrawled on the wall in brown-black blood was a message:

Dearest Holly,
It's been a while and now I'm walking tall once more
But I must confess
What is wrong with Annie Wilkes?

'Oh my God . . . it's addressed to me.'

She stared at it, transfixed, shivering as if a ghost had touched her.

'It's him, Bishop,' she whispered. 'This time it has to be. "Walking tall" was a clue in the letter. It meant he was alive and well.'

There was a darkness rising inside her and she found it hard to pull her eyes away. This was what she had been waiting for, but now that it was right in front of her, she began to feel the fear. Her fingers twisted themselves into a knot as she tried to control her breathing. She felt Bishop's comforting hand on her shoulder: a gentle squeeze. Finally her thoughts pushed through:

'Who is Annie Wilkes?' she said.

'We have no idea.'

She nodded, eyes glued to the message daubed in blood, until Bishop's voice snapped her out of it.

'You want to see the girl's bedroom?'

They retraced their route until they were back in the hall, then trod on the outsides of the steps, the middle of the carpet still holding the faint bloody impressions of the killer's large footprints.

'Be careful up here,' Bishop said. He pivoted over a series of crime scene tags and offered his hand. She took it and followed, clearing the markers, and then they stopped at the end of the corridor by an open door on the far right. Bishop flipped the light and Holly saw pink everywhere. Stuffed animals and stickers. A Disney *Frozen* duvet, with Elsa, Anna and Olaf dolls on shelves. Princess pyjamas laid out on the bed and a glittering tiara on a wooden desk. She wondered if the girl would ever see these toys and clothes again, or would her family buy her new things so she wouldn't have to remember? When Holly had lost her parents, she hadn't been allowed back inside the house and hadn't taken a thing. All her personal items had been picked up by someone else and stored until she turned eighteen. She had given almost all of it to charity shops.

'What's their daughter's name?'

'Kristen.'

'Is she with her sisters?'

'Yes. They're staying with grandparents who live about ten miles away.'

She nodded but had seen enough and led the way downstairs. She couldn't stop herself from going back into the dining room to look at the message on the wall again. The personalisation, the politeness – it had The Animal written all over it – but it was the last sentence that kept spinning in her head:

What is wrong with Annie Wilkes?

Five

Bishop parked at the kerb outside Holly's block of flats in Balham, south London. He had his head down and was frowning as he said:

'Only three of us at the station know your parents were victims of The Animal, but once everyone on the task force sees that message, people are going to ask questions.'

'You think they'll tie it straight to me?'

'It's my gut feeling.' Holly saw him shake his head in disbelief. 'Christ, either it is him, or it's someone who wants us to believe it's him.'

'A copycat?'

'It wouldn't be the first.'

'You don't believe that, do you? You came to me straight from the crime scene. You know it's not a copycat.'

'Holly—'

'There are two dead bodies back there and a message to me. It has to be him.'

'The Animal? The man who everybody else thinks is dead? The man who you saw cremated?'

She didn't rise to the bait.

'We have to wait for forensics before we jump to any conclusions,' he said. 'Without witnesses, CCTV or DNA, we can't prove a thing.'

'If it's him there won't be any forensics. Chief Constable Franks didn't listen to me when I went to him three months ago with the letter The Animal wrote to me—'

'I remember the letter, Holly. The one with the secret code—'

'—telling me he was still alive.'

'*Walking tall* – I get it. It was the term the press used to describe him in prison after you tried to kill him.'

'I was ten, there was never any real threat to him,' she shrugged it off. 'And three months ago, all I had to show was the letter. Now we have a crime scene.'

'Like I said, we need to see what forensics come up with. We can only work on the evidence in front of us.'

'You work on hunches too, just like me.'

'I do, and I'll call the chief tonight and tell him what we found, but that's all I can do at the moment.'

A silence.

It had been a while since he had been inside her flat and she felt she should ask him up for a drink. Their relationship, if she could even call it that, hadn't progressed beyond the occasional drink and a couple of lunches since their last case, but she knew that was down to her. She was the one holding back and stopping it moving forwards. There was something she had to tell Bishop about herself, but she didn't know how. And like most secrets, this one was alive and wanted to get out. She had thought about speaking to him countless times, but a random confession would have been disastrous and the longer she kept it buried the worse the feelings of guilt became, as if she were somehow leading him on.

She realised he was smiling at her. A hint of sadness in his eyes perhaps?

She smiled back and took the initiative:

'Do you want to come up?'

'Sure – that'll be nice.'

Good.

The lift took them to the fifth floor and they went left along the corridor. There was a drop-cloth outside the apartment next door. Her neighbours, Maisie and Vincent Lomax, were having their flat renovated; for the past week workmen had been drilling and hammering, and the communal hallway reeked of fresh paint. She unlocked her front door and the double deadbolts clicked, a security measure she had added since she had received the letter from The Animal. She sometimes felt like a prisoner in her own home and it made her angry it had come to this, but she didn't think she had a choice.

'I should warn you,' she said as she walked inside, 'it's a mess.'

The open-plan kitchen cum living room was in chaos. The walls were covered with hundreds of pages of black-and-white newspaper articles on The Animal and his victims which Holly had collected over the past twenty years. The bookshelves had been stripped empty and all the books, newspaper articles, magazines and police files were scattered over the tables, chairs and the sofa. And where she had run out of room the rest of the books had ended up on the floor, stacked on top of each other, or dumped precariously on either side of the sofa.

She took her shoes off and gauged Bishop's reaction. She knew she had become obsessed with The Animal and living like this was unhealthy, and she'd been half-expecting him to flinch, but he didn't.

'Do you want wine?' she said.

'Red if you have it.'

She went to the kitchen while Bishop skimmed the true crime magazines on top of the TV. He picked up a scrapbook and a yellow writing pad filled with notes.

'Did you write this?'

'The first draft for my thesis at university: "Serial killers through the ages and across the world in three parts. The Killer Next Door, The Mask of Sanity and The Dark Half – Psychology of a Madman". I passed with honours.'

'I certainly hope so.'

A hint of sarcasm there? He surveyed the newspaper clippings stuck to the walls, with their sensationalist front-page headlines: *Victim No.7 – when will the killing end? Will the victims see justice? The Invisible Killer! Psychologists say The Animal will never stop!* And the headline celebrating his death three months ago: *Britain's most horrific killer finally goes to Hell.*

Holly uncorked a Merlot and poured two glasses as she talked:

'How hard do you think it will be to convince everybody else he's alive?'

'I'm not convinced yet, Holly.'

She had hoped he wouldn't say that, but understood his unease. Would the CPS and police authorities feel the same way? They couldn't ignore the possibility. Or could they? What did she really have? Two bodies, a personalised message, a few bloody size-12 footprints and no witnesses.

'*If* he is alive,' Bishop said, 'it means the whole justice system has failed and someone – perhaps several people – has screwed up on a monumental scale.'

He stopped at a framed photo on the dining room table of Holly, smiling for all she was worth, wearing a blue party dress and holding a yellow balloon that said 'Happy Birthday Dad'.

'How old were you here?'

'Seven, eight?'

'Cute.'

There was a booklet hanging from the fireplace. It was highlighted in silver and gold.

'What's this?'

'It's a colour-coded Victim Chart Information Pack.'

'It looks like a Pokémon sticker book.'

'It's just how my head works,' she shrugged. 'It contains the names of The Animal's eighteen victims, their ages, the dates and times of the attacks, where the attacks occurred and the day-count between killings. The MO shifted constantly, there was never any pattern. The only thing that was consistent was his signature – he always stole an item of jewellery from one victim and left it with the next. An important piece of jewellery that he knew would be missed: a silver and garnet engagement ring from the first victim, Raychel Raynes, left at the Martin Smith crime scene. A gold christening crucifix from Martin Smith left in the bedroom of Ernie and Samantha Wellcroft where he took two platinum wedding rings and left them with victim number five, Tip Cullen, etcetera etcetera. The crime scene and photos of the jewellery stolen from each kill are listed chronologically on the radiator.'

'And the mugshots of the men on— is that the toilet door?'

'Yes. They were suspects arrested and released without charge. Four of them confessed to The Animal's crimes, each had mental health problems and were found to have alibis.'

'Autopsy reports?'

'By the Danish bookshelf. There's a couple in the drinks cabinet as well – I ran out of room.'

A large folder on the coffee table caught his attention.

'And what's this?'

'The Bible,' she said matter-of-factly. 'It's a copy of The Animal's sixty-seven-page confession.' She handed him his glass of red wine. 'Cheers.'

'Cheers.'

They clinked glasses.

Her hand went up to her neckline and she touched the silver and enamel butterfly necklace that hung there. The Animal had stolen the necklace from her mother after he had killed her, and Holly thought she would never see it again, so when she was fifteen she had had five green and blue butterflies tattooed on the nape of her neck up to her hairline in the same design. Three months ago, The Animal had agreed to return the necklace to Holly as part of his parole plea as long as she agreed to read his letter. She never took the necklace off.

'And then there's the letter of course,' a hint of sarcasm as she handed him a sheet of paper.

__I__ have wanted to write this for many years now
__k__nowing that in reality I would probably
__n__ever get to see you in person but it was important
__o__therwise I might not have the opportunity to
__w__rite what needed to be said.
__W__hat I did in the past is horrific and shameful.
__H__ow you ever managed to cope, to live and to
__e__merge from the hideous crimes I committed
__r__equired such strength of character and an
__e__nergy that I cannot begin to fathom.

Y_ou are the person I think_
o_f every day when I try my best to_
u_nderstand how I did what I did. Believe me, I_
l_ie awake at night and ask for forgiveness._
I _pray for my redemption knowing how_
v_ery hard it must be for you to live and_
e_njoy your life after bearing witness to what I have done._
J_ustice is blind I know._
E_verybody I have ever known_
s_ays the same thing – find peace within._
S_ome say I should not be forgiven and_
I _can understand why. Most days I_
c_annot forgive myself, but I die in hope._
A_men._
O_r perhaps there is life after death?_
R_edemption for the most twisted_
s_ouls that exist not just on this plane but in_
h_ell itself. The incendiary heat_
o_r sulphurous flames I do not fear. Living_
u_nder Milton's clouds within his epic poem Paradise_
L_ost casts no doubt as to my final resting place._
D_ivine is he who has no fear and_
I _know what will await me. But what awaits you?_
C_herubs?_
A_ngels? Or a Hades type of_
l_imbo inhabited by the demon_
L_ucifer himself?_
Y_ou are not as blameless_
o_r innocent as you might want to think._
U_ncovering the truth about oneself is never pleasant._
H_ave you read of The Furies_

o*f Greek Mythology? Three sisters*
L*iving with vengeance in their hearts.*
L*istening to the voices in their heads until they scream.*
Y*ou would do well to hear their ancient cry as*
I *would shed a tear for their fate rather than my own.*
A*s my final night draws near.*
M*ay the seconds spread for hours*
a*nd my hours for days and may they*
l*ast until*
I *take my final breath which*
v*ery soon will be upon me.*
E*ventually, whether we are a man, woman or child, we*
a*ll die, but it is*
n*ot how, but what we will be remembered for that counts.*
D*id I live out my dreams*
w*hile taking others?*
A*lways. I chose the path of most destruction,*
l*ying, cheating, poisonous, sinister.*
K*illing those who walked with*
i*nnocent blood in their veins.*
N*othing was ever wrong in my head though.*
G*od forgave me as I*
t*ook life after life. Forgive me please, for in God's eyes*
a*m I not your brother too? Simply a lost soul? I will*
l*eave you and this world with nothing but*
l*ove.*
S*ebastian Carstairs x*

'The first letter of every line reveals the hidden message,' Bishop nodded softly. '"*I know where you live Jessica or should I call you Holly. I am alive and walking tall*".'

Six

Holly should have gone to bed when Bishop left, but she couldn't sleep.

She had been nine years old on the day her parents were murdered, and she remembered the smell of blood, the coldness of death and a young female police constable called Yannis Marie who was the first officer at the scene to take care of her. Rereading PC Marie's report tonight, the memories came flooding back stronger than Holly imagined they would. She didn't remember what Yannis looked like, but she remembered holding her hand and the feeling of being safe with this woman.

'And your name is Jessica Ridley,' Yannis had said. 'That's a nice name. Now shall we go over there by the fireplace where it's nice and warm?' Her soft voice made Holly feel sleepy. 'Would you like a drink? Some water or how about a hot chocolate?'

'Hot chocolate,' Holly had said, and she felt her hands gripping the mug she held now.

'I like your dress.'

'It's not mine.'

After discovering her parents' bodies, Holly had run to a house in a nearby village and Mr and Mrs Sayles had wiped the blood off her face, taken her out of her clothes and given her a blue dress to wear from their daughter's wardrobe. Mrs Sayles had given Holly a cardigan as well. It was too big but it was fluffy.

'Well, now that we are settled and clean and have our hot chocolate, do you want to tell me a bit about today, Jessica? About how it started.'

'Okay.'

'Let's go right back to the beginning. What did you have for breakfast?'

'An egg,' she said.

'A boiled egg?'

'Yes.'

'Did your mummy make that for you?'

'I made it myself.'

'Wow – that's impressive. I'm rubbish at cooking.'

The young constable had been so good at getting Holly to relax and talk. Yannis been trained in child trauma, and Holly found out years later this was her first case.

'And then you went to school?'

'Yes.'

'Do you like school?'

'Yes.'

'And what did you do? What lessons did you have today, Jessica?'

'History, Maths and Art.'

'I used to love art, I still draw now. What were you drawing today?'

'I don't remember.'

'That's okay, and did you finish school at three fifteen?'

Holly nodded.

'And then you walked home by yourself?'

'I always do. Raya was supposed to be coming for a sleepover but her mum cancelled it, so she wasn't with me.'

'And is Raya a friend of yours from school?'

'Raya Stephens, yes. She's my best friend.'

Holly took a second. Raya Stephens – like so many details over the years she had forgotten that name. They had been best friends, but she had never seen her again after that day. She wondered what Raya had done, where she was now. She hoped life had been good for Raya.

'What was the weather like when you walked back from school?' Yannis said. 'Was it hot?'

'Yes, it was sunny.'

'And what did you do when you got to your house?'

'I opened the front door and said "Hi, I'm home." I dropped my school satchel on the hall stand and walked through the living room and into the kitchen.'

'There are sliding doors to the kitchen, aren't there? Were they open or closed?'

'Closed. I had to slide them open.'

'Did you hear anything before you went in, Jessica?'

'No, I don't think so.'

'Okay, now this is going to be hard, but I need to ask what you saw when you first opened the sliding doors. Is that okay? What do you remember?'

'I remember seeing red.'

'Red?'

'The room was red all over. On the floor and the table and chairs.'

'And Mummy and Daddy were in the kitchen, weren't they?'

'Yes.'

Her father had been found decapitated on the floor and her mother had been stabbed so hard through her back the blade had come out of the other side and impaled her to the wooden countertop.

'And did you try and talk to them? Your mother and father?'

'No.'

'Did you go over to them to see if they were all right?'

'No.'

'Why not?'

Holly frowned and put the transcript to one side. She remembered the shuddering silence in the kitchen that was so used to noise and the smell of baking that had suddenly been replaced with the smell of blood.

'Jessica? Why didn't you go over to them to see if they were all right?'

Because of the big man with the big hands and the red knife who watched me with such stillness I thought he was dead too.

'Because of him,' she said.

'Him? Who is him?'

'The man.'

'What man? There was someone else there in the kitchen with you?'

Yannis was staring at Holly with the widest eyes.

'Who was there?'

'The man.'

The next few sentences of the transcript had been redacted and Holly had no idea what had been said, but when it resumed they had been joined by a different police officer. His name was DCI Douglas Warren, and he had been the senior officer in charge of The Animal case.

'This is a friend of mine, Jessica. This is another policeman. His name is Douglas.'

'Hello, Jessica,' DCI Warren said.

He was a quick-talker and his voice was high-pitched.

'Do you want to repeat what you told Constable Yannis, young lady. About when you opened the sliding doors to the kitchen. This is very important. You said there was a man there.'

She nodded.

'Is it possible you could describe him to us, because we would very much like to find him.'

'He had short hair and looked like a skull.'

'A skull?'

'Yes.'

'You mean he had a very thin face?' Yannis was holding her hand again.

Holly nodded and said:

'And he got a knife from the wooden block.'

'A knife? When he saw you?'

'Yes.'

'And then what?'

The Animal had walked towards her.

She remembered freezing on the spot and wetting herself, the urine warm and yellow as it ran into her white school socks. And all she could do was stare at his black eyes as he put the knife to her throat. She could feel his breath on her cheek as he kissed her on the forehead and said:

'*I've seen things you haven't.*'

'And then he left,' Holly said. 'He left me alive and I still don't know why.'

Seven

DI Bishop worked while London slept.

Dearest Holly, it's been a while . . .

The direct message to Holly on the wall at the Newsome murder scene bothered him.

It was a call to her. A challenge. And he wondered how she would cope with the pressure in the next few weeks. How many people, cops, SOCO and forensic teams had seen the message? They might not understand the 'walking tall' reference, but they all knew or had heard of Holly and would wonder why this killer had made it so personal. Because it was personal, of course, but hardly anybody knew the truth about Holly, and the implications were huge. He should tell her not to worry. They would get the best team working with her on this, including Craig Thompson and Janet Acton, two detective inspectors whom she had worked with before. Given the brutality of the killings, he would be given as many officers as he needed, he was sure of that.

When Holly had shared the letter with him three months ago, he'd doubted Sebastian Carstairs was still alive. After seeing the message at the crime scene this morning, he was beginning to reconsider. How The Animal, riddled with cancer, could have managed to fool everybody and escape from prison, then reappear well enough to kill again was beyond Bishop. If he *was* free and killing, the first priority would be to catch him, but at the same time they would need to establish how he had escaped and who had helped him. And who had been cremated in his place.

The Sebastian Carstairs files were fanned in disarray on the large mahogany desk in his office, but he wasn't even close to playing catch-up. He took one of the unfamiliar reports and squared off the edges before flicking through the pages to find what he was looking for: the final report compiled by the arresting officer, DCI Douglas Warren.

At around noon on 11 March 1993, The Animal walked into Hammersmith police station and handed himself in. He had completed his mission: to kill one person for each letter of his name and now he was done. Sebastian Carstairs was formally cautioned and arrested, and the interviews began. The process of recording his confession took over three weeks and when DCI Warren was asked by the press how the killer had been throughout, he had replied that The Animal seemed 'very calm, pleasant and cooperative'.

DCI Warren had retired soon after The Animal's case was closed, and Bishop didn't blame him. It was a career high that couldn't be topped. A memoir had followed, along with numerous interviews for true crime documentaries, and he had been awarded an MBE. There was talk of a seat in parliament, a possible peerage, but for some reason the DCI had turned away from the spotlight, saying he would prefer to enjoy the rest of his years in relative obscurity.

His interviews had been pulled out for another airing three

months ago when The Animal had been pronounced dead, and his statements were endlessly regurgitated in the media, but he had flatly refused to cooperate with any new interviews for the press. Bishop could understand that: media scrutiny was a double-edged sword, and DCI Warren had nothing to gain; his memoir had already hit the bestseller charts again.

He picked up the Newsome crime-scene photos and lit a cigarette, drawing on it between sips of whisky. He had seen 'gruesome' many times before on active duty in the Army Air Corps and then Special Forces in Afghanistan, and there'd been no shortage of it since he'd returned to England and joined the Met. To say one got used to it was a lie. You hardened yourself against it, put on a suit of armour, but something nearly always slipped through the cracks.

Mrs Newsome had hazel eyes. Mr Newsome's eyes were blue. Now the corneas were cloudy and opaque like an old camera lens. Everything they had ever seen had been lost forever. He put the photos to one side and started writing a recommendation letter to his superior, Chief Constable Franks, with paper and pen. He wrote in longhand because he knew he needed to choose his words with utmost care and handwritten correspondence seemed to lend itself to a more considered approach than digital.

He began with a brief mention of the Newsomes' young daughter who had found the bodies, then described his own first steps onto the crime scene, the arrival of the coroner, Angela Swan, and the discovery of the message on the wall written in blood. When he had done this, he paused. His whisky needed refilling and he added ice from the freezer.

He read what he had done and took his time on the final paragraph.

We do not have definitive proof that The Animal is responsible for these murders, sir, and I suspect there will be no DNA left at the crime scene, which was his MO throughout his history of kills. However, if by some miracle it is him, the fact that he has somehow eluded death constitutes a grave misjustice along the chain of events that led to his apparent resurrection. Somehow, he has circumvented our judicial system and is once again preying on innocent men and women. His last killing spree cost eighteen lives and today it would seem two more bodies have been added in a new chapter. I believe we must act immediately to capture this individual, as he will no doubt already be planning his next kills. Speed is of the essence and I hope for your full backing to set up an MIT task force to bring The Animal—

He stopped and put a line through *The Animal* – he was being too presumptuous – and instead wrote:

to bring this killer to justice.

He read it twice more, then transcribed it onto his computer and printed it out. Sealed it in an envelope and wrote CLASSIFIED.

Then he picked up the phone.

Eight

The phone rang five times before it was answered by a female voice.

'Hello?'

'Mrs Franks, this is DI Bishop. I'm so sorry to trouble you at this time of night, but is the chief constable available?'

'He is, Bill, hold on one second.'

Her voice was rich and her name was Marjorie, although Bishop never called her that, and informality had no place on the phone tonight. Chief Constable Franks came on and his voice sounded terse.

'We're in bed, what is it, Bishop?'

'We had a double murder today, sir, a husband and wife.'

'I heard.'

'I went to the crime scene.' He chose his words carefully. 'It was highly unusual.'

'Meaning?'

'There is the slimmest of possibilities that there may be some substance to the nightmare scenario we discussed three months ago.'

There was a sharp intake of breath on the line.

'You're talking about The Animal? Sebastian Carstairs?'

'Yes, sir.'

'I don't believe it.'

'I share your scepticism, sir, but I wanted you to be aware of the possibility. If no DNA is found at the crime scene, we cannot presume it's him, so we'll carry on with a standard investigation.'

'Exactly. So why the late-night phone call, DI Bishop?'

'The killer left a message on the wall.'

'A message?'

'It was addressed to Holly and written in blood.'

'What did it say?'

Bishop told him and the response was the inevitable:

'Who the hell is Annie Wilkes?'

'We don't know yet.'

'It's more than likely a copycat, a contact The Animal made during his life in prison or someone he confided his secrets to before he was cremated.'

'We're looking into that now, sir.'

'And Miss Wakefield has been to the crime scene?'

'I took her this afternoon. She's positive it's him.'

The phone went muffled and Bishop knew a hand had been put over the receiver. He heard a muted conversation, a cough, and sudden clarity on the line as the hand was removed:

'In hindsight, you shouldn't have taken her there without consulting me first,' Franks said.

'My apologies, sir, but the message was addressed to her, therefore it would appear whoever this killer is wants her involved.'

'And we must play their game? I know you have a relationship of sorts with Miss Wakefield.'

'Working only, sir.'

Although he wanted more and wasn't sure if his boss believed him.

'But you know her better than anyone else on the murder squad, correct?'

'Yes, sir.'

'Then answer me this. The Animal murdered both of her parents. If he is still alive – which I very much doubt – we can't have her thinking it's him when it might not be. This is a massive conflict of interests and the emotional strain will be huge. Is she stable enough to work this case? Can she be objective?'

'I believe she can, sir. She's a very rational person and I think we need her insight and perspective. Nobody knows killers like she does – and if she can't be objective, I'll take her off the case myself.'

'See that you do. I refuse to believe this is his work, but if it is somehow true it's a bloody disaster. Have the press been informed of the murders?'

'Names of the victims only; no details.'

'I want a media embargo on the message on the wall. Not a word of it gets out. Do I make myself clear?'

'Crystal, sir. I have written my recommendation letter and it will be on your desk first thing in the morning.'

'I want it now,' Franks demanded, his voice brisk. 'Have you made a copy of your report? Has anybody else seen it?'

'No, sir.'

'Don't send it by email, get a private courier to bring the letter to me. And we need to schedule a briefing with Miss Wakefield.'

'At the station?'

'No – I don't want the three of us seen together at the station.

Best if the two of you come by the house tomorrow morning. You have my address?'

'No, sir.'

The chief gave his address and Bishop said goodbye and hung up. He couldn't work out whether Franks liked or disliked Holly, but it was clear he had a grudging admiration for her.

He lit another cigarette. The lighter was a black metal Zippo with a white enamel skull on one side and a red enamel heart on the other. Holly had bought it for him for his birthday in May. He had promised to quit smoking when the lighter fluid ran out.

Bishop deleted the letter he had just typed from his computer. He had already put the finished report to one side ready for the courier and now stared at the original longhand draft. Experience had taught him to always err on the side of caution, so he picked up the pages and burned them until they dissolved into grey ash.

Nine

The West London Coroner's Office occupied an orange-and-brown Victorian brick building with large metal-framed windows in Bagleys Lane, Fulham.

Holly got buzzed in at the door and Bishop was already waiting at reception. A quick hello, a short ride in the lift down one level and they followed the blue line on the floor until they were met by double swing doors. Another corridor, and by now Holly could smell the formalin and chemical cleansers. They passed the morgue where the bodies were kept refrigerated at four degrees and Angela Swan met them at the door to the brightly lit autopsy suite. Tall and gaunt, her grey hair wiry, Angela was smiling although she looked tired.

'Morning, Bishop. Morning, Holly.'

Three stainless steel tables waited for them, all occupied. Another pathologist wearing scrubs and headphones was working at the far table on a body that was covered in blood.

'Drunk-driver car crash,' Angela said. 'Compared to that, our two are incredibly clean. We will go in chronological order as blood spatter indicates the male was killed first.'

She switched the overhead microphone on as she led them to the middle table where a figure lay under a green sheet.

'This is Angela Swan, forensic pathologist for the Greater London area, summarising the post-mortem examination of Mr and Mrs Newsome for DI Bishop of the Metropolitan Serious Crime squad and Holly Wakefield, forensic psychologist. At approximately ten a.m. on Monday, eleventh of August 2019, at the request of the Metropolitan Police I attended the scene of two suspicious deaths near Boreham wood in Hertfordshire. Prior to entering the house, I was shown a digital recording of the crime scene showing the bodies of the deceased: a middle-aged woman and a middle-aged man, both lying in situ in their living room. He was bent over, his head resting on the coffee table, she was lying face down on the carpet adjacent to him. There was considerable blood loss. Photographs were taken under my direction.'

She reached out to the metal table and pulled the green sheet halfway down. John Newsome's skin was pale with blue-veined marbling across his chest and shoulders.

'Our first victim is a middle-aged male; his appearance matches the stated age of fifty-three, with a weight of seventy-nine kilograms and height of one hundred and seventy-nine centimeters. He has grey curly hair, shorter at the front and sides with frontal thinning and balding of the crown. Two vaccination scars on the left upper arm. No tattoos. Rigor mortis was firmly established when both bodies were found. There is only one wound on the victim: on the right side of his neck approximately five centimeters above the clavicle, consistent with sharp force injury. The neck structures were formally dissected when the body was brought here, and full vascular drainage was carried out.'

Holly could see a flap of skin on the right side of John Newsome's neck where Angela had cut through; the pathologist proceeded to open it like the lip of an envelope. The pale muscles underneath became visible and there was a small circular hole in the puckered flesh.

'The weapon was most likely a thin rigid blade with very little give, a bit like a very large knitting needle but much sharper and stronger, I suspect steel, possibly custom made. Did you find the weapon?'

'No.'

'The blade punctured the neck at a downward angle, which would indicate the killer was taller than our victim or standing above him at the time of the attack, or perhaps both. The blade passed cleanly through the sternocleidomastoid muscle and immediately severed the jugular vein, then continued its journey, missing the hyoid bone and thyroid cartilages, but dissecting the anterior omohyoid and the vagus nerve. Note the additional haematoma near the trunk of the vagus nerve and its branches.'

Holly felt herself leaning forward as Angela angled the overhead spotlight.

'Vagal inhibition from a stab to the neck is an exceptionally rare event. There is a tiny, almost circular-shaped cut in the left cervical region, measuring approximately one point five centimetres in diameter.'

'That's the maximum width of our weapon?' Bishop said.

'Yes. The blade then perforated the cervical cartilage at C4 and 5, leaving the carotid artery as well as its main branches untouched, and finally exited at the front of the throat above the fascia, which covers the thyroid gland and the trachea. The trachea and bronchi contained no exudate or blood.

'When the knife was pulled out there would have been severe cerebrospinal fluid leakage, which could possibly indicate either the victim or the killer shifted their bodies. The wound was almost immediately fatal.'

'Cause of death?'

'Exsanguination due to the severing of the jugular vessel, which was complicated by aspiration of blood in the respiratory passage.'

'Are those defensive wounds on his hands?' Bishop said.

'The crescent moon-like impressions and cuts on the lower parts of both palms are, I believe, self-inflicted. The cuts match the victim's own nails exactly, so it appears he clenched his hands into fists when he was first struck – a reflex action, probably, as I believe the victim was taken by surprise and had no idea what hit him. Apart from the hole in his neck, this patient was an otherwise completely healthy male. Shall we move on?'

She replaced the covering and moved to the steel table at the front of the room. The body there was draped in a white sheet which she pulled swiftly back. Holly felt herself flinch.

The woman lay on the gurney, her mouth twisted and her eyes still open. They had a yellow hue and a slightly crystalline appearance and seemed to stare at Holly in dazed agony.

'Victim number two has been identified as Sandra Newsome the wife of the previous victim. Forty-six years old, one hundred and seventy-three centimeters tall, she weighed fifty-two kilograms. Her hair is ash-blonde and long, measuring forty centimeters in length and was pulled into a French braid. No tattoos. A hysterectomy scar with the resultant scar tissue visible and as expected. As per the previous victim, she was stabbed only once, this time through her heart from behind.

'The fatal wound entered the rear of the left side of her back, to the right of the scapula and between the second and third ribs. There is a circular bruise around the injury between the scapula and the spine which would have been the result of the hilt of the unidentified weapon impacting with the flesh. The blade penetrated the two chambers of the right side of the heart, causing damage to the ventricular wall with consequent bleeding around the heart and into the lungs. Perforation of the left pleural cavity is evident, as well as the lung parenchyma, where the weapon completely cut through the bone sections of four ribs along the channels of the wound and tracked to a depth of twenty-eight centimetres before exiting at a slightly upward angle, which means the killer stabbed her low and pushed the blade upwards for maximum damage. The exit wound is on the left of the sternum, with evidence of fibro-cartilage recovered from the blood at the scene of the crime which would indicate small fragments of rib were expelled from the body by the force of the blow. The injury to the large blood vessels and organs inside the body would have resulted in haemorrhagic shock and massive blood loss, which was the cause of death.'

'The bruises around her neck?' Holly said. 'Pre or post-mortem?'

'Pre. Her hyoid bone was fractured – not by the killer's hands, as there is no evidence of finger or thumb impressions, so more likely the crook of his elbow, which makes me think he grabbed her around the throat, then spun her around, semi-strangling her, before he stabbed her. I'm presuming the killer is a he?'

'Highly probable,' said Holly.

'As per the previous victim, there are no defensive wounds. It would appear she didn't have time to react, or perhaps her only reaction was shock and immobilisation at the sight of her dying husband. There was a fresh scaphoid fracture in her left wrist, which occurs most often after a fall onto an outstretched arm. So it would appear he stabbed her and let her drop to the ground. This would also account for the slight bruising on her forehead and carpet fibres we found in her hair. Toxicology showed paracetamol in her stomach; no alcohol was detected in either victim.'

'Time of death?'

'Between eight-thirty and midnight on Sunday evening.'

Angela flipped the spotlight off.

'Do we know who this killer is yet?'

'No,' said Bishop.

'Well let me fill in some blanks. The weapon he's using will be thin and have a scalpel-like sharpness. Because of its shape it will be easy to conceal, so I'll be interested to see what it looks like when you find it. There were no hesitation marks on either of the victims, therefore I would be very surprised if these were his first kills. This killer knows his anatomy and he's very precise; neither of the wounds were survivable even with immediate assistance. Death would have been rapid: thirty seconds for him, less than a minute for her.'

Ten

It took Holly and Bishop over an hour to drive to Henley-on-Thames in south Oxfordshire, a town that had survived the Black Death and was now famous for the Henley Regatta boat race.

The chief constable's house was large and imposing – a Georgian mansion with courtyard and gardens to match. Bishop parked on the gravel driveway behind four other cars. When Holly got out, she took in the surroundings, but Bishop was pensive.

'Looks like we're not the only guests this morning,' he said.

They made their way up the stone steps to the red door. Bishop knocked.

'Have you been here before?' Holly said.

'No.'

The door was opened by a small and precise man dressed like a bank manager. He smiled courteously:

'Please come through. The others are already in the drawing room.'

Holly wondered who was waiting for them as the man led

them along the corridor, past the kitchen and through a room with a Steinway piano. Another corridor and he knocked on a set of double doors at the end. He didn't wait for a response, or if there was one, Holly didn't hear it. The man opened the doors halfway and stood in the entrance.

'Miss Wakefield and DI Bishop, sir.'

He stepped aside and ushered them into the drawing room, which was painted dark blue and had cherrywood floors. There were shelves lined with books, bronzes on plinths and the obligatory oil on canvas landscapes on the walls. Three men in armchairs by the fireplace swivelled at their entrance and their conversation ground to a halt. Chief Constable Franks stood up. In his sixties with white hair, he was sun-tanned with an unremarkable face, but his shoulders seemed hunched as if under extraordinary pressure.

'Ah, good,' he said and smiled, but it didn't make it to his eyes. 'Drinks for our guests, please, Stefan. Coffee and tea?'

'That's fine – thank you,' Holly and Bishop both said.

Stefan nodded and departed.

'DI Bishop, you are no doubt familiar with everyone here,' Franks said, 'but let me introduce Miss Wakefield. Holly, this is Chief Superintendent Bashir from the commissioner's office.'

The man was tall and thin with thick dark hair and eyebrows to match. His eyes were almost black and his voice strong and well-educated.

'Miss Wakefield, a pleasure to meet you.'

'Chief Superintendent,' she said, and shook his hand. The grip lasted a little longer than was customary and her hand felt warm when she pulled it back to her side.

Franks said: 'And this is DCI Warren, the man responsible

for capturing The Animal back in 1993. Retired now, but the Superintendent thought it appropriate he should be here.'

DCI Warren was a shrunken man in his late seventies. He wobbled like an infant when he took a step towards Holly and his hand trembled in hers:

'Good morning,' he said.

'It's a pleasure to meet you, sir. I've read your memoir several times.'

For the briefest moment Holly wondered if the man recognised her as the nine-year-old girl he had stood next to after her parents' bodies had been found, but that would be impossible. The old man wiped at his mouth with a handkerchief, and stared at her with glazed eyes as if his thoughts were elsewhere.

'Take a seat, please,' Franks said. So they did, in chairs that had been positioned in readiness. Holly was content to stay silent as Bishop small-talked with the others until the drinks arrived, but she could sense his discomfort. As Stefan was leaving, Franks said:

'Close the door behind you, thank you.'

The door closed and Chief Constable Franks cleared his throat.

'I called Superintendent Bashir after I spoke to you last night, DI Bishop,' Franks said. 'I voiced your concerns and he in turn spoke to Commissioner Reeman. Superintendent Bashir?'

Without seeming to hurry, Bashir gazed contemplatively at Holly and Bishop.

'Yesterday's murder of John and Sandra Newsome is rather troubling. I believe you have just come from the coroner's office?'

'That's correct, sir,' Bishop said.

'What are her thoughts?'

'Whoever the killer is, these are not his first kills. The knife-work is too confident.'

'And the forensic results?'

'Nothing as yet; forensics are still processing evidence gathered at the crime scene.'

'Good. And the message on the wall was addressed to a *Holly* – possibly you, Miss Wakefield?'

'Yes, it would appear that way,' she said.

'Miss Wakefield has helped us on several cases in the past, sir,' Bishop said. 'We think the killer might be challenging her.'

'Challenging her?' Bashir said. 'You mean *catch me if you can*?'

'Something like that.'

Bashir gave Holly a curious look.

'A very cruel thing to do, considering your situation.'

'My situation?' Holly said.

'Chief Constable Franks informed me of your connection to The Animal, Miss Wakefield, that your parents were both victims in his bloody crusade.'

Holly shot Chief Franks a look. What was done was done and he met her gaze unwaveringly.

'And now here you are,' Bashir continued, 'fighting the good fight for us against a copycat who is taunting you by leaving obscene messages.'

'A copycat?'

'Of course. The commissioner and I are both adamant the murder of Mr and Mrs Newsome was carried out by a fanatical individual who simply wants his ten seconds of notoriety. Use The Animal's moniker "Walking Tall" in a message on the victim's wall and he's instantly front-page news.'

'With all due respect, Superintendent, I don't believe we're dealing with a copycat here,' Holly said.

Bashir glanced at Chief Franks, then back to Holly. Incredulity turned to amusement.

'Yes, the chief has informed me of your elaborate hypothesis that The Animal is somehow alive. Quite frankly I don't understand.'

'This isn't some wild conspiracy theory, sir. The Animal wrote a letter to me before his parole hearing that had a hidden message—'

'Which has also been brought to my attention. A cruel hoax from an evil man destined to die. And then yesterday you saw your name in that message on the wall, like a clarion call from an old adversary, and alarm bells rang in your head. And now you think this man somehow fooled everybody, escaped from one of the most secure prisons in England and cheated death like a modern-day Lazarus. You don't seriously believe that, do you?'

'As a matter of fact, I do.'

Out of the corner of her eye she saw Chief Franks' shoulders tighten.

'I was under the impression you went to his funeral, Miss Wakefield.'

'I did.'

'Therefore you were a witness to his incineration?'

'I was.'

'Then may I suggest that you should be wary of the harm that could come from clinging to this fantasy that Sebastian Carstairs is still alive. We all need enemies, they fuel our fire and make us stronger, but I can assure you, your enemy is dead.'

'You're wrong, sir. He is smarter than anyone I know, and I believe he is killing again, and the only reason he was caught last time was because he finished his mission and handed himself in.'

'Excuse me?'

'He killed eighteen people and handed himself in. That's the only reason he stopped killing.'

'DCI Warren would have caught him,' said Bashir.

'I don't think so.'

It was the sarcasm that stung and she saw Bashir bristle and heard Franks say:

'Stay in line please, Miss Wakefield.'

'I'm sorry, but I won't.' She raised her voice and continued: 'You all have to listen to me. You have no idea what you are up against!'

'I was there, Miss Wakefield,' Bashir's voice matched hers. 'I was there in the blood and the mess with DCI Warren at some of the original crime scenes. We both saw things that I wish we never had: mutilated bodies and burnings and drownings, and a man whose face and throat looked like Swiss cheese after he had been forced to drink acid, so please do not lecture me on us having no idea what that man was capable of!' He reached out a hand and gently touched DCI Warren's arm. There was obviously a bond between them and Holly wondered how far back it went.

'Do you have any idea how ridiculous you sound?' he asked. 'What if I told you Fred West had suddenly come back to life and was killing young women again – would you believe me? Or the Moors Murderers, Myra Hindley and Ian Brady? Hindley died of pneumonia in 2002 and Brady of lung cancer in 2017. Sebastian Carstairs had cancer as well, and he died from complications at 11.37 p.m. on May thirteenth of this year, and was cremated the day after. The coroner signed off on his autopsy, which was witnessed by the Broadmoor Chief Medical Officer. I have a copy of The Animal's death certificate in my office, I'm thinking of having it framed. Would you like a copy?'

'No!'

'Really? Then what will it take to convince you he is dead? What would you have me do? Exhume the body? Well we can't, because he was cremated.'

'You don't understand. When I went into that house yesterday . . . It was as if I had . . .'

'Had what?'

She paused, unable to find the words. Bashir shook his head dismissively.

'I have given you ample time to express your views, Miss Wakefield, which I was gracious enough to listen to. Now please, the man is dead and you should move on.' He turned to DI Bishop, his voice cold:

'DI Bishop, you will head up the investigation into the Newsome murders and this will become your priority. Understood?'

'Yes, sir.'

'Commissioner Reeman has assured me you shall have all necessary resources of Her Majesty's Government to apprehend this killer and take him off the streets without delay. Chief Constable Franks will keep me up to date on your progress.' He took a breath. 'Now, I believe it is time for us to take our leave.' He helped DCI Warren from his chair and held onto the frail man's arm as he led him away, but DCI Warren didn't want to go yet. He stood his ground next to Holly and blinked as if under the gaze of bright lights.

'Why you?' he said softly.

Bashir paused, a rather unpleasant look on his face.

'What are you asking her, Douglas?' he said.

'The woman. Why her?'

Holly stood up and leaned forward slightly.

'Why me, what, sir?'

'Why do you think The Animal is still alive?'

It was a question she had asked herself every day for the past three months and she shook her head wilfully. She was exhausted by lack of sleep and tired through worry and stress; if she was wrong, she was wrong, and deep down she knew she had no proof, yet she still clung to an odd faith in her gut instinct.

'Because when I went into that house yesterday, I felt scared. And I don't scare easily, not any more.' She could feel the hairs rising on her arms. 'It was as if I had stepped back in time. The same feeling, the same smell, the same memories – and I'm not paranoid, though some people might think that of me. My head hasn't figured it all out yet, but my gut is screaming at me, and it wasn't just the murders and the message on the wall, it was the fact that I know this killer as well as he knows himself. I could feel him, and I want to run away, trust me, I really do, because he is so dangerous, but I know he wants me to be part of this, and I don't think I have a choice.'

DCI Warren blinked rapidly and looked away. Bashir pulled firmly at his arm, ready to leave.

'Superintendent, I know there's not much to go on,' Holly pleaded, 'but if we start investigating now and if information comes to light through the normal channels of the investigation that The Animal *is* somehow alive, then at least we'll be ahead of the game. His first mission was to kill eighteen people, a victim for each letter of his name, and now he wants something else.'

'What?'

'I don't know.'

Bashir smiled slightly, then raised a hand in dismissal:

'Goodbye, Miss Wakefield.'

He headed to the door with DCI Warren beside him. Holly shouted at their backs:

'Why are you not taking this seriously?'

'Holly, please,' Chief Franks said softly. 'I do believe the matter is closed. The Animal has not risen from the grave.'

'Well I hope you're right, Chief Franks, I really do, because if he is alive, and if he isn't stopped more men and women will die and their children will be left on their own, without parents, just like I was, and nobody should have to go through that and we have to stop him!' She paused and took a shallow breath. Her eyes were cloudy with tears and she wiped at them clumsily.

As Bashir opened the door she heard his voice echo back to her:

'You cannot live your life chasing a ghost, Miss Wakefield.'

Eleven

Bishop drove. The traffic heading into London had slowed to a crawl.

Holly was all cried out.

'They're idiots,' she said. 'Just wait for the body count to mount up and then they'll be sorry. Then they'll . . .'

'They'll what, Holly? Is that what you want? Dead bodies? Orphans?'

'No,' a beat. 'I'm sorry. Of course not, but that's what's going to happen.'

'You cannot let emotion get in the way of a case, Holly. Rule number one.'

She shook her head. She was angry at herself, angry at Bishop, angry at everyone.

'I'm sorry,' she said. 'That wasn't me back there.'

'It was you and it was good to get it out because now you can be more objective.'

'I just wish they had listened. They didn't even give me a chance. I thought they would at least be open to the possibility.'

'Look – for the time being we forget about The Animal

and just concentrate on what we have in front of us, okay? We investigate the Newsome murders like we would any other homicide.'

'So we have to act as if Superintendent Bashir is right?' she said. 'That this murder was the work of a copycat?'

'Yes.'

'You don't believe that, do you?'

He didn't answer, but she let it go.

'So the letter The Animal wrote to me was just a cruel joke, and my name on the wall was what? A set-up? A coincidence? You don't like coincidences.'

'You're right, I don't, but I can't see any way out of this.'

'It was how my mother was killed,' Holly said.

'Huh?'

'My mother and Sandra Newsome were both stabbed from behind between the ribs. Maybe it's another way of getting my attention.'

Silence for a while. Holly watched Bishop take out a cigarette. He played with it for a while but decided against it.

'Why was DCI Warren there?' she said. 'Why parade him in front of us like that?'

'Maybe Bashir wanted to prove a point.'

'What point? The old man didn't even know where he was. Did you know he was like that?'

'I'd heard rumours. He's got vascular dementia and the police benevolent fund is helping him. He's in a care home, I think – or carers visit his home; I forget which.'

'Could we talk to him?'

'And ask him what? Questions about The Animal? Now I understand why he's stayed away from the press all these years. Put him in front of a camera and who knows what he'd say.'

'He might know something.'

Bishop shook his head and decided the cigarette was a good idea after all.

'So that's it? Case closed?' Holly said.

'There is no case.'

She was staring at the road ahead. The atmosphere was fucking freezing.

'Holly?'

'What?'

'Do you want to work the Newsome murder with me or not?'

'Yes.'

'Good.'

His phone beeped with a text. He read it and his brow furrowed.

'Shit,' he said.

'What is it?'

'It's Chief Franks. He wants us to go back.'

Twelve

Stefan opened the front door, but there was no smile this time and no offer of drinks.

He led them through to the drawing room where Chief Franks was standing facing the fireplace with his back to them. There was some paper smoking in the grate and Holly wondered what had been burned. Chief Franks ran a hand through his silver hair and turned suddenly.

'I'm removing you both from the Newsome case.'

'What?' said Bishop.

'DI Thompson will take over command. As of now, Miss Wakefield, your services will no longer be required. Yes, I know the rug has been seemingly pulled from under your feet,' he said, 'but the commissioner is adamant The Animal is dead and I believe your involvement in the case may muddy the waters.'

'Sir, with all due respect, how the hell can we help catch this killer if we're not even involved?' Bishop protested. 'And what if Holly is right? What if—'

'We had seven sightings of The Animal last week,' Franks

said. 'Three in Liverpool, three in London, and one on a British Airways flight from Venice to Gatwick. Do you know what these sightings had in common?'

'No.'

'They all occurred within one hour of each other. People want conspiracies, and it is our responsibility not to feed them. What happens if we tell the public a DI in the Met Police force and a psychologist from King's College think The Animal might still be alive? What will be the response? Will they laugh? Will your rumour be dismissed? Or will it make the rounds on social media where it will no doubt find a home with some of the more gullible members of the general public? And what will happen then? Will the public feel fear, anger, confusion? At the moment the public feel safe. We cannot risk undermining that sense of security. As far as this administration is concerned, Sebastian Carstairs is nothing more than ashes. I felt duty-bound to mention your theory to Commissioner Reeman, but she is adamant that we cannot be seen to be wasting resources hunting a man who died three months ago.'

'Then what do we do?' Bishop said.

'I'm removing you from the case,' Chief Franks said sharply. 'But not the investigation.'

Holly watched him closely. His shoulders seemed to have relaxed, but a part of him remained hesitant.

'I have been given direct orders that we cannot launch an official police investigation into Sebastian Carstairs, but I see no reason why we cannot conduct a secret one. DI Thompson will be the face of the inquiry for the Newsome killings, but behind the scenes you will look for evidence – solid proof, not "gut instincts" and supposition – that The Animal is still alive and responsible. I want daily updates, and you will report to me here rather than at the station. No one else can know what you are working on. This is an inquiry that must be carried out in absolute secrecy.'

'It can't just be the two of us, sir,' Bishop said. 'We'll need a team of at least twenty officers.'

'That's not going to happen. For one thing we don't have the manpower or the resources, and even if we did, we can't risk this leaking to the media. Twenty officers means twenty wives, husbands or partners, not to mention friends and colleagues,' Franks said. 'We can't have this case being discussed in the canteen or over a beer after work. If Chief Superintendent Bashir were to get wind of this, heads would roll. So it will be just the two of you working the case, and that's my final offer. Will you accept those terms?'

When Holly had assisted the Metropolitan Police on previous cases she had been part of a huge team of experienced women and men. Without their help, this task was going to be nearly impossible. She knew Bishop would feel the same, but what else could they do?

'Yes,' she said.

'DI Bishop?'

'Yes, sir.'

Chief Franks seemed satisfied.

'I want to make it clear I understand you will be working under considerable limitations, but I have faith in you both,' he said.

It was the first time Holly had heard Franks be so candid and she felt herself flush with a certain amount of pride.

'Thompson will ask questions,' Bishop said. 'He'll wonder why I'm not working the Newsome murders.'

'Then we tell him you've been assigned to another inquiry. How many murder cases do you have on your desk at the moment?'

'About thirty.'

'Hand them all over to CID.'

'Then what do I do?'

'Cold case files.'

'Cold cases?'

'Yes. Your new assignment will be under the guise of a cold case task force. You will have access to all The Animal's files along with a dozen or so unsolved cases going back to the early 1990s, the height of his reign of terror. If anybody asks, your job is to ascertain whether he was responsible for any of these unsolved murders, tie up a few loose ends. In reality, you will be investigating the Newsomes' murder from your unique perspective. For obvious reasons you can't be anywhere near the station incident room.'

'Then where do we work from?'

'The east wing of the station is currently undergoing renovation and staff have been relocated for the duration. The gym in the basement is being used as a storage space for the old furniture, but it has its own separate entrance at the back of the building. You can set up your office in there. There are still builders on site, but they won't have access to the basement. You should be able to come and go without anybody seeing you. I cannot emphasise how important it is that your work is kept secret. Never talk about the case outside of here or that room. Understood?'

'Yes,' they responded in unison.

'What will you need?'

Bishop said, 'Sebastian Carstairs was pronounced dead in

his bed at Broadmoor. If he is alive, then he must have had help from someone inside the prison. We need the names of the prison guards he came in contact with and how often were they rotated, who he shared cells with, where he ate, how many times he was in solitary confinement. And we'll need the hospital files where Sebastian Carstairs had his chemotherapy, along with the names of all of the nurses and doctors who treated him, and the security team who escorted him to and from the prison.'

'I'll arrange it.'

'I think it's important to study all of the original letters Sebastian Carstairs received in prison,' Holly said. 'There would have been hundreds over the years from fans and deluded women – any one of them could have assisted in his escape. There may be something in the letters: secret notes or instructions. It might be an idea to access the tape recordings of his therapy sessions as well. I've read the summary in his file, but I need to know exactly what was said in each session. I don't know how many therapists he got through, but he's incredibly manipulative and one of them could have been coerced, so we'll need their names too.'

'Bishop?'

'I want to be kept up to date with DI Thompson's investigation,' Bishop said. 'His team may unearth something from the Newsome murders that could help us – we can't be kept in the dark.'

'I'm no longer overseeing the Newsome case,' Franks said quietly. 'Superintendent Bashir has taken a personal interest, so access to those files will be limited for me. I can't be seen to be barging in and asking too many questions. I'll see what I can do, but it won't be easy.'

'Sebastian Carstairs has a sister called Cassandra,' Bishop said, frowning. 'She went to his funeral, so there's a chance she might still be living in England. We'll want to make contact with her. We'll need her National Insurance number, driver's licence and bank details.'

'Tread carefully with her. Who knows where her loyalties lie.'

'And perhaps most importantly, we need to find out who Annie Wilkes is,' Holly said.

'I think I've found that out already.' And there was a note of optimism in Chief Franks' voice. 'If it is who I believe it is, Wilkes was her maiden name,' he said, 'which was why she wasn't listed as such in the police files. Her married name is Annie Jacobs.'

'So who is she?'

'Annie Jacobs is a double-murderer. She killed her brother and his wife and now she's in New Hall Prison for the criminally insane.'

Thirteen

Bishop found parking on Worlidge Street, about two hundred metres from Hammersmith police station.

The sun was hot and the London streets busy with tourists and workers out for an early lunch. They made their way around to the rear of the police station, which looked like a 1970s block of flats: concrete, with a lot of square wood cladding. A short flight of steps led to a double-door made of tinted glass that unlocked and opened to the smell of fresh paint. A circular saw buzzed from behind one of the closed doors with a sound that put Holly's teeth on edge, and from somewhere a radio played.

The lift at the end of the corridor was out of order so they took the stairs. Two flights down, the stairwell opened onto a pitch-black corridor. There was no light switch. Bishop took a step forward and a strip light in the ceiling came on. Another step and another light and Holly noticed the lights went off behind them as they passed room after empty room until they reached the door at the end of the corridor marked GYM. Bishop removed the padlock and pushed it open. The space was low-ceilinged, musty and cramped. Dust, dirt and damp stains on the walls with dozens of mismatched steel filing cabinets, broken chairs and desks stacked on top of each other. To the far right, a few dumbbells and barbells had been left on black mats next to an empty water cooler. There was one narrow window in the far wall: a strip of frosted glass near the ceiling which looked out onto the pavement and Holly could see people's feet as they walked past.

'We really are in the basement,' she said.

'We should move some of this stuff around. Clean it up a bit.'

'No. The clean-up can await. Let's get started.'

They grabbed two desks and two unbroken chairs and sat facing each other in the centre of the room. They had sandwiches for lunch, hooked up their computers, helped themselves to a wireless printer from the abandoned Vice squad offices on the third floor as well as a stapler, pens, pencils and highlighters, boxes of A4 paper and drawing pins.

Bishop filled up the water cooler then said:

'I'll be back in a minute.'

After he left, Holly took out her own files and scrapbooks on The Animal from her backpack and put them in order on her desk. She had brought the framed photo from the dining room table of her wearing the blue party dress and holding a yellow balloon that said 'Happy Birthday Dad', and put it by the computer.

She found a whiteboard on wheels in a room along the hall, grabbed a Sharpie and wrote *John Newsome / Sandra Newsome – Sunday, 11 August 2019*. Then she wrote *Annie Wilkes* underneath and put a question mark by her name.

Chief Constable Franks had given them the Annie Wilkes file and she spent the next thirty minutes reading through it.

When Bishop came back he brought with him a kettle, mugs, sugar, milk, tea, coffee and hot chocolate. He set everything on the desk by the wall and put the kettle on.

'Coffee?'

'Please.'

They sat opposite each other and sipped from their charity-shop mugs. A few seconds of quiet in their new surroundings until there was a knock at the door. It opened and a private courier entered, wheeling in a dozen boxes of evidence marked *cold case.*

'Twelve boxes for DI Bishop?'

'That's right,' said Bishop, 'just put them over by the wall. Do I need to sign something?'

'Jesus, this place is dismal,' the courier said as he held out a clipboard for Bishop to sign. 'Why are you down here?'

'Cutbacks,' Bishop said.

The courier left and Bishop locked the door.

They sifted through the boxes until they found the Carstairs files. There were six in all that they carried over to their desks and the two of them began to rifle through the contents.

Bishop looked up from the file in front of him. 'Regardless of the outcome of this investigation, to be successful we have to work on the basis that The Animal *is* alive and *is* killing again.'

'Agreed.'

'I think the best way to tackle this is to split up,' Bishop said. 'One of us should concentrate on Carstairs, while the other looks into Annie Wilkes. I'll take Carstairs: talk to the prison, hospital and security guards to see if there are any holes in their security that The Animal would have been able to exploit and somehow escape. Also, someone was cremated on the day of the funeral and if it wasn't The Animal we need to find out who it was.'

Holly nodded.

'Then I'll try and find out why The Animal is so interested in Annie Wilkes,' she said. 'Let's start an incident board.'

They stuck up all eighteen of the victim files in chronological order from left to right on the wall below the frosted window and walking feet: crime scene reports, autopsy notes and photos of the pieces of jewellery stolen from each victim. Holly's hands were cold as she taped her mother and father's photos to the wall. She touched a finger to her lips and kissed them both before she turned away and watched Bishop place a photo of The Animal in the centre of the wall.

It was a police photo from 2016. He was gaunt with a protruding jaw and cheekbones and short blond hair. His eyes were dark, almost black and even now as Holly stared at them they seemed to pierce right through her. There was an emptiness, a vacancy within, but nothing to give any indication of what he was. No tell-tale sign of psychopathy, just a steady neutral gaze that contradicted the murderous thoughts that spun inside his head.

'There was never a pattern found with any of his victims,' Holly said. 'He used a variety of disguises to make it more difficult for anyone who saw him to identify him. Different hair colours, different wigs, different costumes as well. SOCO found about a dozen outfits in one of his houses: he masqueraded as a plumber, a carpenter, a security guard and a policeman, to name a few.'

'A policeman?'

'It's not uncommon for serial killers to dress as authority figures. It feeds their ego, but also makes it easier to access property, and victims will automatically place a certain amount of trust in someone in uniform.' She stood, Sharpie in hand, surveying the photos of the victims. 'Each kill method was slightly different, and the only part of his signature that was the same was that he always stole a piece of jewellery.'

'So he would have taken something from the Newsomes?'

'If he's keeping to the same signature, and I think it would be hard for him to stop that now. If it's The Animal, he'll want us to know it's him.'

'So we need to do an inventory of all the jewellery they owned?'

'Yes.'

'It should be under their home insurance, I'll get on to it. And this was the case with every murder?'

'Apart from one.'

She went to the board and pulled down a photo of a silver bracelet with the word *amore* engraved on it. She passed it to Bishop, who stared at it and frowned.

'I don't remember ever seeing this bracelet in the inventory.'

'That's because it's not there. The bracelet was taken from victim number sixteen, Lucy Le Bas, the cardiac physiologist. She was the only victim whose piece of jewellery has never been recovered.'

'So this bracelet should have been found with victims number seventeen and eighteen?'

'My parents,' Holly said.

'How many times did they search the property?'

'Three, according to the police report. The house has been renovated since the murders so there's no way anyone would find it now.'

Bishop handed the photo back and went to the whiteboard.

'Let's assume the Newsomes are his first kills since he became active again,' he said. 'What's interesting is the message on the wall. Was there ever anything like that at any of the other crime scenes?'

'Only one. Victim number eleven – Tibor Slovenski.' She rifled through the file on the desk and handed it over.

'He was an Armenian chef in Shoreditch. Thursday nights he locked up the restaurant by himself, but on the twenty-third of September 1989 he never made it home. When the owner came to open the restaurant the next morning the front door was unlocked and Tibor was stuffed in the oven. He had been stabbed once in the chest and both his hands had been amputated and were glued to the taps in the bathroom.'

'Glued?'

'Page thirteen for the photos. They were positioned as if he was turning the taps on or off, as if they were somehow still attached to his body.'

'And the message?'

'*To kill you must first remove your fear.* It was written on the bathroom mirror in fat from the deep fat fryer. He wrote it as a direct response to one of the questions that had been asked about him in the press. "How does The Animal find it so easy to kill?" He wanted people to understand him. He thought he was educating them.'

'So he read the newspapers?'

'Religiously, and he'll be doing the same now.'

Bishop rifled through the rest of the files on the desk.

'Physiology, prison records, diet – I want the oncology reports.'

'They're here.' Holly handed them over.

'Thank you.' A quick skim: 'Gary Fitzroy was the cancer specialist who treated him for his chemo.'

Holly saw him make a note and she pulled out a bag of USB sticks from a box. There were sheets of paper with a list of psychologists' names, some from different departments, different prisons and even different parts of the world.

'What are those?' Bishop said.

'Interviews with The Animal's doctors and shrinks.'

She put them to one side, opened a folder and found a series of dark photographs of a living room and bedroom. Resting on every surface and hanging from the walls were dozens of tiny wind-up tin toys that looked almost alive in the photos. There were soldiers and Zeppelins and boxers on springs, and Oriental merchants and clowns and Easter bunnies that had silver-blue eggs in their baskets. They were all old with chipped paint and broken limbs.

She turned one of the photos over. On the back was written:

Late nineteenth-century German lithographic tin toys found at
320 Kilbourne Road, Sebastian Carstairs' final residence.

She had never seen anything like this in the cases she'd worked on and studied, so she asked Bishop about them.

He squinted at the photos and pulled a face.

'I have no idea,' he said. 'What are they?'

'It says they're nineteenth-century German tin lithograph toys. They were found at The Animal's house after he was arrested. It was a passion of his, apparently. It says here he had similar toys when he was a kid.'

'That might explain a few things.'

A few bundles of handwritten letters tied together with

string caught her attention. Some of the envelopes were decorated with red crayon hearts. She opened the first one, started reading:

'You should see some of this,' she said frowning: '"I feel as though I know you. Please marry me and I will help you become the man I know you can be." And here's another: "You were young once, a child, and I see that innocence in you still. Let me capture it for you and show everyone what a lover you are – not a killer."'

'Seriously?' said Bishop.

'Richard Ramirez murdered at least thirteen people in the mid 1990s in California and ended up marrying a prison groupie called Doreen Lioy while he was behind bars. She wrote over seventy-five letters to him. Here's another one: "I love you, Sebastian, and together we could have beautiful children and I would never cheat on you." My God, he must have over a dozen offers of marriage in here.'

'I'm doing something wrong, aren't I?'

It made her smile, then he said:

'Let's talk about Annie Wilkes.'

Holly picked up the file Chief Franks had given her and passed it over.

'She was diagnosed with bipolar disorder when she was fourteen,' she said, 'and was found guilty of murdering her brother, Len Wilkes, and his wife, Colette, in 1993. She stabbed them both multiple times with a kitchen knife.'

'Did she have a history of violence?'

'Only against herself. Several suicide attempts when she was a kid, then her mother and father took her to Ossington.'

'What's that?'

'It's a bit like Wetherington or The Priory. A self-help

and self-admittance hospital for people with mental health problems. She had ECT, was released and her psychiatrist prescribed her gabapentin, which is an anti-epileptic, and Clozapine, which is an antipsychotic. After her parents died, she was arrested a dozen or so times for possession of cannabis. No overtly aggressive behaviour noted unless she was off her meds.'

'Who was her doctor?'

'A psychiatrist called Derek Martin. He still takes care of her now and visits her once a week in New Hall Prison.'

'What about Annie's husband?'

'Ex-husband. She took his name and the two of them got divorced after six months.'

'Where is he now?'

'Got killed in a car crash on the M3 coming out of London, that was in 1991.'

'And then two years later she kills her brother and his wife.'

'In the police report it says Annie had been evicted from her flat for not paying the rent and was staying with her brother. According to the neighbours she'd been sleeping there for two weeks. Toxicology found drugs in her blood, sleeping pills and MDMA. She would have been as high as a kite when she killed them. Her defence lawyers and psychiatrist have always maintained her innocence and said she blacked out and woke up after taking some sleeping pills, remembered finding the bloody knife, but instead of calling the police, she cleaned it and went back to sleep.'

'Great defence. Where is New Hall?'

'Yorkshire. I've made an appointment to see her tomorrow morning, and I'll talk to Derek Martin afterwards. I'll get the train from Euston tonight.'

'And Cassandra,' he said. 'Carstairs' sister. We have an out-of-date phone number, no National Insurance number, no tax records and no driver's licence.'

'Do we have a photo?'

Holly had seen her at the funeral, had even spoken to her briefly, but the woman had been wearing a veil and she wouldn't have been able to identify her.

'This is all we've got from the police records,' Bishop said as he handed Holly a single black-and-white photograph of Cassandra. It had come to the Met via Border Force from Germany and had the words *zwolf Jahre alt* (twelve years old) written on the back. She was small and blonde with a mouth that looked uncomfortable smiling.

'There's also these,' he said, and handed over a stack of old newspapers. 'The press didn't exactly make life easy for her.'

The Most Hated Woman in Britain was one tabloid headline. *Animal's sister – Is she as mad as her brother?* Read another. There were photos of her beneath the stories, invariably shying away from the cameras and in most of them she looked as if she had been crying.

'She's probably been in hiding all these years,' Holly said. 'And I don't blame her. How old would she be now?'

'Fifty-seven.'

His brow was furrowed and she wondered what he was thinking.

'Bishop?'

He still didn't look sure, but he said:

'I want to ask Max to help us find Cassandra.'

'Max? What happened to the two-person rule?'

'He specialises in surveillance and can be trusted. Are you okay with him being here?'

Max had been Special Forces with Bishop in Afghanistan. Bishop had brought him to watch over Holly on the Pickford case and he had ended up saving her life.

'How is he?' she said.

'On drugs, paranoid and broke.'

'Bring him in.'

She checked her watch.

'I have to leave. I'll be back tomorrow afternoon.'

Fourteen

Holly caught a taxi to Euston station.

The train journey to York took four hours and dinner consisted of a sandwich from a vending machine. In the hotel she lay on the bed. She had numbered the USB sticks of The Animal's therapy sessions and plugged the first into her Mac. It appeared on screen with a date: 11.12.15. She pressed play. A few seconds of silence, followed by static, then:

'. . . I saw the devil and I ran towards it.'

'Why did you run towards him?'

Two voices.

She stopped the recording.

The first voice was guttural and soft, but she recognised The Animal immediately. The German accent was there, very slight, and sometimes he sounded almost American. The second voice was English, nasal, and a couple of octaves higher. She started the recording again:

'Him? You think the devil is a him?'

'The devil is whomever you want it to be,' The Animal said. 'That's the thing about the devil. To me he could be a friend who comforts me in times of need. To you he could be the bogeyman or the shadow by the door when you turn the lights off at night. Do you get scared at night, Hedley?'

Hedley?

She stopped the tape and referenced the list of psychiatrists and found the name Hedley Phelps. She circled it and went into the hospital files she had brought with her. There were a few details about his employment record and she pulled out a small postcard-sized photo. Hedley Phelps looked like an overstuffed kid. He seemed quite the character dressed in a white suit with a trilby hat on his head, his pudgy hands folded expectantly in his lap. On his breast pocket was a name tag that said, unsurprisingly, Hedley Phelps. There was an address in Mayfair, a high-end residential area of London, with his mobile number and his emergency contact was listed as his wife, Sylvia Phelps. Holly checked her watch – it was nine o'clock and she gave him a call on his mobile that went straight to voicemail. She left a message asking him to call her about Sebastian Carstairs and their cold case investigations, then went back to the USB recording:

'Do you get scared at night, Hedley?'

'Sometimes,' Hedley said, and there was a nervous cough, 'but we need to talk about you, not me, Sebastian.'

'Then let's talk. I have very little conversation with anybody else in here. What shall we talk about? Schrödinger's cat or Pavlov's dogs?'

'You like animals?'

'Cats are too wilful to control, so I prefer dogs. I love their obedience and their willingness to suffer. Have you ever killed a dog?'

'No.'

'When you strangle a dog, it doesn't understand what's going on. It thinks this is another form of love. Everything is love at the end of the day.'

'Everything?'

'Yes, but you need passion first. You lack passion, Hedley. Don't be offended, it's an observation, that's all. Whenever I see you, you walk very slowly as if you are never in a hurry. Your shoulders are rounded, your neck strained downwards, staring at the floor or at your feet. Are you ashamed of yourself?'

'Ashamed? No, I don't—'

'You walk like a child. It's a social awkwardness. You rarely make eye contact and when you do it's fleeting. Do you ever stare upwards at the horizon or the sky? Are you depressed?'

'No.'

'Are you still having problems with Sylvia?'

'She and I have talked about things, but I feel as though she's not being honest with me.'

'About the affair she had?'

'Yes.'

'Do you think she's still seeing the other man? What was his name? Brian?

'Brandon.'

'That's right, Brandon. That's a strong name. He sounds like a movie star.'

'He's not a movie star, Sebastian, he's a gym instructor. Can we not talk about this?'

Holly paused the recording and took a second. It was intriguing. It was as if Sebastian was conducting the session, as if he were the therapist. Starting again:

'I'm sorry, Hedley. These sessions help me so much and I love helping you in return, you're a good friend to me in here.

I just want to help. I want to find the old Hedley that you've talked about. The happy Hedley. I want to know what drives you to get out of bed in the mornings?'

'My work.'

'There needs to be more than that. And that's the difference between us. What got me out of bed every morning was my passion.'

'For your work?'

'For my killing. As heinous as that sounds to you and to the rest of the world, that was my passion. My personality was swallowed up by my passion, my whole life was. When I killed my first victim I told her I loved her. It gave me shivers when I said it.'

'You've never told me that before.'

'I want to share these things with you. Insights into my life, into what has made me into me. It's important to say these things out loud sometimes. What was your relationship like with your parents?'

'My mother was good to me. She was a good woman. My father was cold and hostile. He scared me.'

'Did you ever think about killing him?'

'No, of course not. I'm not . . .'

'We all have anger, Hedley, and it's nothing to be ashamed of. I wanted to kill my father when I was eight years old, that's how I felt in those days. He died and then it was just myself and my sister.'

'Did you always get on with Cassandra?'

'Yes. She looked up to me. She would play with me and our toys.'

'Teddy bears, dolls? What did you play with?'

'Our toys were made of tin.'

'Tin?'

Holly had brought the photo of the tin toys with her and she stared at them curiously as she carried on listening.

'Lithographic tin,' Sebastian said. 'It's a very German thing. Beautifully made and very realistic.'

'I'd like to see these tin toys, Sebastian.'

'I still have some, kept somewhere safe. When we were children, we would spend hours with them, making up stories and adventures.'

'What sort of adventures?'

'Escapism I think you'd call it now. I had a tin soldier called Wagner. He used to go everywhere with me. He used to protect me.'

'Protect you?'

'From my father.'

Holly's phone rang. It was Bishop.

She paused the recording.

'You got there safe?' he said.

'I did and am enjoying strong tea on a good mattress.'

'Sounds like heaven.'

'Are you still in the basement?'

'I've just had a quick workout with the dumbbells. Combining crime fighting with fitness – what could possibly go wrong?'

She smiled: 'What have you found out?'

'Initial conversations went pretty much as expected: according to the prison there is no chance in hell that he could have escaped and no chance in hell that he could have faked the cancer and somehow survived. Tomorrow I'm planning to drive over to Broadmoor and the Phoenix Hospital and chat with the security team and the doctors. You always get better answers face-to-face. How about you?'

'I'm listening to the recordings of The Animal's therapy sessions with his lead therapist, Hedley Phelps. I put in a call and left him a message, I think we should set up a meeting with him.'

'Okay. What does The Animal talk about?'

'Killing dogs and playing with his tin toys and sister. There are a few more recordings to listen to, I'll get through what I can, then I'll call it a night.'

'All right, I'll see you tomorrow.'

'Drive safe, Bishop.'

She had said it automatically, but felt a bit silly afterwards.

'I will do, I promise. Night, Holly.'

Fifteen

Holly's pillow was crunched beneath her head and the only light in the bedroom was from the computer. It illuminated her face in a soft blue.

She was making her way through the USB sticks. Some had recorded sessions with other therapists that were short and held no new information, two of them had been blank and two had recordings of a woman's voice dictating an editorial piece on the safety of environmental practices in the USA, and one of the legal rights of a book deal in Europe. Holly's eyes were closing as she listened to another one.

The Animal and Hedley talking again:

'Tell me more about Wagner, your tin toy soldier.'

'Wagner was always with me. Even though he was made of tin he was so strong. He comforted me, like a pacifier – I think that's what they call them in America.'

'He calmed you down?'

'Calmed me down when my father was close. I used to take him everywhere with me.'

'As a child.'

'As an adult as well.'

'Did you take him with you when you started killing?'

'Every time. I brought him here with me today to meet you.'

There was the rifling of a paper bag and The Animal said:

'Here he is.'

'Oh, wow.'

'You can hold him.'

'Really? Thank you.'

'But be careful, he's very special to me.'

'Of course.'

A few seconds of silence and in her mind Holly could see The Animal handing over the tin toy to Hedley. It was like an exchange or an emotional bribe.

'He looks so lifelike,' Hedley said.

'He has seen everything I have. He watched me kill, he watched me as I watched them.'

'Them?'

'My victims.'

A few more seconds of silence then the paper rifled again and Hedley said:

'Thank you, Sebastian, that showed a great level of trust.'

'Because I do trust you, Hedley. I trust you more than you know.'

The recording stopped then started almost immediately, but now it was a different conversation and a different energy.

'How do you know when someone is dead?' Hedley said.

'Their whole body just relaxes. I used to call them rag dolls. When the rag doll's arms and legs flop, that's when you know. I used to like to hurt people and I had no remorse. I could have done it over and over again without it bothering me.'

'Did you think of yourself as an assassin?'

'You make it sound so exotic. I was just a serial killer.'

'You still are?'

'Of course not. I wanted to stop and that was why I handed myself in. I knew I was doing terrible things, and the good voice was trying to talk to me and convince me to stop and then there was always the other voice. The bad voice.'

'Which we've talked about many times, Sebastian. Is that voice still there? Does it still reach out to you?'

'No. That voice is quiet now, and working with you and these therapy sessions have changed my outlook on life, on people and on what I've done. The drugs which you prescribe for me have – how should I say – curbed my appetite beyond all recognition. I don't really know how they work, and perhaps I don't need to, but I feel different now, more than I have ever felt. I feel changed, more alive, does that make sense?'

'It does, Sebastian, and that's wonderful to hear.'

'When I was first brought to this prison my mindset was so different and if I had been let out I would have killed again. In those days, had you unshackled me, I would have killed you. Now we can sit here with no restraints and no guards, that's incredible progress.'

'It is.'

'Looking back objectively, the killing was never anything personal and people used to get that wrong. It was simply a compulsion that needed to be acted on. It was what I dreamed about. Stabbing people, strangling them, suffocating them.'

'Always up close and personal?'

'I wanted to talk to them just before they left, I always wanted to say goodbye.'

'What did you want them to think as they died?'

Holly sat up in bed. An image of her mother and father swam in her mind.

'I wanted them to think of me. I wanted them to see me, feel me and smell me. I saw surprise, shock, fear. I've seen so many emotions in people's eyes, I've seen everything and then I've watched the blankness come over them. I always stayed until it left. Until they went limp.'

'Like rag dolls.'

'Like rag dolls.'

'Rag dolls,' Holly said under her breath and slid off the bed and turned the kettle on. She sat by the desk and listened to the voices that now sounded unnaturally loud in the dark room.

'I shudder at my past, Hedley,' The Animal said. 'In those days I used to enjoy what I did because I used to think of it as my job. How bizarre is that? Do you enjoy your job?'

'I do. It's very fulfilling. And especially with a patient like you, I'm getting the results that I've been trained for and I'm helping someone change.'

'You should get an award, Hedley, for the way you've helped me.'

'No, no, I'm not interested in any accolades.'

'Recognition then for your hard work? Your research on me should be rewarded. I could help you. Perhaps you could write a book? We could write a book. Together. About me, about how you have changed me.'

'I don't know. It's—'

'It's what? You don't think you deserve this, Hedley? Well, you do.'

'Perhaps a conversation for another day. Right now, can we talk about your father again?'

'The man who smelled of salt?'

Sebastian had been born in the old town of Lüneburg, about fifty kilometres south-east of Hamburg, that had been built on a salt-dome which was the town's original source of income.

'My father spent ten hours a day in the salt mines. Every night before he walked into the house he took his boots off outside and shook his jacket, but he still smelled of salt and the dirty brown crystals followed him wherever he went. He had salt in his hair, in the pores of his skin. His breath smelled of salt and his hands were as hard as rock with callouses the size of conkers. His hands were always raw and used to crack and bleed and we would rub cream into them at night.'

'We?'

'Cassandra and I. It was a ritual we had to follow every night.'

'That ended with sexual abuse.'

'Yes. My father and mother left their mark on both of us. It's amazing what you can get used to when you're a child, the pain and the violence.'

Holly emptied a sachet of hot chocolate into a cup and added a mini-pot of UHT milk.

'And this was when you were very young?'

'Five or six years old. I don't remember a day *not* being abused. They are the only memories I have of my childhood. I used to hide in the bed when he got home, with Wagner, my tin toy, and I would hold him under the covers with me and I would pretend that he was me and I was him.'

'Did it help?'

'Sometimes.'

'Were the assaults worse when your father drank?'

'It made no difference. He was mean either way.'

'Was it easy emotionally to leave your father, despite the fact he abused you?'

'I think I would have killed him if I had stayed.'

'But you let him live. Did you ever let any of your victims go?'

'Once.'

'Who?'

'I never killed children,' Sebastian said. 'Children were special to me.'

The kettle started to whistle. Holly turned it off and poured the hot water into the cup. She stirred the hot chocolate slowly. Listening carefully.

'Children are beautiful.'

'But children grow up to be adults, Sebastian.'

'Yes.'

'And adults are different?'

'Because adults have a choice. You can choose to come in here, to dress nicely, to go home and beat your wife and children or to not beat your wife and children. A child doesn't get that opportunity. A child will sit at home and wait to be loved. A child will fall asleep at the top of the stairs and hope that his father will notice him when he walks past and leaves the house for work. Because they know no better, children will love you unconditionally. Regardless of the outcome, the child will always love you.'

'The child you let go. Do you remember who it was?'

'I did a lot of research into who I was going to kill. I owed it to them to be thorough, but the girl wasn't supposed to be there.'

'It was a girl?'

Holly shivered and her whole body went cold.

'A girl who is a woman now. She'll be in her thirties, her mid-thirties.'

'Do you think she will remember you?'

'She thinks of me every day, she won't be able to help herself,' said Sebastian.

Sixteen

The Animal didn't have nightmares, but the next morning he woke with a start at the sound of a voice.

He had been dreaming he was a child again and back in his old house in Lüneburg, and he had been visiting the salt mine with his father. The first time his father had taken him there he had been five years old. Down in the jerky cage, through the shafts and labyrinthine passageways, past the underground lake and the dozens of statues and the chapel carved out of rock salt by the miners. His father had left him in the darkness and given him a piece of rock salt to suck on. Sebastian had pretended it was sugar and sometimes the silver and brown granules actually tasted sweet on his tongue until it made him sick. To this day, whenever he thought of his father he could taste the salt like angry bile in the back of his throat.

When his father came home from work he would sit in his favourite chair and lick the salt off his lips while he and Cassandra rubbed the cream into his cracked and bleeding hands. Some nights his father would stare straight ahead as if in a daze and others his empty-pool eyes would sway from side to side, from child to child as he decided which one to take. His mother would watch from the lounge leather sofa, pretending to be asleep, but Sebastian could always see the glint of her slitted eyes in the firelight, watching them with dark thoughts in her head. And if she decided to join them she would take off all of her jewellery, piece by piece: rings, necklaces and bangles, and lay them on the side table and smile an empty smile. And Sebastian would stare at the jewellery as it sparkled in the firelight and wonder what it meant.

Rubbing the cream in faster and faster until it was done and then his father would pull himself from the chair and take one of their hands and lead them away, and if it wasn't him, Sebastian would sit and watch his sister disappear into the room with no name and if it was him he would try and walk with his shoulders back and his head high to show his sister he had no fear, although inside he was already melting.

When it was done Sebastian would come back outside to the living room holding his mother's hand and he would go to bed with no words and put Wagner under his pillow. And very soon his sister would come and lie next to him and whisper:

'Thank you.'

And they would hold hands and bury their heads into each other and say:

'If they can't see us, they can't find us.'

Over and over again until their tears dried on the pillows and they both fell sound asleep.

'What did you say?'

There was the voice again. The voice that had woken The Animal from his dream, and for a split second he was disorientated and didn't know who the voice belonged to or where he was. He had been with his sister and Wagner and—

'Hello?' The voice said. 'My wife, my wife . . . I can't hear her any more. Why won't you talk to me?'

The Animal opened his eyes. An old man and an old woman were tied to chairs by their hands and feet under a dim ceiling light in the centre of the bedroom. The old man twitched slightly but the woman was motionless. The Animal watched them from the shadows, sitting on the floor with his back to the wall.

'My wife . . .' the old man said.

'Your wife is a rag doll.'

'A what?'

'A rag doll. A *stoffpuppe*, a Margarete Steiff.'

'I don't understand.' The old man coughed. 'You must talk to me. I thought you might need help. I can help.'

'Help?'

'Yes, help. You were talking about salt. About how salt smelled. I didn't know salt was like that.'

'You didn't know?'

'No.'

'Sweat. Tears. And the sea,' The Animal said.

'What?'

'That's where salt is most abundant.'

The Animal stood up and the change in the man was immediate.

'Please let me see my wife,' he whimpered. 'Please. She is diabetic and needs her pills. I don't know what to do. I can't . . . I can't bear it . . .' Somehow he managed to shuffle his feet and the chair scraped back a few inches. 'Look – I don't understand. Why won't you let me see her? And you? I want to see you. Why do you hide in the shadows?'

'I don't like the light.'
'Two men talking to each other. I should be able to see you.'
'Is that what we are?' The Animal said. 'Two men talking?'
And he felt the rage coming upon him.

Seventeen

'My name is Harriet, but the inmates call me Rex. As in T-Rex.'

The female guard at New Hall Prison who walked with Holly down the dimly lit corridor was stocky and strong. She had her sleeves rolled up to show off the tattoos on her forearms. Holly had informed the warden why she was there and Rex had volunteered to oversee and make the introductions.

'Annie Wilkes is in lockdown again,' Rex said. 'She's got a cell to herself, but she's not getting much peace at night after her transfer from maximum security. She's back in the Rivendell Wing – inmates at risk of self-harm and suicide – we have to keep them away from the general prison population. We've got a lot of "screamers" in there who stay awake making all sorts of racket until their meds kick in. I do a ten-hour shift, twelve at the weekend, and I'm shattered when I come off the clock. The place is a madhouse – pardon the pun.'

'Will she be sedated?'

Rex checked her watch.

'Nope. Meds are at nine thirty, after chow. She'll be fine.' She raised her voice to the camera in the wall: 'Open door three.'

A loud buzz and the metal door slid to one side. A new corridor.

The noise from the screaming and cursing women was horrendous.

'Eventually they exhaust themselves, but it's like this every morning and every night.'

'Anything I should know about her?'

'Give her this.' She handed Holly a cooking book. It was well-worn and used. 'She's a keen baker and it will make her more amenable. Our specialist unit has its own private kitchen for convicts to use and Annie helps grow vegetables in the garden. She's doing an NVQ in hairdressing, but her eyesight's shit so I wouldn't trust her to cut you a bob. We don't consider her dangerous to anybody other than herself, but don't provoke her. She wanted to meet you in her cell, it's her comfort zone, but I'll be outside and the door will be kept open.'

'Thank you, Rex.'

They stopped at a wall that had been repainted so many times the surface looked like pale glue.

'Open two-two-five!'

A metallic clunk and the door unlocked. Rex grabbed the latch and slid it to the left and Holly stepped inside.

Annie Wilkes sat on her bed with a pillow clutched to her stomach. She was overweight, her eyesight was failing and she wore massive glasses that made her eyes seem unnaturally large.

'Hi, Annie, my name is Holly. Thank you so much for agreeing to talk to me today.'

The bug eyes stared back at her.

'I've forgotten why you're here,' Annie said. Her voice was surprisingly delicate.

'I'm a counsellor and psychotherapist.'

'I've already got a shrink, Derek Martin, he's been looking after me for years. I like Derek. I have a girl-crush on him. I don't need to talk to another one.'

Rex poked her head around the door.

'Be nice to our guest, Annie. She's come all the way from London to see you.'

'I brought you something,' Holly said and handed her the cooking book.

Annie inspected it carefully. Blinked at a few of the colour photos.

'I like that one . . . I like that one . . . that's a pretty picture . . .'

'Rex tells me you're a good baker?'

'I make a mean crust pastry. You can sit if you'd like.'

Holly did, on the only chair in the cell by the washbasin. The room was sparse and the same blue-glue as the corridor. On a stand beside the bed was a copy of *Alice in Wonderland*.

'How many times have you read that book?' Holly said.

'I read bits of it every day. Have done for the last ten years.'

'Who's your favourite character?'

'The dormouse, because he gets to sleep. I have anxiety. I'm scared of pretty much everything and everyone. I worry about what I eat for breakfast and what I'm going to do in the afternoon after my nap. But I'm wearing my big-girl pants today so I'm trying not to worry about you.'

'You don't have to worry about me, Annie. I know you have bipolar disorder and I know it's not your fault. I know how sensitive you are.'

'I get manic and depressive at the same time. The voices in

my head are my stupid emotions. Most people don't understand and that's when I get angry because I can't express how I feel.'

'Like something's going to snap inside of you?'

'Yes.'

'But you're not suicidal now, are you?'

'Not now, and that's why Derek is so good. He's really helped and I'm a functioning member of the prison society. I had manic episodes and I was depressed when I first came here. I wanted to die and I had the motivation to make it happen. Mix anger and energy and that's a bad combo. Like fries and mayo. Do you like fries and mayo?'

'I've never tried it.'

'Don't waste a day. I'm a ketchup girl.'

'And how long have you been here now, Annie?'

The eyes went wider behind the glasses.

'Rex?' she said.

'Twenty-six years,' came the voice from the corridor.

'Do you remember why you're here?' Holly said.

'They said I killed my brother and his wife.'

'That's right. Would it be okay for me to ask you a few questions about that?'

'Ask me whatever you want. My brain was like sherbet back then and it's still fuzzy on a lot of things. I used to get blackouts, so it's hard to say if it's my memory you'll be listening to or what all the other people have told me happened. One thing I can tell you though is I didn't kill 'em.'

'No?'

'You don't kill what you love, do you?'

'No, you don't. And you loved your brother?'

'Len always made me laugh. Colette was a skinny little

thing, she was French. She would cook for us and make fresh croissants. If she saw me baking now she'd be proud of me.'

'So you were living with them?'

'Yes.'

'And you had a blackout on the day of the murder?'

Annie shrugged her heavy shoulders.

'Annie?'

'According to the doctors. They said I was high on MDMA when I stabbed them. How many times, Rex?'

'Forty-two and thirty-three.'

'They said I stabbed my brother forty-two times, and Colette thirty-three times.'

'And do you remember what happened to the knife?'

'According to the lawyers I picked it up, cleaned it and put it back in the kitchen. Now why would I do that?'

'I don't know.'

'If I'd have killed them I wouldn't have put it back in the rack now, would I?'

Her breathing suddenly became laboured.

'Do you need some water, Annie?' Holly said.

'How long, Rex?'

'Twenty minutes and you get your pills,' Rex said.

'Twenty minutes. I have to stick to my routine and that's important. After my pills I come back here for quiet time, recess and physical activity, which for me means lying on the bed, then TV time, study recreation time and group therapy. Then it's visitor hours, but you're my visitor today, then tonight it's movie night – what is it tonight, Rex?'

'*Sleepless in Seattle.*'

'Have I seen that?'

'Yep.'

'And then lights out. Repeat, repeat, repeat.'

'I won't interrupt your routine,' Holly said. She watched the woman for some time and wondered if she had killed Len and Colette. Blackouts, memory loss. It was always possible.

'Did you ever have any friends come over to the house, Annie?'

'Friends? I didn't have too many friends back then. If I did, I don't remember them.'

'What about your brother? Or maybe Colette? Did they ever have people visit?'

'Sometimes. What do you mean?'

'Someone who came inside the house maybe a week or two before the murder. Maybe you talked to them or saw them? Would you remember something like that?'

Annie screwed her eyes up. She made a guttural noise, concentrating hard. Then . . .

'No.' A beat. 'How long, Rex?' she said.

'Eighteen minutes. You okay, Annie?'

'I think I'm done here, Rex.'

Rex appeared at the door and gave Holly a nod.

Disappointed, Holly stood up. Then she reached into her jacket and took out a photo.

'Can I show you a photo, please, Annie?'

Annie squirmed and shot a look at Rex.

'You don't have to look at it if you're not comfortable,' the guard said.

'Is it a photo of my brother or Colette?'

'No, it's some writing on a wall,' Holly said.

Annie took the photo, squinted at it and removed her glasses. She held it an inch from her eyes with fingers that were red with flaking skin at the knuckles. She kept it there for a good minute, moving it from left to right and back again.

'And your name is Holly?'

'That's right.'

'So why is my name there with you and who wrote my name?'

'We think it was written by a man called Sebastian Carstairs.'

Annie's face shifted slightly. Her next words were timid and barely audible:

'*The Animal*.'

'You remember him?' Holly said. 'He killed a lot of people many years ago.'

'Why does he want to know what's wrong with me?'

'I don't know, Annie. That's what we're trying to find out.'

'Is he a friend of yours?'

'No.'

She stared at Holly with her big fish eyes.

'There's nothing wrong with me, Holly Wakefield. There's nothing wrong with me. I'm *Walking tall*.'

Holly felt shivers on her arm.

'What did you say? Annie? What did you just say?'

'I don't owe you an explanation. I don't owe you shit. I am not here for your entertainment! What are you going to do? Put me in prison? I'm already here! There is nothing wrong with me! Twenty-six years, right, Rex?'

'Come on now, Annie, deep breaths, don't go there.' To Holly through gritted teeth: 'You need to leave now.'

Rex handed the photo back and Holly exited the cell and walked fast along the corridor.

An alarm went off and two guards hurtled past her. Above the banging and the raging noise, all Holly could hear was Annie shouting:

'THERE IS NOTHING WRONG WITH ME!'

Eighteen

'I have always maintained Annie's innocence and so has she.'

Annie's psychiatrist, Derek Martin, made tea for them both, then sat. Not behind his desk in the prison's east wing, but on the sofa, an arm's length from Holly. He was a timid man, very thin, with elegant fingers that he steepled as he spoke.

'I've put in five appeals against her conviction, the first one dating back to the day of her sentencing. It didn't even make it past the judge, let alone the Court of Appeal. Nor did appeals number two or three, or four. Number five made it past the judge and we were both hopeful for a while, but that was four years ago and, without new evidence, the answer is always going to be the same. No appeal and no new inquiry.'

'Have you contacted the Criminal Cases Review Commission?'

'I have. As far as I'm concerned there has been a terrible miscarriage of justice, yet again there seems to be complete apathy on their part.' He took a sip of his tea. 'I won't stop trying, of course, but part of me believes Annie will be spending the rest of her life here at New Hall, which in a way will be a relief.'

'What do you mean?'

'She has become institutionalised. She has no space of her own, no choice where to go, what to eat or who to spend time with. She has chronic health conditions: anxiety, depression, hypervigilance and a disabling combination of social withdrawal and aggression. How could she possibly cope if she was released? She has never been what we would consider a normally operating person, and now she's stuck in this hideous slow-death that none of us can fix. What was your opinion of her, Holly?'

'I liked her,' Holly said.

'Do you think she's a killer?'

'I don't know. I'd have to talk to her more and examine—'

'But what is your gut telling you?' the man said softly.

She knew Derek was searching for support, but she had to be careful. It was, however, a question she had been asking herself ever since she had met Wilkes. She wanted to believe the woman who loved baking, who wore almost comedic-sized glasses and who loved the dormouse in *Alice in Wonderland* was innocent, but she also knew there was reasonable doubt. She had no alibi for the time of the murders, and no other suspects were ever brought forward. However . . .

'My gut is telling me I should trust her,' Holly finally said.

Derek smiled for the first time.

'Thank you for saying that. Would you like more tea?'

'Please, thank you.'

He poured as he spoke:

'You mentioned you wanted to see Annie because of a case you're working on? Can you be more specific?'

'I can't tell you who it involves, but . . .'

She removed the photo of the writing on the wall from

her jacket and passed it over. Derek took it and stared at it, frowning.

'What is this?'

'It was found at a crime scene, written in blood on one of the walls.'

'*What is wrong with Annie Wilkes*?' he whispered. And then his body straightened and his eyes seemed more alert.

'Somebody knows something,' he said. 'Annie may have an ally at last.'

Holly shuddered at the thought.

Nineteen

As Holly was leaving the prison, Bishop emerged from the basement incident room tired and somewhat anxious.

For the past two hours he had been running police checks on their people of interest: Gary Fitzroy, the Phoenix Hospital oncologist who administered the chemotherapy to The Animal, Hedley Phelps, The Animal's therapist, Cassandra, his sister, and Evan Wright and Michael Levan – the Broadmoor security team. None of them had any convictions and all the police checks came back clean.

The security team were from a company called Securi-Check, who were based in London and had contracts with Broadmoor, Belmarsh and Wormwood Scrubs. The two men appointed to The Animal's detail were in their thirties, seemed affable and eager to talk. They had worked for the same private security firm for the past ten years and explained their transport routine as follows:

Sebastian Carstairs was chaperoned to and from Broadmoor to the Phoenix Hospital by both guards during his cancer treatments. After his treatment was over, he was allowed to go to the toilet to freshen up.

'Did he go by himself?'

'Yes.'

Then he was put back in his wheelchair and pushed from the ward along the corridor to the Two Palms Café on Level Two of the hospital, where he was given a cold drink and a biscuit. Sometimes he wanted neither and preferred to sit with a cold towel covering his head and sometimes he just wanted to leave. Whatever his decision, the security guards escorted him to their van where he was loaded inside and taken back to Broadmoor. The journey time was ninety-three minutes and they never stopped anywhere on the way to or from the prison. Once back at Broadmoor, The Animal was signed in, frisked, put through the metal detector and wheeled to B Ward where he was taken to his cell and given pills to help him sleep and ease his pain. If the pain was too much he was moved to the infirmary in the east wing of the prison and was always given a room to himself. There was a duty nurse on-call twenty-four hours a day, but according to them he never asked for much except the occasional Doxepin sleeping pill.

The circuitous route of taking him to the Phoenix Hospital for treatment and then bringing him back to prison was repeated one day a week for fourteen weeks, so fourteen trips in total.

'How close did you stay to him on the detail?' Bishop said.

'Close. In the oncology ward he had a room to himself and before he was allowed inside we searched the place, even though it had been modified.'

'Modified how?'

'All non-essential items were removed. We had to make sure

nothing was left that could be used as a weapon. There was only one bed and we checked under the sheets and the mattress and in the pillows. There was a single plastic chair opposite the bed that was bolted down and we felt through the lining of the curtains by the windows.'

'What floor was he on?'

'Third floor – a thirty-five-foot drop onto concrete below and the window only opened six inches. There was one adjoining room, but we always made sure it was locked and one of us stood with our backs to it before the doctor came around and started the treatment.'

'That was Doctor Gary Fitzroy, right?'

'Yeah, that's right.'

'Was the doctor searched?'

'No.'

'Did The Animal have any other visitors?'

'His sister came in a few times.'

'Cassandra?'

'Yes. The first time she only stayed for maybe five, ten minutes and then she left, but as the weeks progressed she stayed longer.'

'Tell me about her. What did they talk about?'

'I don't know. They always spoke in German, so we didn't understand.'

'The conversations weren't recorded, were they?'

'Not by us, but I'm sure the hospital has CCTV.'

'I'll check. Did anybody else visit him?'

'There was a priest. He was a chaplain from a London parish. Greek, I think, and he brought a Bible with him and used to read from it and he would play with his rosary constantly, spinning the beads in his hand.'

'How often did he visit?'

'He was here for every chemo session. He would say hello to us, say hello to Sebastian and then sit in the chair.'

'Did they talk?'

'No idea, we were outside the room by then and the door was always shut, so we couldn't hear. On the last day of treatment the priest brought two women with him, they looked like his wife and daughter. After the treatment was done they took Sebastian into the chapel and gave him his final blessing and then they all left. The women were upset, heads down and weeping. The older one especially. She wouldn't stop crying – never seen anything like it, and I've seen a lot of the bereaved over the years.'

'Did you ever get the two women's names?'

'No, but the hospital will have a record, they would have had to sign in.'

'So when the treatment began you weren't in the room?'

'No, we went into the corridor, but we could always look inside.'

'Was he kept handcuffed?'

'No. We removed them when he was settled. He wasn't going anywhere and the doctors prefer treating patients hands-free in case there's an emergency and someone has to be moved in seconds.'

'Did The Animal ever talk to you, acknowledge you?'

'Never.'

'And he never mentioned any of his past crimes?'

'No.'

'Were there any changes in his appearance?'

'He lost a shedload of weight, but chemo can do that to you. His hair got thin, his gums were receding and his teeth were loose from the chemo.'

'His teeth?'

'Yeah, on his last day of treatment he pulled one out and threw it at us.'

Twenty

It took Bishop an hour to drive to the Phoenix Hospital in Essex and he arrived just before twelve o'clock. The senior oncologist, Gary Fitzroy, was waiting for him and the two sat facing each other over the doctor's desk.

'In one way, Sebastian was already dead by the time we spotted the cancer, because it had already progressed to stage four,' Gary said. 'We thought the chemo might prolong his life, but at the end of the day it's down to quality of life, and he was an incredibly sick man.'

'Was it discovered during a routine check-up?'

'Apparently he complained of chest and lower back pains at Broadmoor. They thought it was just an excuse for him to get out of solitary confinement, but when they sent his bloods and we looked at his AFP markers we saw the guy was riddled with it.'

'What's AFP?'

'Alpha-fetoprotein. It's a tumour marker for liver cancer. It started in his pancreas and spread to his liver and brain. I was surprised he wasn't in more pain.'

'So Broadmoor did the initial tests?'

'They drew the blood and we worked from what they gave us.' He checked the files. 'Mary Cochran sent us the samples and signed off on them.'

'Who's she?'

'One of the nurses at Broadmoor. I've known her for years.'

'And how did Sebastian cope with the chemo?'

'Like most people. He was sick and had a few moments when he seemed angry, but he kept it inside and always maintained his composure. He was given adjuvant and neoadjuvant chemo, and according to the notes after twelve weeks of treatment the doctors realised it was having very little effect on the tumours, and they were doubtful if longevity of life was at all possible. The side effects were as one might have expected, and after being told there was no change in the tumours, Sebastian stated he wanted the chemotherapy to stop.'

'There were no other treatments available?'

'No. We gave him weeks to live and true to our word he was dead within fourteen days.'

'And you knew who the patient was?'

'Hard not to know, there was security everywhere when he first came in. We were curious, someone asked the right questions and suddenly it wasn't a secret any more, but he needed the security, not to protect other patients, but to protect himself. Once word got out, people here were mad as hell he was getting first-class treatment. They thought it was a misuse of NHS money – and I don't blame them. There's a long waiting list for chemo and when a serial killer gets it, it means someone else goes without. A lot of people wanted him to suffer.'

'Did you?'

'Look – I didn't judge him, I was just here to hook him up to the machines and read the charts.'

'What about visitors during his treatment? I heard his sister came to see him.'

'That's right.'

'Were they affectionate with each other?'

'She held his hand a couple of times, but mostly she would sit on the chair by the foot of his bed. She brought a book with her and would read.'

'Really?'

'It's not uncommon. Depending on the drugs, the treatments can last between one and six hours. A lot of visitors bring something to read. It's more about the patient having a companion, they don't need to talk to each other constantly.'

'Do you remember what the book was?'

'No.'

'Did she ever give him any gifts? Flowers, photographs, a card?'

'Not that I saw, but you'd have to check with the hospital administrators. I'll be honest, Sebastian was kind of frosty towards her, I wouldn't have guessed they were related, and when he decided to stop treatment, he told me he didn't want his sister anywhere near him.'

'Do you know why?'

'He said he didn't want her to see him in his final days. She tried to call him on the phone to come here, but I was told not to accept her calls.'

'Is that common behaviour?'

'Every person reacts differently, you can never predict.'

'And there was a priest who came to see him as well. Do you have a record of his name?'

'Reverend Michael Theopolis. Whenever I came into the room to check on Sebastian the priest would either be quoting from the Bible or describing his church and what it meant to him. He seemed like a proud man. Old and weak as a kitten, but proud of his church. On the last day of Sebastian's treatment the priest was accompanied by two women. They looked religious too, dressed in black, and I thought they might all be part of the same church.'

'Did they sign in?'

'They had to – hold on . . .' Gary pulled out the visitor log and read from it.

'Ana and Maria Theopolis.'

'The same last name?'

'Yes. One was older, a larger woman, the other was younger, I thought maybe the priest's wife and daughter.'

'And they had never come in before?'

'Not until the last day.'

'Did you hear what they talked about?'

'I heard them but I didn't understand them. They all spoke Greek.'

'The security detail said there might be some CCTV of Sebastian getting his treatment?'

'I can find out for you, and if there is some I can have it sent over.'

'Thank you.' Bishop paused a beat, then said: 'And you can't fake the symptoms of cancer, can you?'

'Fake it? Why would anyone want to fake cancer?'

'Sorry, it sounds absurd, but I have to ask.'

'Well, there are a few cases of it happening – not just cancer but other diseases. It's called Munchausen's syndrome – it's a psychological disorder where someone pretends to be ill or deliberately produces symptoms of illness in themselves to get sympathy.'

'Or in the case of criminals to avoid jail time or claim compassionate release from prison,' Bishop added. Again he paused for a second, then: 'So say a person didn't have cancer and for whatever reason you still gave them chemo treatment – what would happen to them?'

'That would never happen.'

'Indulge me.'

'Okay. Well, even if you didn't have cancer, the drugs would still affect you adversely and different drugs would cause different side effects.'

'So you would become sick?'

'Absolutely. You could get an infection if your white blood cell count was reduced because of your deteriorating immune system. If your red cell count was reduced you'd get tired and incredibly sick: nosebleeds, bleeding gums, hair loss, nausea, effects on the nervous system, kidney damage, hearing loss – I mean, the list goes on and on, but that couldn't have happened in this case.'

'Why not?'

'He couldn't have faked it. Like I said, his AFP markers were off the charts.'

Bishop felt himself sag slightly. He had had an idea, but it was obviously not feasible. He changed tack.

'Did you ever talk to Sebastian yourself?' he said.

'You mean have a conversation?'

Bishop nodded.

'No. I said what I say to every one of my patients when I first meet them. I introduce myself, then explain what I'm going to do as I do it. I don't think he even looked at me. And to be honest, I couldn't think of a single thing to say to him.'

'And he never spoke about the past, the murders he committed? No names were ever mentioned to you?'

'Never.'

Twenty-One

By the time Bishop was back at the basement Gary Fitzroy had already emailed over the CCTV from the hospital.

There were jump-cuts in the footage, where cameras had missed The Animal on certain corridors, but it was easy to put together an overall view.

Sebastian Carstairs was suffering, there was no doubt about that. He looked ill when he was pushed into the oncology ward, and looked sick when they hooked him up to the cannula that pumped the intravenous Oxaliplatin into the vein in his arm for three hours every week. Bishop took a clean screenshot of The Animal and printed it off.

The priest who had visited him was tall, thin and bearded and clutched his rosary beads every time he entered the hospital as if they were a life-support. He normally arrived about an hour after the start of the treatment and either sat in the chair opposite or on the end of Sebastian's bed. The two barely spoke and when they did, it was the priest who did the talking. Sometimes he would stand at the foot of the bed, hands gesticulating wildly, the Bible in his hand, and other times he would lean close to The Animal and whisper. Throughout it all The Animal seemed to watch him with half-open eyes, his face expressionless. The priest always waited until the treatment was finished and then he would say a prayer before he left.

According to the hospital reception paperwork, Michael Theopolis was the Reverend Father at the Greek Orthodox church on the Trinity Road just outside of Wood Green. His home address in Palmers Green was listed, along with his telephone number. Bishop called, an answer machine kicked in and he left his number.

The two women who accompanied the Reverend Father on the final visit, Ana and Maria Theopolis, shared the same address as the priest. One appeared a good deal older than the other, so it made sense they were his wife and daughter as the oncologist had suggested. Both women had thick, dark, wavy hair with olive skin and dark eyes.

On the final day of Sebastian's chemo the pair arrived twenty-five minutes before the end of the treatment. They each gave the priest two kisses and a hug as they entered the room. The older woman spoke with the priest while the younger woman stayed seated on the chair. Five minutes before the session ended the three of them held hands around the bed and said what Bishop thought could be interpreted as a group prayer.

The video then showed Gary Fitzroy entering and disconnecting the cannula from The Animal's wrist as the security team came in behind and watched. Sebastian was helped into the wheelchair and one of the team pushed him from the room and along the corridor. They stopped at the Two Palms Café and sat at a table. The security detail sat one table away. The Greek women stayed by Sebastian's side and the priest bought them all tea. They sat there for fifteen minutes until Sebastian signalled he was ready to leave and he was wheeled into the chapel and the priest and two women followed.

After less than five minutes, The Animal was pushed out by the Reverend Father and the security team took over and led him away. The priest and the two women watched Sebastian and his escort for the briefest moment and then turned and walked in the opposite direction. They held hands and the older woman rested her head upon the priest's shoulder as they exited.

Bishop lit a cigarette and called Broadmoor. He asked if the priest Michael Theopolis and the two women, Ana and Maria Theopolis, had ever visited The Animal in his last two weeks at the prison.

'Yes, two women using that name came to Broadmoor the day before he died.'

'With the priest?'

'No. Just the two women.'

'The priest didn't come?'

'No.'

'Do you have security footage?'

'We can send it over.'

'Thank you.'

Bishop searched through the paperwork. He found the phone number the two women had left, but it turned out to be a pay-as-you-go and had been disconnected. Bishop understood that; in high-profile cases, prison guards and hospital staff sometimes leaked contact details to the press, so perhaps the two women were simply being cautious. Or perhaps they had something to hide.

He called Mary Cochran at Broadmoor, the nurse who had

taken Sebastian Carstairs' blood samples, and she explained it was a straightforward procedure done every week at the prison. Bloods were taken on Monday and Tuesday and sent to the various hospitals around the country that were catering for the individual prisoners. She sealed the bloods herself and the courier picked them up from the fridge at the same time every Wednesday.

Bishop stubbed out his cigarette and clicked on the flash drive labelled *Cassandra*.

The hospital CCTV was crackly but he could see The Animal's sister was a fine-looking woman with light eyes and a thick mane of blonde hair, tall with ski-slope Germanic cheekbones and jawline. Her interaction with her brother at the hospital was as the oncologist, Gary Fitzroy, had described. There was very little communication or familiarity between them and she seemed content to sit on the chair opposite the bed and read a book while her brother received his chemo. Bishop enlarged the frame. The book was *Das Parfum* by Patrick Süskind. Cassandra never stayed longer than twenty minutes at each session and she never came in contact with the priest as she had always departed by the time he arrived. When she signed in at the Phoenix Hospital, she had given her address as Hampstead, but had left no street name or flat number, and no telephone details.

According to the file the police had on her, Cassandra Carstairs was fifty-seven years old. She had three other addresses that had been listed over the last twenty years, but each of the telephone numbers given was out of service. Her National Insurance number gave a separate address, but again the telephone number was out of date and there were no records of her with HMRC since 2005, which meant she hadn't paid taxes for the past fourteen years. She could have been paid in cash of course and maybe that's how she survived, but the fact that she had come to visit her brother gave Bishop hope that she might still be working and living in the UK.

He made a call to the Passport Office in London and they confirmed the last record they had of her was when she travelled to England in April 1991. He checked the property in Twickenham her brother had put her in, but it was now owned by a housing conglomerate. He could find no other records of her anywhere, which seemed strange; although with very few controls inside the Schengen Area, she could have easily gone back to Germany after visiting her brother and then slipped through to another European country leaving no trace whatsoever.

She was off the radar, that was for sure, and he had already hit a stumbling block.

He printed off headshots from the CCTV of Cassandra, Michael, Ana and Maria Theopolis and stuck them up on the incident board. He stared at them for a while, then left the basement and made his way to the front of the police station.

He took the lift to the fourth floor, went along a corridor and entered the incident room. One morning spent alone in the basement and he realised how much he missed the bustle of a working police squad. There were forty-five officers assigned to the Newsome case, men and women who shared the same relaxed manner as himself, with an air of quiet assurance common among those who had spent many years on the force. He sat on the edge of a desk and watched them working and listened to the phones and the ping of messages. His eyes were drawn to the incident board and the enlarged photos of John and Sandra Newsome's bodies. He wondered if he and Holly really were chasing a ghost.

'Hey, sir, where have you been? I thought you'd be knee-deep in this.'

It was Sergeant Ambrose. Big smile, big blue eyes.

'Got seconded to some cold cases,' Bishop said. 'How's it going here?'

'Tough. We might have one lead though: the next-door neighbours have a little girl who was supposed to be asleep but says she was awake and watching the rain and saw a car parked a little way up from the house.'

'Did she get the registration?'

'No, sir, she's only six. There's a sketch artist over there now, but we're not holding our breath.'

'Is Thompson around?'

'Upstairs with the brass. He should be down in a minute.'

He waited until Thompson arrived. The DI was a bull-chested ex-footballer in his fifties, with short-cropped blond hair and a red face.

'You got a minute?' Bishop said.

'Sure, let's go in the office.'

'How about the canteen?'

They both had black coffee on the table in front of them and Thompson had bought himself an apple. It was red and sounded soft when he bit into it.

'How's the Newsome case going?' Bishop said.

'We've got a girl who says she saw a car.'

'Ambrose told me. Anything else?'

'We're working our way through a dozen or so suspects with violent MOs who have been released way too early, and we're still running forensics, but so far the place was clean. Whoever did it was very careful.'

'Any ideas about the message on the wall?'

'It was written in the victims' blood. Annie Wilkes was convicted of killing her brother and sister-in-law twenty-five years ago, but we can't see a connection. Looks like the killer is playing silly buggers and trying to waste our time.' Thompson paused, then said: 'The name Holly,' he said. 'We thought it might be your Holly to start with.'

'My Holly?'

'Wakefield.'

Bishop gave Thompson a thin smile.

'There are a lot of Hollys out there,' he said.

'Yeah, that's what we figured. It's a common enough name and we think it might be the killer's girlfriend or partner, maybe an ex. Whoever she is, it's a message to her so we need to find her. It's not much to go on, but we're running the name through the database to see if we get any hits.'

Thompson downed his coffee and looked ready to leave but said:

'So, you want to tell me what's going on, Bill?'

'What do you mean?'

'I thought the Newsome case was yours, but it was handed to me, no explanation given. Then all of a sudden you're king of the cold case files, where no self-respecting DI wants to find himself. Did you piss somebody off, or are you thinking of taking early retirement?'

'None of the above.'

'And now you come into the incident room and want to talk, but away from the others, so here we are, having coffee, three tables removed from anybody else.'

'What are you, a detective?'

'Apparently. Come on, talk to me.'

'It's complicated,' Bishop said. 'The moment I can, I will, but right now I can't, so just trust me. Superintendent Bashir is overseeing the Newsome murder, right?'

'I was just in the meeting with him.'

'I need a favour.'

Thompson scowled and took another bite of the apple.

'This is all a bit too cloak-and-dagger, Bill,' he said. 'I don't like cloak-and-dagger, I like transparency.'

'I know you do,' Bishop said.

'What do you need?'

'Have you done the home inventory of the Newsomes' property yet?'

'You think this was a robbery?'

'I want to know if the killer took any jewellery,' Bishop said.

Twenty-Two

There was a faint haze of blue smoke from Bishop's cigarettes when Holly returned to the basement.

'So what is wrong with Annie Wilkes?' was Bishop's first question.

She crossed to her desk and slumped in the chair. She had been on the train for four hours from Yorkshire, had skipped breakfast and was hungry and already tired.

'Annie's disturbed on a lot of levels – and I don't blame her,' she said. 'She believes she's innocent and her psychiatrist agrees.'

'Derek Martin?'

'Yes. She can't remember a lot of things, but she knew who The Animal was. She got agitated when I showed her the photo of the message on the wall.'

'There has to be a connection between her and The Animal, otherwise why use her name? They never knew each other? Never met each other?'

'No.'

'She didn't write to him in prison?'

'She hasn't written to anyone. Derek told me she's received

about thirty letters over the years from men and women; a few journalists wanting a story and some people threatening to kill her.'

'Do you have a list of those people?'

'Here,' she handed over a pad and watched as he stared at the names. He rubbed his eyes and handed it back.

'You want a coffee?' he said.

'Please.'

He got up and went for the kettle. Switched it on and prepped two clean mugs.

'Maybe Annie is innocent?' he said. 'The Animal wrote: *But I must confess*, so maybe he is confessing to killing Len and Colette Wilkes.'

'It's plausible. The crimes were particularly brutal. No other DNA was found at the crime scene other than Annie's, so he left no trace, which was his usual MO.'

'Okay, but if it was The Animal, why would he confess now, twenty-six years after the fact?' Bishop brooded for a while as he thought it through. 'Unless of course The Animal is messing with us and the writing on the wall means nothing. I mean, we're talking as if we can trust him, Holly.'

'I know that's dangerous, but I think we can. The message means something to him, otherwise he wouldn't have written it, therefore it should mean something to us.'

'Then there is also the logistical problem of his health.'

'What do you mean?'

'The guy was sick. Hair falling was out, he lost his teeth, the whole lot.'

'There are only two possible scenarios for The Animal to be out there killing again, Bishop. One – he had cancer and somehow beat it . . .'

'Not possible.'

'Two – he faked his cancer.'

'Impossible, according to his oncologist. And even if he somehow managed it, he would still have become very sick from the treatment.'

'But he would have survived it. Then it would simply be a question of lying low, recovering from the effects of the chemo until he had the strength to start killing again.'

'Either way, it doesn't add up,' he said.

'Don't lose faith, Bishop.'

'I'm not, I'm not.'

She watched him run a hand through his hair. He wasn't looking at her. He seemed to be staring past her.

'Who were the officers who arrested Annie Wilkes?' she said.

'DI Pattison and Sergeant Harnham.' Bishop picked up the file. 'Harnham died of a heart attack five years ago, so it's DI Pattison we need to see.'

Twenty-Three

'My name's DI Bishop and this is Holly Wakefield. We'd like to talk to you about Annie Wilkes, if we could.'

They had arrived in Streatham, south London, at a Victorian terraced house. Bishop had already called ahead and spoken to DI Joseph Pattison and he knew they were coming, but he still looked a little shell-shocked.

'I don't remember much about that case,' he said. 'It was so long ago.'

'It will only take a few minutes.'

'My wife's shopping, you'll have to be gone by the time she gets back. We can go in the garden.'

He led them through the house. The back door was already open and Holly and Bishop sat in the shade of a tree on a wooden bench. DI Pattison sat on an old plastic chair opposite.

'Tell me about her arrest,' Bishop said.

'Haven't you read the file?'

'Humour me.'

'Dispatch told me there had been a disturbance at the house, so I drove there with Sergeant Harnham. When we arrived at the property it was quiet—'

'Six o'clock in the evening?'

'Something like that. It was the neighbour who called the police, so we followed normal procedure. Knocked on the door: no response. Then we went around the back of the house and had a look through the windows. We saw a foot on the floor, poking out from behind a wall in the hallway so we broke down the door.'

'You didn't call for back-up?'

'We both ran in thinking it might have been a heart attack or something, but when we got to the hallway and saw all the blood, we knew it was murder.'

'And Len and Colette Wilkes were lying side by side?'

'If that's what it says in the file, yes. Sergeant Harnham puked up in the downstairs toilet, I remember that. I think it was his first murder, and I radioed for an ambulance and the coroner.'

'You didn't check for a pulse in either of the victims?'

'God no!' He looked horrified. 'There was no way either of them were alive.'

'And at this point the front door was still locked, wasn't it?'

'I think so.'

'So let me get this straight – you broke down the back door to gain entry and there were two mutilated bodies on the ground? Did you ever think about checking out the rest of the house to make sure the killer wasn't still inside?'

'Afterwards I did, but the whole house was so quiet and we were both in such shock that we didn't think it was possible anyone else was there.'

'But Annie was upstairs, wasn't she?'

'Yes.' He took a moment and shook his head. 'We didn't hear her come down the stairs behind us and all of a sudden she was next to us. She scared the shit out of me. She was like something out of a horror movie. She had long black hair and was as pale as a ghost and was wearing a white nightdress, a frilly one, and there was blood over her hands and arms and her eyes were glassy, I knew she was high on something.'

'What did you do?'

'I think I asked her something like – "who are you?" And she told me her name and then I asked her about the blood on her. She said she had washed the blood off the knife and "put it back in the rack where it belonged".'

'You remember those exact words?'

'I'll never forget them. The prosecution must have repeated that phrase to the jury fifty times during the trial, but it was the fact she was so casual about it that made me feel uneasy, you know? Like she was telling me dinner was in the oven, or she'd just hung the washing out.'

'And then she saw the bodies?'

'Yep.'

'How did she react?' said Holly.

He turned to look at her and she could almost see his thoughts.

'She started screaming,' he said, 'and she ran over to her brother and held him, so we both tried to pull her off. She was stronger than we thought, but somehow we managed to carry her away and then we handcuffed her. She wouldn't stop struggling, so we had to hold her down and it was horrible, because I knelt on her back and I thought I felt one of her ribs crack and then she seemed to quiet down and just sobbed. We stayed like that until the ambulance came.' He took a moment and shifted in his seat. 'She wouldn't let go of my leg. She kept asking me not to leave her, and she wanted to see her brother and sister-in-law again, and she was still crying. It was the hardest thing I ever did, trying to coax her to let go of me so the ambulance crew could check her out, just in case she had been a victim too, but—'

'But what?'

He took a breath.

'Even when they were looking after her she kept saying, "The knife is back in the rack, the knife is back in the rack. I cleaned it and put it back."'

'So she was booked and charged with murder?' said Bishop.

'That's right, and then DCI Warren came in and took over.'

'Why?'

'He was the poster boy for the Met. The guy who was on the hunt for The Animal. You remember him?'

'Sure,' said Bishop. 'And nobody ever thought about opening an investigation or looking for anybody else?'

'No. I mean, she practically confessed.' His eyes flickered over to Holly. 'Christ, how much more do you need?'

'You know she's bipolar?' Holly said.

'I found that out during the trial. But when I first saw her, no, of course I didn't know. Toxicology said she was high on drugs at the time of the murder: MDMA and sleeping pills. The defence claimed she had a history of blackouts and that she'd had one that day and couldn't remember anything, but the jury didn't buy it.'

'And who conducted the search of the premises?'

'We all did. The forensics team came in and looked at everything, and myself and PC Harnham followed procedure to the letter. We had to give up our uniforms because they were covered in blood, so they were taken away and used in the trial. They took Annie's nightdress and SOCO went through all the knives in the kitchen and found one with traces of blood on it; tests confirmed it matched the victims' blood and it had Annie's prints on it. The coroner concluded it was the murder weapon, so it was a bit of an open-and-shut case.'

'And did you think she was guilty?'

'Yes.'

'She has always claimed her innocence.'

'I spent another sixteen years on the force and ended up arresting over eighty murderers and every single one of them said the same thing. Christ, even Ted Bundy claimed he was innocent!'

'No,' Holly said. 'He never said that.'

Twenty-Four

They caught a late lunch, mulled over what Pattison had said, then headed back to the basement office.

Holly went over to the incident board and the photo of the blonde woman from the Phoenix Hospital CCTV caught her attention.

'Is this Cassandra?'

'Yes, and we got confirmation she visited her brother at the hospital during his chemo, so there's a good chance she'll still be living over here.'

Holly scrutinised the photo and took in the facial features of Sebastian's sister and tried to match them to the woman she had seen three months ago at the funeral. She couldn't, as the woman had been wearing a veil, but at least they had a face to go with the name now. There was also a profile photo of an elderly man with a curly black beard. He wore black priest's robes with a purple stole that hung around his neck with the ends draping down the front. Below him was a photo of two women with dark hair and dark eyes.

'Talk me through the others,' Holly said.

'The man is a Greek Orthodox reverend by the name of Michael Theopolis. He visited The Animal during his chemo treatments at the hospital.'

'What do we know about him?'

'Not much yet. I've already put in a call to his church and left a message.'

'And the women with him?'

'Ana and Maria Theopolis, his wife and daughter. They came with him on the last visit to the hospital and visited Sebastian at Broadmoor prison as well. Would you put Sebastian Carstairs down as the religious type?'

'Definitely not.'

'He mentions God in the letter he wrote to you.'

'A lot of killers talk about God and having their souls saved. Personally, I think they do it to annoy their victims' families. God can forgive you for coveting your neighbour's wife, or lusting after Susan from marketing, so therefore he can forgive me for killing, torturing and raping your child. I'm not a big believer in the Lord, but if he does exist I hope he's choosy. I wouldn't mind seeing Brad Pitt up there, but I wouldn't want to see The Animal in Heaven.'

She saw Bishop smile as he said:

'You might want to look at this, Mrs Pitt. It's the CCTV of Ana and Maria Theopolis visiting The Animal at Broadmoor the day before he died.'

They watched the clip. The footage was unedited, so Bishop had to fast-forward at certain points, but they saw the two Greek women when they entered the prison, were searched, then let through and into the waiting area. From there a prison guard escorted them along several corridors until they entered a large room with six hospital beds, all of which were empty apart from the one in the far corner by the window.

'Where is this?' Holly said.

'The east wing of the prison infirmary.'

'Is there sound?'

'No.'

The camera switched angles and Holly got her first look at The Animal in bed. Riddled with cancer, she barely recognised him. Although he was tall, he was half his size, his eyes sunken and grey and the sloping dome of his head was nearly bald.

When the two women came to his side, his eyes flickered, but he seemed too weak to talk. He half-raised a hand as if in greeting, then dropped it and the two women sat either side of the bed. Each held one of Sebastian's hands. The younger one was talking, her body gently rocking back and forth and the older one had her head buried in the blanket by Sebastian's waist. After a few minutes, both women kissed him on the cheek and hugged him and the younger woman gently ran a comb through what was left of the killer's hair.

Holly felt suddenly angry.

'Why the hell do they care so much?' she said.

Twenty-Five

The Reverend Michael Theopolis's house was on St George's Road in Palmers Green, north London.

They knocked on the front door. There was no reply for a while and then the old woman from the CCTV opened the door. She was so frail and bent over Bishop had to crouch down to make eye contact.

'Maria Theopolis?' he said.

She stared at him suspiciously. He asked about her husband and daughter, but the woman said something in Greek and waved him away. She kept repeating the words in Greek and waving her right hand until she shut the door.

As they retreated down the path, the door opened again and a young Greek boy of about nine or ten took a step towards them.

'Are you looking for Uncle Michael and my mother?'

'Ana Theopolis? Yes, we are,' said Bishop.

'My uncle is away, but you'll find Ana at the church. Just follow the road. It's a half-mile on the right.'

'Thank you.'

The church was larger than Holly had imagined and more modern. The roof was flat and covered in plastic sheeting and scaffolding.

Inside were pews covered with purple cushions, and on the walls hung icons of Christ and the Holy Family. There were about thirty people present who spoke in hushed voices. Holly thought a ceremony had just finished, so they kept their distance until some of the people started to file past them on their way out and she spotted Ana. She saw them too and approached with a smile.

'Good afternoon,' she said. 'Were you here for the service?'

'No, we weren't,' Bishop said. 'We've just come from your mother's house, and a young boy said we could find you here. Ana Theopolis?'

'Yes, that was my son.'

Bishop showed his warrant card.

The smile dropped but came back a few seconds later and she said:

'Police, how can I help?'

'We're looking for your father.'

'He's not here, but come through, we can have coffee.'

She led them into a kitchen at the back of the church and made strong coffee in small cups. They sat on sofas as they talked:

'Where is he, Miss Theopolis?' Bishop said.

'Ana, please. My father is on sabbatical – he's gone back to Greece.'

'Do you have his contact details?'

'We do, but he'll be at the Monastery of the Holy Trinity in Meteora, so it will be hard to contact him.'

'And when will he be back?'

'The sabbatical lasts for three months. Is there something I can help with?'

Bishop stayed silent for a second and Holly stepped in.

'We'd like to talk to him about Sebastian Carstairs.'

'Yes?'

'Your father visited Sebastian while he was going through his chemotherapy at the Phoenix Hospital. Did he often visit prisoners?'

'There are inmates there who have reached out to him in the past and he would go there to hold talks and prayers.'

'Did you ever meet Sebastian?'

'Twice, both times with my mother. My father asked us to accompany him to the hospital when Sebastian was going through his last bout of chemotherapy, and then we visited him again at Broadmoor just before he passed away.'

'Had you been to Broadmoor before?'

'No.'

'And this time your father didn't go with you?'

She took a second, then:

'No, he was on sabbatical by then, so he sent us in his place. I don't understand, has he done something wrong?'

'No, not at all.'

'Then what is this about?'

'We're investigating cold case files,' Holly said. 'Unsolved murders that date back to the years Sebastian Carstairs was most active in his killing. We're trying to ascertain if he had anything to do with them, so we're talking to everybody who had any contact with Sebastian in his last few months to see if he ever confessed to any other homicides that we don't know about.'

'Confessed?'

'Yes.'

'No. He was very ill, he barely spoke. My mother and I were there simply to comfort him in his final hours.'

'And he never talked to you?' said Holly.

'About what?'

'About his crimes.'

'No.'

'He didn't mention any names to you from the past, men, women or children?'

Ana flinched at the word *children* and said:

'No, and if he ever spoke to my mother she would not have understood him: she doesn't speak or understand English. I can call her, if you like, and get her to come here. I can translate your questions to her.'

'No, that's fine,' said Bishop. It looked as though he was about to say something else, but Holly kept going:

'And you were aware of who Sebastian was?' she said.

'Yes.'

'*The Animal*, the press called him. He killed at least eighteen people that we know about. Did he ever mention the names John and Sandra Newsome? They were a husband and wife who were murdered last weekend and the style of killing was very similar to the murders Sebastian committed in the eighties and nineties.'

'No,' Ana said, her face suddenly pale.

Holly felt Bishop shoot her a look out of the corner of her eye.

'Are you sure?' she said.

'Yes. I would tell you. Look, I know he did wrong in the past, but my father offered him salvation, and when Sebastian repented, I believed him. We all did. He was a changed man. Would you have had him executed, like they do in America? He was convicted of his crimes and punished by the law and forgiven his sins by my father and God. When we were with him he was a gentle man, full of remorse and compassion.'

'So he did speak to you?'

'Sometimes,' she paused, her voice almost a whisper. 'He said he was sorry.'

'Sorry?'

'Yes.'

'And that was it? How do you know he was sorry?' Holly said.

'Because he wouldn't lie. He wasn't like that, and my father and I weren't the only ones who were there for him.'

'What do you mean?'

'His therapist came to talk to us.'

'Hedley Phelps?' Bishop said, suddenly engaged again. 'You knew him?'

'Yes. He was treating Sebastian and helping him through his problems. Hedley is a wonderful man.'

'How did you meet him?'

'He came to the church about a year ago and talked to us about Sebastian. He said the man wanted help and needed someone to talk to. Hedley arranged the meetings for my father.'

'And upon meeting Sebastian, your father accepted him and who he was?'

'My father was never one to turn anyone away. It's easy to judge someone by their past actions, even if those actions are murder. Sebastian simply wanted a chance at forgiveness.'

Bishop took a moment then:

'Are you here every day?'

'Seven days a week. We're having the roof renovated, so it's best if I'm here anyway. With my father away, I am the one who has to deal with the council regarding the permits.'

'We appreciate your time, Ana,' Bishop said, and stood up to signal the meeting was over, but Holly wasn't done yet.

'Why were you so affectionate towards Sebastian?' she said.

'What do you mean?'

'We've seen the prison CCTV video. You were holding his hand, kissing him, combing his hair. Why?'

'He was about to die,' and there were tears in Ana's eyes when she spoke. 'How would you like to die, Miss Wakefield? In a cold, hard prison bed by yourself? Or with people attending to you, holding your hand and telling you, you are loved?'

Twenty-Six

'You shouldn't have mentioned the Newsome case, Holly.'

They were back in the basement. Bishop was making coffee but Holly had declined. She sat at her desk, bit her lip and let him talk.

'That's classified information,' he said. 'You made it too personal and you pushed too hard with your questions. I understand your frustration, but we have to maintain our neutrality.' He watched her with some sympathy. 'Ana Theopolis really got under your skin, didn't she?'

'God forgave The Animal for killing eighteen people and her father in all his priestly wisdom forgave him too? Yes, the whole conversation bugged the hell out of me.'

'We've found a Greek translator to talk to the mother,' he said. 'They're going to pick her up this afternoon and ask her the same questions. Do you want to be present?'

'No.'

She heard his phone buzz with a text. He read it and said: 'Back in a minute.'

For the next hour, Holly stared gloomily at the computer

screen as she sifted through various documents. It was a long and drawn-out task and the basement room darkened as she worked.

She called Hedley Phelps again and got the same voicemail so left the same message, then she called Broadmoor prison and her mood wasn't improved when she was informed Hedley Phelps was on vacation. They said he was due three weeks' annual leave and left ten days ago. She asked if they knew whether he had left the country and they said he was more likely staying at home in Mayfair. Holly checked the address she already had and asked if there was a number for his home? Yes, there was. She took it down and checked her notes. His wife's name was Sylvia. She called the number and got their answer machine and Holly left a message. Within a minute Sylvia called her back.

'How can I help?' the woman said. Her voice was sharp and quick.

'Thank you for getting back to me, Mrs Phelps. I'm working with the Met Police and we're trying to get hold of your husband—'

'He moved out.'

'Oh, I'm sorry to hear that.'

'I'm not. We're going through a divorce.'

'Do you know where he's staying?'

'I wrote it down somewhere, I'm not sure where, but he's supposed to be here tomorrow morning to pick up the last of his things, so why don't you come over and you can talk to him then?'

'What time would be good?'

'Ten-ish?'

'Okay, thank you, I'll see you both at about ten.'

The line went dead. Holly sipped her coffee. It tasted rotten.

There was one more USB stick from the therapy sessions so she slotted it into her Mac. There was a recording of music from the radio for the first twenty minutes, classic eighties tunes which eventually stopped and then The Animal was speaking with Hedley again. It seemed to be halfway through a session:

'It started out as childhood curiosity when I was eleven or twelve years old,' Sebastian said. 'Just to see what it looked like to cut open live animals, and then I didn't want to stop.'

'And was there pleasure in cutting open the animals?'

'Yes, but nothing sexual. It was never sexual. It was just power and control. The killing was simply a means to the end. I didn't enjoy it when I first began, but I grew to like it. I want to make it clear I have never blamed anything else for my behaviour, not my parents, my upbringing, or drugs. It was me, wholly me, and I take full responsibility.'

'So who are you, Sebastian?'

'Just a regular psychopath.'

Holly shook her head. He was so casual, as if he were discussing football scores or a shopping list.

'Do you have emotions, Sebastian?'

'Is madness an emotion? Perhaps it's the seventh sense?'

The conversation stopped and it went back to the recording of eighties music from the radio, then the sound levels went to zero. Holly adjusted them but there seemed to be nothing more and then very faintly she thought she heard the sound of someone crying. She turned up the volume.

'I'm sorry,' whispered a voice.

She couldn't be sure if it was Hedley or . . . ?

'I'm so sad,' said the soft voice.

It *was* Hedley.

'Come here. Come here. Let me hold you, Hedley. Let me comfort you.'

Then there was silence as though something had gone wrong with the recording. It came back with a hiss and the voices began again, but now the intimacy had been shattered, and Holly could almost hear the two men smiling as if they had shared a joke she wasn't privy to.

'You tell me, Hedley.'

'I don't know.'

'I have had publishers contact me over the years. I could help you, Hedley. Everybody wants to know about me, and you hold the key. A book deal. You would make a fortune. You could live your life on the lecture circuit: *The Man Who Tamed The Animal*!'

'Stop it,' Hedley laughed. 'You're making me blush.'

'But this could be your chance. Perhaps Sylvia would want you back? I bet she would. Hedley Phelps – famous author – *The Animal Tamer.* She would be all over you!'

'Well, I mean . . .'

'She's jealous of you, that's the problem. She's a journalist, and what is a journalist? A novelist who never had the guts to try.'

'Maybe you're right, maybe she is jealous of me. There were times when she wouldn't even read anything I had written.'

'But did you read her boring editorials?'

'Of course.'

'Well, there you go then. This is your time now, Hedley. Embrace it.' A pause. 'Look at us. We are both growing so much with these sessions.'

Then Sebastian laughed and Hedley joined in. Hesitantly at first, as if not fully understanding the joke, and then the voices began to blur and echo as if Holly were hearing the exact same conversation from more than one separate recording played at the same time and she couldn't make out the words. She used a sound enhancer app to modify the audio and saved the cleaned-up version. Then she adjusted the volume levels of the speaker and pressed play again.

The voices were still jumbled and there was static.

She manipulated the filter until gradually there was less static, then she replayed the recording once more.

Nothing. It was as if the conversation had somehow been deleted.

She readjusted the settings, then pressed play again. Hedley and The Animal were talking once more, but it was so hushed it was hard to hear, as if they were whispering. Hedley seemed to be crying and the sound had a strange, compressed quality, more like an electronic sound. After a while it seemed as if the recording was over, then there was a very faint woman's voice. A distorted phrase that repeated itself again and again as if on a loop. Holly leaned forward at the table trying to hear, but it was hard. The words were so faint, she wasn't sure if it was real or not. She went back to the beginning and increased the volume to the maximum setting, then sat there straining to hear, her hands a little twitchy. Again she adjusted the controls and suddenly the woman's voice came through loud and clear, almost sing-song:

'I have cookies, just come out of the oven! You want one?'

She stopped the recording. Stared at her screen without doing anything, beginning to doubt what she'd heard. Then she rewound the last few seconds and pressed play again.

'I have cookies, just come out of the oven! You want one?'

It was a stark contrast to what she had been listening to and the voice was somehow familiar and intimate, as if from a TV commercial. She played it several times, slightly baffled, and was about to play it again when the office door suddenly banged open. Holly jumped and spun in her seat.

A man was standing in the doorway.

Twenty-Seven

The man was over six feet tall and wore jeans, a T-shirt and a hoodie. He was in his late forties, had a black beard streaked white and dark circles under his eyes.

It was Max. Bishop's friend and ex-Special Forces.

'I make you jump?' he said.

She realised she was holding her breath, let it go and managed a smile.

'Hi Max, good to see you again. You okay?'

'Living the dream.'

He peeled out a cigarette. Magicked a lighter from nowhere and lit it before taking a drink from Bishop's cold coffee mug.

'Where's the big guy?'

'He'll be back in a minute.'

'Do I get a desk?'

'Go for it.'

He dragged one of the spare desks across the room and she watched him unload his backpack: a sleeping bag, a mug, a toothbrush and toothpaste, six packets of cigarettes, half a packet of sliced white bread and a toaster. He held up the toaster and bread.

'Where do I put this?'

'Over by the coffee and tea. You want a cup?'

'Tea please. Milk and three sugars.'

Holly put the kettle on. Max took in the room and walked over to the incident board. He made his way from left to right, stopping at the various crime scenes. Victim number one: Raychel Raynes. Victim number two: Martin Smith. Victims number three and four: Ernie and Samantha Wellcroft.

'They were all murdered by the same guy?'

'Sebastian Carstairs.'

'The Animal? I remember reading about him.'

Number five: Tip Cullen. Number six: Rory Anglesey. He paused at the next, whispering her name:

'Ma Baker?'

'Michelle "Ma" Baker,' Holly said. 'She was victim number seven. She was a fashion stylist from Essex who was strangled and drowned in her bathtub on January twenty-seventh, 1988.'

Max nodded and kept walking. Carlos Villaverde was next – the photos depicted multiple stab wounds to his stomach, then it was another woman and Max lingered on her face, drawn to one of her alive and smiling next to a horse. She was beautiful.

'That was Jana Wurdel, a horse groomer. She was stabbed to death on April ninth 1988 at her home in Bristol. She has a son who's fifty-three now. Then it was Luigi Bonomi, an Italian somalier,' Holly said. 'He was the last victim from 1988, and then in 1989 The Animal only killed one person, Tibor Slovenski, a chef, on September twenty-third.'

'Why did he only kill once that year?'

'We don't know. He never gave a reason. Victims number twelve and thirteen were Ken Whitehead and Ray Grimmet, a gay couple from Southbourne in Dorset. Each had their commitment rings stolen. They were made of white gold, set with seven precious stones in the colours of the rainbow.'

'You seem to know an awful lot about this killer,' Max said, and Holly wondered what he was thinking. He passed Martina Jong, a librarian who had been hanged by a belt in her own bedroom, Fred Cracknell who had been beaten to death with a billiard cue and the gruesome crime scene photos of Lucy Le Bas, victim number sixteen, whose throat had been cut from ear to ear.

Holly flinched as Max reached the end of the board and stared at the photos of her dead parents, victims seventeen and eighteen. He reached up and took a copy of the letter The Animal had written to Holly and read through it, transfixed. He didn't ask why it was addressed to her, instead he read out loud: '"*The Furies . . . Listening to the voices until they scream.*"'

'Greek mythology. They were three sisters: Alecto, Megaera, and Tisiphone. They punished wrongdoers. Liars, thieves, murderers.'

He nodded as if to say he understood, then:

'I thought The Animal was dead?'

Holly was about to answer when Bishop came back in.

He walked straight to the incident board and stuck up an 8x10 photo of an orange coral necklace underneath Sandra Newsome's picture.

'DI Thompson just confirmed this necklace is not accounted for in the house inventory.'

'It was stolen from Sandra Newsome on the night of the murder?' Holly said. 'Was anything else taken?'

'That was it.'

She forced her eyes from the photo back to Bishop and cleared her throat.

'It fits the MO and now it fits the signature,' she said softly.

There was a long-drawn-out silence and then Max said:

'You guys want to tell me what's going on?'

Bishop briefed him extensively about what was needed and why they had brought him in.

'You'd better read this,' he said, and handed Max a file.

As Bishop carried on talking, Holly watched Max's reaction. At first, he had a dazed expression on his face as he flicked through the report and listened at the same time, then he seemed to straighten in his chair as he got through one cigarette after another. There was something jumpy about his mouth and Holly wondered how bad his addiction was. Bishop's directions were succinct and to the point and at the end of the instructions he swore Max to secrecy.

Max nodded, finished reading and looked up.

'And you both think The Animal's still alive?' he said.

'We do.'

'So I just roll with that, right? You're both fucking crazy, the guy's in the ozone layer, but what the hell, I've got nowhere else to be. When does the rest of the cavalry get here?'

'It's just us,' said Bishop.

'Just us,' Max said softly. 'So this is unofficial then?'

'Yes. Are you in?'

'I brought my sleeping bag, right.'

'Good,' said Bishop. 'Holly and I will fill you in on some more of the details now. Holly?'

'Sebastian Carstairs was born in Germany on ninth November 1959. His father had been a salt-miner, his mother a nurse, and he has a younger sister called Cassandra. Like Sebastian, Cassandra never married and has no children.'

'And she's still alive?'

'Yes. When Sebastian was captured his medical records were subpoenaed from his childhood home and there seemed to have been a history of sexual and mental abuse from the father and mother to both children, with accounts of beatings and bruises before the age of ten. Sebastian inherited his father's height and strong build and competed as a wrestler at junior level and when he turned sixteen he joined the Bundeswehr.'

'What's that?'

'Germany's federal armed forces.'

'So he's ex-military?'

Bishop nodded and handed the one official photo of Sebastian from Germany, which was his army barracks ID when he had been first recruited. His face had been more rounded back then, but the underlying cheekbones and jawline were as clear as his eyes.

'He spent two years training with the army,' Holly said, 'but at the sudden death of his mother, he returned home. After the funeral he took Cassandra with him and the pair moved west and settled in a town called Lorrach in south-west Germany, close to the French and Swiss borders. They cut off all links with their father, who according to medical records died from throat cancer in a hospital near Düsseldorf in 1979. In his will he left a considerable sum of money to both of his children, which had been paid out to the family because of the insurance claim from the accidental death of their mother. At this time, Sebastian worked construction on building sites and property development. There are a few reports of him getting into fights, and one report of him strangling a dog, but that was never proved and he was never prosecuted. He moved to the UK in 1982.

'He lived in rented accommodation in Hounslow for the first six months while he looked for a house to invest in. In 1983, property deeds show he bought a flat in Hounslow and paid cash. He rented it out, took a home equity loan and purchased another flat in Wimbledon where he lived by himself. Over the next three years he bought four other properties, all around London, all of which he leased. During this period, Sebastian was never arrested, never got into trouble and appeared to be a model citizen.'

'When did he make his first kill?'

'February thirteenth, 1986,' Holly said, 'and her name was Raychel Raynes.'

Twenty-Eight

'Raychel Raynes was twenty-one years old and lived in the town of Reading.'

Bishop passed over a clipped folder to Max as Holly carried on talking:

'She had been out jogging on the evening of thirteenth February and failed to return home. On Valentine's Day her body was found by a dog walker, hidden in some bushes off a bike trail east of the town centre. She had been strangled and hit three times on the head with a large piece of flint that was recovered at the scene. The police thought it was a random and unorganised attack, but they couldn't have been further from the truth. The autopsy of Raychel Raynes showed she had not been sexually assaulted, indicating the attacker was not a lust killer or incited by sexual urges. However, the death had been particularly violent.

'She had been strangled to the point of unconsciousness, then resuscitated, then rendered unconscious again and the process had been repeated a dozen or so times, evidenced by the enormous amount of petechial haemorrhaging on her neck, lips, cheeks and whites of her eyes. Then, when the killer had had enough of this, he finished her off by hitting her three times with a heavy flint in the face. The killing was estimated to have taken up to fifteen minutes and the cruelty of the kill made national headlines.

'A manhunt followed throughout the local area and thousands of people were interviewed. According to Raychel's family, a silver and garnet ring had been stolen from their daughter's finger during the attack. When the search expanded to encompass the rest of the UK, it included pawn shops, charity shops and local auction houses. After three months the ring had not been found, there were no principal suspects and all of the secondary suspects had been interviewed and released.'

'When was victim number two killed?' Max said.

'Just over one year later, on thirty-first March 1987. This time it was in Chatham, Kent and the victim was a thirty-five-year-old man named Martin Smith. He was found in his council flat with his throat cut, his left hand nailed to the floor and his left foot amputated and left upside down in the kitchen sink. He had been dead for over a week.'

'Jesus.' Max took a new folder from Bishop. 'How did they link the victims?'

'The coroner found a small silver ring with a garnet stone circling the iron nail that had been hammered through the victim's palm.'

'That was the first victim's ring? Raychel Raynes's?'

'Correct. It was identified by her parents. And this is where The Animal's signature became apparent. Do you know the difference between an MO and a signature?'

Max shook his head and put the files down.

'The MO, or Modus Operandi, is the method used to

commit the crime. In this instance The Animal will do extensive research on his victims, attack when he knows they are alone or vulnerable, most often later in the day, and he will always wear gloves and leave no forensics. His method adapted slightly with each victim as he became more experienced. His signature, which fuelled his emotional and psychological needs, always stayed the same with every single kill. He would steal a piece of jewellery from one victim and leave it with the next, so as to claim the previous kill.'

'So why was he so obsessed with jewellery?'

'We don't know why.'

'So he leaves the garnet ring with Martin, and then what does he take from him?'

'A gold crucifix necklace which was left with victims number three and four.'

Holly went through the paperwork on her desk and handed Max the next file but he didn't bother opening it.

'They were husband and wife, Ernie and Samantha Wellcroft who lived in Morton in Essex,' Holly said. 'He stole two platinum wedding rings from them.'

'Right,' Max said. 'And left them with victim number five. Cut to today – that's why you guys got all excited at the coral necklace on the incident board? Correct?'

'Exactly,' Holly said. She glanced at the final file but pushed it aside, her hands suddenly sweaty.

'You got a smoke?' she said to Bishop. Both Max and Bishop offered, but she took one from Bishop, sat back at the table and lit up. She tapped the ash into a saucer and stared at the file in her hands. A photo of her mother and father was stapled to the front page. Not a crime scene photo, but one from their wedding day, before Holly had been born. It was a black-and-white print and her parents were staring at each other and smiling as if they knew all the secrets of the world.

'Holly?'

Her head jerked up.

'Sorry,' she said. 'Where were we?'

'Eighteen bodies so far,' Bishop said. He knew what she had been looking at and she saw the concern in his eyes. He gave her an 'are you okay?' nod. No words necessary. It made her feel better. She nodded back that she was.

'Twenty if we include Sandra and John Newsome,' she said.

'The two new bodies on the whiteboard?' Max said.

'That's correct.'

'With the missing coral necklace. So who's he going to kill next?'

'We don't know, and it's impossible to predict,' sighed Holly.

Bishop took a more optimistic view: 'During the twenty-six years he spent locked up, a lot of things changed to tip the balance in our favour. There's been a huge increase in CCTV and everyone has a mobile phone with a camera, which means his victim selection and surveillance has to be handled even more carefully. Obviously he won't be using his real name, so if he has credit cards they will be either stolen or faked, as will his driver's licence. If he has a bank account, or several, which I highly suspect, it will be under a different name or perhaps under a dummy corporation. He will need cash to survive though, it's just a question of where he's getting it from.'

'How could he have set all those things up from prison? Bank accounts and stuff?'

'He was wealthy and owned numerous properties in the nineties,' Holly said. 'He might well have squirrelled some of that money into hidden accounts before he was put away. We think the majority of his property was passed on to his sister after he was incarcerated.'

'So she's helping him out?'

'Maybe, but she seems to have disappeared off the map as well.'

Max raised his hand as if in school. He had gone back to that dazed look.

'Yes, Max?' said Holly.

'Were you ever his shrink?'

'No.'

'Then why did he write the message on the wall to you at the Newsomes' crime scene, and why did he write you that personal letter?'

She didn't think Max would have asked that question, but he had, so . . .

'He killed my parents.'

Max looked a little stunned.

'Your parents were two of his victims?'

'The last two. Numbers seventeen and eighteen.'

He swivelled in his seat as his eyes followed the body count on the incident board. After a short time he lowered his gaze and turned back to her.

'That's some crazy shit,' he said.

Holly almost smiled. And then she did smile and for some reason she suddenly laughed at the absurdity of the statement.

'Yeah, Max, it was some crazy shit.'

She shot a look at Bishop as if to say: Are you sure he's okay to work on this? Bishop gave her a patient nod.

'And you want me to help find him?' Max said.

'Find her first,' said Bishop, and pointed to the photo of Cassandra.

'The sister? Okay. Give me whatcha got.'

Holly handed over a thin file.

'She was born in 1962 and after moving to Lorrach in 1983 with her brother, she studied as a veterinarian, then she moved to the UK in April 1991 and Sebastian set her up in one of his properties in Twickenham. A year later she was working as a vet in a pet shop off the high street. There's a contact telephone number for her that she gave to her employer twenty-six years ago, but that's no longer in service.'

'Did she ever visit her brother in prison?'

'Initially she wanted nothing to do with him. The press tracked her down and took her apart, wrote stories about her, and she consequently lost her job at the pet shop and seemingly disappeared. Whether she went into hiding or left the country, we don't know,' Holly said. 'However, she attended his funeral three months ago, so there's a chance she's still living in London. We have the address of another pet shop in Hampstead from ten years ago and another old telephone number—'

'That's fine,' Max cut her off. 'If she's here, I'll find her.'

And he took the file and left the room.

There were a few seconds of silence before Holly said:

'Is he going to be okay?'

'He'll be fine.' A beat. 'Are you okay?'

Holly nodded, then turned to her computer.

'I want you to listen to this tape. There's something on there.'

Twenty-Nine

They were at the chief's house in Henley-on-Thames and all three sat in the same room as the day before.

Holly had just played Bishop and Franks the tape and the chief was incredulous.

'The Animal is offering Phelps a bloody book deal! Is that even ethical?'

'It happens,' Holly said. 'Therapists can cash in if they have their patient's permission. It's not that that bothers me though, it's the manipulation we're witnessing. The sessions between Hedley Phelps and Sebastian seem to go way beyond the parameters of normal therapy.' Holly shook her head, frowning. 'The conversations are too personal.'

'Surely that happens sometimes?'

'It does – but it's not healthy.'

'Have you talked to Phelps?'

'He's on three weeks' leave from Broadmoor,' Holly said. 'We've left messages for him, but he's not getting back to us.

I spoke to his wife, who said he'd moved out because they're going through a divorce, but she didn't have his new address on her. We're going to pay her a visit tomorrow morning.'

'Good.'

'There are some other words and phrases on the tape that seem strange, but there's too much static and I'm hoping someone from IT can clean it up for us.'

'Leave it with me,' Franks said. 'What did you find out about Annie Wilkes?'

'She's bipolar and has no recollection of the murder other than what she's read about in the newspapers and what she heard at the trial.'

'So the whole message could be a misdirection?'

'That's why we want to compare the handwriting on the wall to a message The Animal wrote at the murder scene of victim number eleven.' Bishop handed over the two photographs. Franks barely glanced at them before placing them on the table.

'Is that it?'

'The killer stole Sandra Newsome's necklace which fits The Animal's MO, but yes, for the moment, that's it.'

'I managed to get hold of DI Thompson's initial report on the Newsome murders,' Franks said. 'I can summarise the most important detail: Forensics found a hair upstairs in the daughter's bedroom on her duvet. They ran it through the system and the DNA matches a convicted paedophile called Thomas Kincaid.'

'A paedophile?' Holly said incredulously.

'They have his DNA at the murder scene,' Franks said. 'For all intents and purposes it appears as though they have identified the killer and your search for The Animal is over.'

'Whoever killed the Newsomes was not a paedophile. He left a six-year-old girl untouched upstairs . . .'

'Thomas Kincaid likes boys—'

'You said he was convicted,' Bishop said. 'I'm presuming he's out now?'

Franks handed him a file and he duly passed it to Holly. She skimmed through the pages as she listened to the chief. There was a probation photo from last year. Kincaid was five foot ten inches tall, thickset, possibly a bodybuilder with a mountain-man type beard and heavy eyebrows.

'He spent twelve years in Broadmoor for killing a fifteen-year-old boy and was released nine months ago,' Chief Franks said. 'He's still on probation, and when Thompson and the team went to pick him up this afternoon from his designated house, he wasn't there. The landlord said she hadn't seen him since Sunday afternoon – the day of the murder.'

'Why would he write a message to me and why would he ask about Annie Wilkes?'

'I don't know about Wilkes, but he was on B wing for eight years in Broadmoor, the same wing as The Animal, so they would have had contact. The Animal could have told him about you, The Animal could have asked him to carry on killing on his behalf. Thompson and the team are hot for this Kincaid character: DNA at the scene, he disappeared the day of the murder – it's all very convincing.'

'Convincing perhaps, but circumstantial. I don't think we should be this hasty, sir,' said Bishop. 'I'll admit the scenario Thompson's painted fits together nicely, and everything we've come up with is a little vague at the moment, but there are leads we need to follow up on from the hospital, and most importantly, this tape recording with his therapist.'

'You're clutching at straws, both of you.'

'What else can we do?'

'Sir,' Holly said, 'I know we're still feeling our way in the dark and I know there's not much to go on—'

'I shouldn't have done this,' the chief said. 'The two of you working this case alone was an impossible task. I was a bloody fool for even starting it. I should shut the whole thing down now before it gets out of hand.'

'It won't.'

Franks didn't look convinced.

'Give us another forty-eight hours to see what we can come up with,' Holly pleaded.

She watched him carefully. There was nothing more she could do.

'Fine,' the chief said under his breath. 'Hopefully by then Thomas Kincaid will be in custody and this nightmare will be over.'

He took the recording and two photographs and left the room. 'See yourselves out.'

Thirty

It was almost closing time when Holly and Bishop met Max at the Lyric pub off Great Windmill Street in Soho.

The Victorian alehouse was small, dark and cramped, and they pushed past the heaving bodies to find Max in a corner with a table he had saved. He had an empty pint glass in front of him, but Holly didn't think that was the only one he'd had.

She and Max small-talked while Bishop made a phone call and when Bishop hung up, Max took orders and made his way to the bar. Bishop shifted in his seat and his knee bumped into Holly's. She didn't move and neither did he.

'I've read Thomas Kincaid's file,' she said. 'It's definitely not him. He doesn't have the psychopathy for this type of crime, or any of the other traits of a serial killer.'

'One of his hairs was found at the scene.'

'Secondary or tertiary DNA transference. Kincaid could have come in contact with the killer, something as simple as a handshake or touching the same door handle, the DNA is transferred and left at the crime scene.'

'I know you're good at this, Holly, but I want to know if

you have for one second entertained the idea that you might be wrong and The Animal is floating in the ozone layer like Max said?'

She hadn't.

'Do you think I'm wrong? Do you think it's Kincaid?'

'I don't know, but as a policeman I have to be open to the possibility of the evidence in front of me, that's all I'm saying.'

'I get that. But give me anyone except Kincaid.'

He smiled.

'I'll try. Has Phelps got back to you yet?'

'No.' She dialled the therapist's number again. A few rings and his voicemail picked up:

'*Hello, this is Hedley. I'm not available, but don't worry. You can leave a message and I will get back to you as soon as I can.*'

'Hello, Hedley,' said Holly. 'It's Holly Wakefield again. I know you're on holiday but DI Bishop and myself have been trying to reach you at your office and at home. We have some questions regarding one of your patients, Sebastian Carstairs. We're going to meet your wife at the house in Mayfair at around ten tomorrow morning, she said we could talk to you there. You can call me back on this number or if it's easier you can email me – holly-kick-sass@gmail.com. Thank you.'

She hung up. Bishop stared at her.

'Holly-kick-sass?'

'Holly-kick-sass, yeah, you know: "I'm sassy" – a throwback to one of my affirmation courses.'

'Not Holly-kicks-*ass*?'

'You can interpret it any way you want, DI Bishop.'

She smiled as Max returned brandishing three pints. Two ales and a Guinness for Holly.

'Thanks, Max,' she said.

He raised his glass to her and then to Bishop.

'To old times,' he said.

'To old times,' said Bishop. 'And to new.'

They all chinked glasses.

There was a long pause from both men as they drank and Holly had a sudden mental image of the two of them side by side in the harsh desert landscape, hunkered down in the sand with the constant rat-a-tat-tat of gunfire.

'How did the meeting go?' Max asked Bishop.

'They found someone else's DNA at the crime scene.'

'Case closed then?'

'Not yet,' said Holly. 'We're doing more research. How's the hunt for Cassandra going?'

Max shrugged, then said:

'I did some research on you, Holly.'

'Really?'

'Hard to find much, but I know you have a nickname – the *psychopath whisperer*.'

It had been a phrase coined by a journalist in a newspaper article written about her after the Pickford case late last year.

'Yes,' she said. 'Don't believe everything you read.'

'I'm curious though. Why do what you do? Why spend your time looking inside people's heads?'

Bishop stood and his chair scraped back.

'You guys chat,' he said. 'I'll be back in a minute.'

He headed to the toilets, and Holly took a sip of her drink. Max was still waiting for her to answer. He wasn't blinking, as if he had all the time in the world.

'It's complicated,' she said.

'Don't bullshit me. I'm helping you guys because of Bishop, but I want to know who I'm working with.'

'You already know my parents were murdered by a serial killer, and when I was a kid I wanted to know why, so I kept going with that thought and it carried me through my foster home, then through college and took me into teaching criminal psychology, and now I work at Wetherington Hospital most days of the week and help the police in my spare time.'

'Wetherington – is that a nuthouse?'

'Pretty much.'

'Do you see other serial killers there?'

'Some.'

'So every time you walk inside those walls you're remembering the pain of your past?'

She'd never heard it put like that but . . .

'Yes, I suppose I am. There's something about them that still fascinates me. We think they're evil, but in their eyes they're the heroes of their own stories. They're just regular people doing what they love to do.'

'Can you fix them?'

'No. You can control them with drugs, but only if you can catch them. And I really want to catch this one.'

'If he's alive.'

'He's alive.'

'So when we catch him, this invisible man, he gets hauled into a cell and doped up for the rest of his life?'

'Something like that.'

'We could always kill him first.'

Max's eyes were crystal clear but there was something else going on behind them.

'I tried that once already,' she said quietly. 'When I was ten years old.'

'You what?'

'At the end of his trial, I tried to kill Sebastian Carstairs.'

'You tried to kill The Animal when you were ten years old? What did you do? Hit him in the bollocks with a hockey stick?'

Holly laughed.

'I stabbed him.'

'Where? In the toe?'

'In the chest, you arse.'

Max laughed. It sounded like a bark.

'You've got a bit of anger inside you, haven't you?' he said.

'Not any more.'

'It's always there, Holly.'

She watched him finish his pint and stare at the empty glass.

'I was brought up in the foster system too,' he said. 'Dad left before I was born. Mum couldn't cope. I was six years old when she gave me up. We all have our stories, don't we? My foster parents did good by me and I did good by them. I was an unruly little bastard, to be honest, but they gave as good as they got and kept me on the straight and narrow. I needed discipline, so I went into the military after I left school.'

Bishop was heading back. He got stuck at the bar talking to a woman and Holly's eyes lingered over him:

'What was it like, working with him in Afghanistan?' she said.

'With Bill? I'd have died for him and he would have died for me. It's as simple as that. That's what I loved about the army. It's difficult coming back onto civvy street. It's hard to trust people when the stakes aren't so high.'

'Why did you leave?'

'I woke up one morning and the uniform didn't fit any more, let's just leave it at that.'

'Are you coping?'

'Sometimes.'

Bishop returned and sat.

'What did I miss?' he said.

Max smiled:

'Holly tried to kill The Animal when she was ten years old. She hit him with a stapler.'

'Shut up, you dick,' said Holly, but she couldn't stop laughing.

'Ah, now the real Holly is coming out to play,' said Max as he smiled. 'This is going to be a long night. I need a piss. I'll get another round on the way back. Same again, Holly?'

'Go on then.'

She watched him walk towards the bar.

'How is he still so steady on his feet?'

'Max can drink.'

'I'm glad he's with us, Bishop.'

'Yeah,' said Bishop. 'So am I.'

She felt a sudden chill and looked around the bar. People's faces were indistinct in the shadows of the low lighting.

'The Animal,' she said.

'What about him?'

'I just get the feeling he's closer than we think.'

Thirty-One

It was early in the morning of Thursday, 15 August, and The Animal was following his usual routine. He drank two cups of strong black coffee, then did thirty minutes of exercise: a series of yoga movements, lunges and press-ups. He did the press-ups on fists that had been hardened by the concrete of the prison floor. He was sweating when he finished.

He showered and shaved and made himself a breakfast of scrambled eggs and bacon, wearing a towel around his waist. After he ate, he washed the plates, saucepan and utensils and put them away in their cupboards. He poured the remains of a carton of milk down the sink, and collected the rest of the food from the fridge and put it in a black bin liner.

His suit and shirt jacket were hanging on the back of the front door, along with a dark grey trilby, and he had already ironed his trousers. He dressed quickly, took a seat on the sofa and made two phone calls. The first was to C&G Furniture, a small family-owned business in east London. He didn't have the catalogue with him, but he had made detailed notes on a piece of paper and held it in his hand as the call was answered:

'Country and Garden Furniture, how can I help?'

'Oh, hello,' Sebastian said. 'Is Geoff there, please?'

'Hold the line, I'll transfer you.'

A few seconds passed.

'This is Geoff. How can I help?' The voice was pleasant, not overly friendly.

'Geoff, we spoke last week – my order number is three-seven-two-four.'

'Three-seven-two-four? Hold on a second.'

'It was for an oak table.'

'Yes, here we are. One oak table from the farmhouse range with four white shabby-chic chairs to match.'

'That's the one. And delivery is tomorrow morning, I believe?'

'Let me check the driver's log. Yes – delivery is scheduled for Friday the sixteenth, at nine thirty in the morning to the Access Self-Storage Facility in Wembley, that's HA9 0JD, unit 11.'

'Correct. I'm storing the furniture there for a while. And the table is solid oak, isn't it?'

'Just as you ordered, sir.'

'Not oak veneer.'

'No, sir.'

'It's very important I have the real thing.'

'Of course, sir.'

'That's wonderful, thank you. I'll need five litres of white paint as well.'

'Gloss or matt?'

'Matt. It's for the interior.'

'And which white would you like?'

'Yes, it's funny isn't it. White is white really, but you have all sorts to choose from. I'm stuck between stone white and dove white.'

'Both are very popular, sir. Is there natural lighting where you'll be decorating?'

'No, it's an enclosed space. There are no windows at all.'

'Then may I suggest dove white? It's a little more subtle and the blue undertones will reflect what light there is and amplify it.'

'Yes, I like that, you've sold me on the dove white. Five litres then, please, and some brushes, a roller and a drop-cloth. I'll pay for the paint and the other sundries, cash on delivery.'

'Perfect. I'm stuck in the main office tomorrow, so the driver will be Tom.'

'And will he help me unload? I broke my ankle three days ago in a skiing accident and I'm a bit wobbly on the crutches.'

'There'll be two of them in the van, I'm not sure who the other one will be, but they'll unload and carry everything inside for you.'

'Thank you, Geoff, I really appreciate your help.'

'My pleasure, sir.'

Sebastian hung up and lit a cigarette. He savoured every breath as the smoke drifted lazily across the room. Once finished, he dialled another number.

'Is that Jakub, from AA Movers?' he said, when he heard the Polish accent answer the phone.

'Yes.'

'I believe one of my colleagues spoke to you yesterday, I'm a representative from the Wellness Charity, I want to re-confirm the moving van will be with me tomorrow at ten thirty in the morning.'

'Address?'

'The Access Self-Storage Facility in Wembley, unit 11 – that's HA9 0JD.'

'Ten thirty. We'll be there. And the address we're going to?'

'I'll call you later with the details,' said Sebastian.

He hung up and walked into the bathroom. In the sink was what looked like a misshapen power drill with a heavy-duty trigger. The drill bit had no teeth but was a circular tube, about four inches long and with the diameter of a one-pence piece. There was blood, hair and dark matter all along the tube and The Animal ran it under the tap and washed it until the stainless-steel bolt was mirror-clean. He dried it methodically with a towel then went into the bedroom.

He ignored the two dead bodies that lay stretched out on the floor.

Instead, he stared at the message on the wall he had written in blood:

Do you remember their smiles, Holly?
What would you give to see them one more time?

He pulled out a postcard-sized photo of Holly from his jacket pocket. It had been taken two days ago. He stuck it on the wall above the message with a drawing pin. Stepped back and stared. He straightened it carefully. Making it perfect.

Then he put the strange-looking drill inside a black sports bag on the bed, and packed a book that he was looking forward to reading. Today was a day to relax because the following few days were going to be very busy.

There was a knock on the front door. It was unexpected, but tentative so didn't alarm him.

He carried the bag through and left it behind the sofa, then checked the peephole. It was a woman he hadn't seen before. She had curly dark hair and was holding a baby. He contemplated for a moment, but could see she was about to knock again so he smoothed down his shirt, angled the trilby on his head and opened the door. They stared at each other for a while as he waited for her to speak.

'Hi,' she said. 'I'm sorry to trouble you but I barely got any sleep last night because of the dog.'

'The dog?'

'Your dog was barking until the early hours. I wasn't sure if you were aware of it, if you were out? But this little one was up and then she managed to sleep through it, but I couldn't, and I don't want to be rude, but would you be able to try and persuade him not to bark at night?'

The pleading in her eyes was intense. It had been so long since he had seen a woman this close, since he had smelled a woman this close.

'I'm sorry,' he said. 'I was taking care of it for my wife – but well, we've just separated, she's been having an affair and she took the dog back home with her very early this morning.'

'Oh, I'm so sorry, that's . . .'

'Awkward early-morning doorway conversation?'

He chanced a smile.

'It was inevitable perhaps,' he said, 'our marriage breaking down. I work long hours and I'm addicted to my job. Are you married?'

'Yes.'

'That's nice.' He licked his lips. 'And who's this little one?' he said.

'Flora.'

'Hello, Flora. You're a lovely creature, aren't you? What is she, twelve, fourteen months?'

'Fourteen. Did you – do you and your wife have any children?'

'Three. All grown up now. Two are at university and the eldest is a palaeontologist at the Natural History Museum. What about you, Flora?' And he waved at the baby. 'What do you want to be when you grow up? Do you want to look at old fossils in the mud? Or perhaps you could be a lawyer or maybe even a policewoman and catch the bad guys?' He smiled again and the mother in the corridor smiled with him.

'We'll have to see,' she said. 'I'm Anita by the way, I'm at number twenty-four, I didn't catch your name?'

'I'm Hedley, Hedley Phelps. I'm a psychiatrist I don't really know this area very well. The infidelity and the separation has all come as a bit of a shock to me.'

'Of course. It must be so hard.'

She didn't know where to look and it made him feel warm inside.

'Well, it's been lovely to meet you, Hedley,' she said, 'and if you need showing around or want me to tell you the best places to go shopping, just let me know.'

'Thank you. I might take you up on that, Anita.' He put a hand on the door. 'I'd better get ready for work now,' he suggested quietly. 'Have a lovely day.'

'And you. Bye.'

After he closed the door, he leaned against it and counted for thirty seconds. Then he opened it to make sure she was gone. For some reason the woman had reminded him of Holly. It was the eyes, it had to be: chestnut brown, chocolate and cherry, and he felt the aching pain again. He put his thumb and index finger inside his mouth, past his tongue and towards his molars. Then he tugged firmly.

There was a sharp snap and he pulled out a rotten tooth, root and all.

Thirty-Two

Holly stood outside her brother's grey cell door in Wetherington Hospital.

She had woken when it was still dark, having slept badly, with a pounding heart and the sweat of anxiety. The dawn was crimson when she made herself breakfast and drank coffee, then she had showered and dressed. She knew she had to see her brother so didn't question the impulse and drove the three miles from her flat to the Hospital on the Cromwell Road. Even though she worked here four or five days a week, she only saw Lee sporadically now. Sometimes she enjoyed their talks, other times not, and as she walked the sterile corridor to the pale grey door she now faced, her emotions were guarded. She gave a nod to the security camera, the door lock flashed green and she entered.

The cell was twelve-by-twelve feet and the same colour as the door. There was a single bed, a toilet, two chairs and a fold-up table. Lee was lying on the bed with his arms across his chest. He was two years her senior and had the faintest red hair, almost blond, that had been thinning for as long as she could remember.

'The Animal is still alive,' Holly said and sat at the table.

He dragged himself into the seat opposite. His face was pale and wraith-like and his eyes were a crystal blue.

She had brought him a pack of cigarettes and he opened them like a greedy kid with a chocolate bar.

'You want one?' he said.

She nodded.

He took out two cigarettes and lit them both. Handed her one and contemplated his own.

'I told you he was still alive the last time you came to see me,' he said.

'You said he will always be alive, I thought you were being metaphorical.' A beat. 'They don't believe me: the police, the commissioner.'

'What about your friend, DI Bishop?'

'He believes me. We're working the case by ourselves.'

'He's following your lead? What some people do for love. That's a dangerous thing, the policeman who doesn't really know anything about you.'

'He knows more than most people.'

'Does he know about me?'

'He knows you exist.'

'Does he? This is going to end badly,' he said.

'Who for?'

'One of us. All of us. Everybody?'

She was suddenly irritated with him. They had known each other longer than anybody else, but sometimes she felt like a stranger. He always seemed intent on finding a weakness in her armour and sometimes she was curious as to what he really thought of her. The inevitable cigarette in her hand. The mood she brought into the room.

'Do you still dream of Mum and Dad?' she said.

'Every night.'

'Do they still talk to you?'

'They don't talk to me, they say one word: *kaleidoscope*.'

'Kaleidoscope, I remember. Like the toy we used to have when we were kids,' she said. 'Look through the eyepiece, twist one end and the coloured beads and mirrors make rainbows.'

'Something like that.'

'Don't go all cold on me.'

'I'm not going cold,' he said. He uncrumpled a bit of tinfoil from his pocket and tapped his cigarette.

'I just feel as though I'm wasting my time.'

'What does that mean?'

'With you, with this. You're blinded by your quest for love, Holly. Your need to be wanted. You won't ever find a replacement for Mum and Dad, but I think you've found one for me – and that should be celebrated.'

'Bishop?'

'Who else?'

'It's not as if—'

'Sometimes you have to leap before you look.'

'I will never leave you, Lee.'

'You've been saying that for decades, but maybe it's time you did.'

'And do what?'

'Follow a different path. Get rid of your blunted emotions and open your eyes to the new hope.'

'I am open to it, but I can't forget the past.'

'Come off it, we've all got a past! The difference is, I don't live there any more.'

'Christ, you're being a dick!'

'Christ, you've still got so much anger!'

She sat back. All her energy had been taken and he leaned forward and stared at her through the haze of smoke:

'What is that you're wearing?'

'What?'

Her hands went around her neck to the butterfly necklace.

'It was Mum's.'

'I thought The Animal stole it.'

'I got it back.'

'It suits you. You remind me of her.'

And Lee started to laugh. Crazy laughs that rocked his body until he had tears running down his cheeks. Eventually the fit subsided and he wiped his eyes and blew his nose.

'Are you done?' she said.

'Sorry, I needed that.'

'I didn't want to get into this today, Lee. I wanted to have a quiet talk, that's all. Can we change the subject?'

'Up to you.'

'How are you feeling with the new drugs?' she said.

'Shit. Tired. Familiar faces everywhere but I can't see a bloody thing.'

'You can see me.'

'And how long will that last? What am I to you, Holly?' he said.

'I told you I don't want to talk about this.'

'Answer the question.'

'Fine, then be more specific.'

'How many times have people stared at me and only seen the wall behind me? Read the blackboard I was standing in front of when we were kids as if there was a massive hole through my body. The silence inside of me.' He trailed off and shook his head.

'When will I get to feel good, Holly? You help other people with mental illnesses but you don't see them. You don't see what I see, what I have seen, and you will never be able to. You cannot see through my eyes. Ever. And no matter how loud I shout, no matter how much I cry and how much I reach out to whoever is there, the silence will always be louder than everything and nobody will ever hear me. Never. I look at you and I can hear you. Like a tap dripping on a hard surface. You are noise, you always have been, Holly, and always will be. I'm just the silence on the other side of the room. The silence that nobody ever hears.'

'I hear you, Lee.'

'That's because you have no choice.'

For several seconds neither of them spoke and then she stood up. She'd had enough. She stared at his blank eyes and felt so sad she didn't know what to do. There was a sudden knock on the door and Lee stubbed out his cigarette.

'It's not for me,' he said.

Thirty-Three

Dr Bernstein's office was as neat as he was.

In his sixties, Bernstein was a slight, small man, impeccably dressed and his manner was amiable but sharp. He was one of the chief physicians at Wetherington and had been Holly's counsellor for as long as she could remember.

Bernstein was the one who had helped her pick up the pieces of her shattered life after her parents had been killed. During that time Holly had been placed in foster care, and although smiling people were constantly talking to her, and she was always warm and the police fussed over her and gave her whatever she asked for, she didn't really understand what was going on.

Bernstein had helped her understand that her mother and father were dead and that the big man with the bony hands was responsible. And at ten years old, Holly realised she had only one thing to do for the rest of her life – and that was to kill the man who had taken her parents' lives. It wouldn't bring them back, but it would fill the gap that was getting bigger inside her every day.

She had no idea how to kill anyone, so at first she simply imagined what it might be like. Do I shoot him like on the TV? No – I don't have a gun. Do I strangle him? No – my hands are too small. The ideas came and went with every day, and the more she fantasised about it, the more real it became, until she could almost taste it and it was the only thing she thought about. She wanted to stab him in the heart like her mother had been stabbed and finally, after weeks of attempts and practice runs in her foster home using a small knife and fruit from the garden, she thought she was ready.

On the day the trial ended, before the verdict was announced, The Animal was paraded in front of the press on the way to the courtroom. Holly walked into the building with the tiny fruit knife hidden in her sock. She watched him walk towards her as if in slow motion, then broke away from her guardian and struck. The tiny blade flashed and The Animal smiled as the knife embedded in his chest, then he held on to her gently and took her down to the floor with him.

'I've been waiting for you, Jessica,' he had whispered in her ear.

Then he let her go and she felt adult hands grabbing her and pulling her away. The Animal had spent six hours in surgery. Six centimetres lower and the blade would have severed his aortic valve and killed him outright, but he survived. The Crown Court wanted to charge her with attempted murder. Her lawyer pleaded down to manslaughter and because of the extenuating circumstances of Holly being a victim and only ten years old, the judge threw the case out of court.

After that episode, Dr Bernstein saw her through her psychiatric evaluation with the Child and Adolescent Mental Health Services and Holly spent the next seven years attending therapy sessions with him discussing her anger, depression and anxiety. She had been a cutter back then. The first time had been with a razor blade on the left forearm. It had felt like slicing open a lump of ham. The zing of pain a second after the cut and then the blood. A stupid amateur mistake. The cut was too deep and too obvious. It would show and need stitches. To this day in front of Dr Bernstein she would always unconsciously pull down her shirtsleeves, and she caught herself doing it now.

He had helped her channel her energies and her life into finding out why people killed, and she got a degree in criminal psychology from Bristol University. He brought her into the fold at Wetherington Hospital and mentored her through her first series of patients and as her confidence grew she began to teach criminal psychology at King's College one day a week. She had been tested mentally over the past two years working with the Met, coming up against killers who had opened the doors of her past, but she had come through stronger and wiser.

Dr Bernstein watched her closely. He smiled cordially as he leaned back in his chair and crossed his legs.

'I hear you're working on another case with the police,' he said. 'How is it?'

Her talk with Bishop about the possibility of her being wrong about The Animal being alive and Thomas Kincaid being the killer had unnerved her slightly.

'I don't know if I'm doing the right thing. I'm trusting my gut instinct. But other people are trusting me too and I'm starting to doubt myself. I'm keeping the past alive and I don't know if that's good.'

'It depends which part of your past. We all doubt ourselves, but if you're looking for the truth, that's all that matters. Are you getting enough sleep?'

'Sleep is sporadic, but the pills help.'

'How about the idea we talked about of separating the sanctity of your home from the workplace? Work is merely a set of tasks that need to be undertaken in a certain environment and home is your safe space.'

'It's not entirely going to plan. This new case is very personal to me.'

'They're all personal to you, Holly. I just want to make sure you're coping.' He stared at her, unblinking. 'It's another murder, isn't it?'

'Yes.'

He pulled himself to his desk. He scribbled a note and sounded subdued when he said:

'Are you exercising? Going to the gym?'

'Three times a week, and I'm walking as well.'

Her thoughts drifted. She put a hand to her necklace again and memories of her mother flashed by in an instant: beautiful woman, dead woman, beautiful woman, dead woman. And then she heard Bernstein say:

'Holly?'

'Sorry?'

'I asked if you wanted to talk about Lee?'

'Do we have to?'

'No. How was he behaving today?'

'Annoying and a bit shouty.'

He nodded slightly and pulled out a prescription pad. Wrote something quickly and handed it over.

'If it gets too much, twice a day with water after food. When do you think the case will be finished?'

'That's impossible to say.'

'Well, if you need to talk, I'm here.'

'Thank you, Dr Bernstein, I appreciate it.'

'I'll see you again next week, Holly.'

She was walking towards the hospital exit when she thought she saw The Animal.

A flash of his face and then the hulking shadow turned along the corridor. He was wearing a doctor's white jacket and walking away from her. She followed, her stomach in knots, her hands sweaty. How had he got past security and how long had he been following her? If he was at Wetherington, had he also been to King's College? Was her presence there placing her students in danger? She looked around for security, but there was no one else in sight. She quickened her pace, almost lost him around a corner and then he was right in front of her. She reached out and touched his shoulder, not knowing what she would be able to do.

The man turned and his blue eyes stared at her, and she could see the terrible intelligence working inside. And then he smiled and it wasn't The Animal. It was one of the orderlies she had seen before but couldn't remember his name.

'Sorry,' she said, and hurried on past.

Thirty-Four

Holly and Bishop were driving through Mayfair.

The streets were wide and the cars shiny as they headed towards Hedley Phelps' flat. Holly was upset after her conversation with Lee and worried about where this case was taking her. Imagining she had seen The Animal at Wetherington Hospital was simply ridiculous.

'The Greek translator interviewed Maria Theopolis,' Bishop said. 'She concurred with everything her daughter said.'

'Any news from Michael Theopolis in Greece?'

'Not yet.'

'Can we have some music?'

Bishop turned the radio on. Classic FM. She felt his eyes on her as he said: 'You okay?'

She glanced at him quickly then switched her focus back to the road.

'Trying to put everything together in my head, that's all.'

He reached over and squeezed her arm.

'If you ever need to talk, I'm here for you. You know that, right?'

There were no complications with Bishop and she managed a smile.

'Thank you,' she said.

'There's a file on the back seat about Hedley Phelps, you might want to take a look.'

She reached around and grabbed it. It was thin, only three or four pages inside and she began to read:

'He was at Bristol University, same as me,' Holly said. 'He studied therapies, complimentary medicine and pharmacology.'

'Same years?'

'No, he left in 2001, I began in 2002, we just missed each other. Then he got a placement over in the States at the Haven Behavioral Hospital in Philadelphia. It's not for criminals – mainly older patients who need a little help. He spent six years in Philadelphia and got married to Sylvia Collins in 2009, she's a British journalist originally from Birmingham. They moved back to the UK in 2012 and settled in London the same year.' She turned a page.

'He began working at Broadmoor in 2013, specialising in prisoner rehabilitation. He believes the criminal system has its priorities back to front. He thinks we should take money away from prisons and build more hospitals to help killers, because putting psychopaths away doesn't stop their disorder, it simply creates more of it.'

'What do you think?'

'It's a controversial opinion. On one hand he's right, but on the other, we can never cure psychopathy, and if psychopaths are a different breed to us, which they are, then the real question is: are they evolving faster than our ability to deal with them?'

'From a layman's point of view, Hedley Phelps does seem

to have taken an incredibly unhealthy interest in his infamous client,' Bishop said.

'Some therapists fall into that trap. A part of them wants to be close to the notoriety, which makes them feel special and fuels their ego, so there's a bit of narcissism involved, and others on a deeper level want to be part of the dark fantasy that their patient talks to them about.'

'Would they ever commit to the violence? Join forces or become partners with them?'

Holly sat up slowly in her seat.

'You mean something similar to Helsinki syndrome, where the captive falls for the kidnapper?'

'Yes.'

'I can't imagine Hedley Phelps committing any murders, but . . . Did he have any other patients at Broadmoor?'

'Six, all murderers who are still behind bars. And according to this he had a private clinic in Westminster that closed last year.'

'Does it say why?'

'No, it doesn't give any more details. Do you think he'll talk to us?'

'I don't see why not,' Holly said. 'I'm sure he thinks The Animal is dead so he wouldn't be betraying a confidence, but he might not divulge their entire relationship.'

'What do you mean?'

'The recordings we listened to are incredibly intimate, and that worries me.'

A few minutes past ten o'clock and they arrived at an expensive street in central London. Georgian houses, all white with stone steps and front doors between pillars. Bishop pulled over and parked.

‘Let’s see what Hedley Phelps has to say for himself,’ he said.

The large terraced house had been split into four flats and Hedley Phelps and his wife lived on the second floor. Bishop pressed the buzzer. A few seconds passed then they heard the tinny sound of a female voice:

‘Hello?’

‘Mrs Sylvia Phelps?’ Bishop said.

‘Yes.’

‘This is DI Bishop from the Metropolitan Police and Holly Wakefield. I believe the two of you spoke yesterday?’

‘Yes, that’s right, but Hedley isn’t here.’

‘I thought he was supposed to come over at ten to pick up some things,’ Holly said.

‘He was, but he hasn’t showed. I called him and he didn’t pick up.’

‘Mrs Phelps, can we come up?’ Bishop said. ‘It would be very helpful.’

‘Can I see some ID, please?’

There was a camera by the buzzer and he flashed his warrant card. A pause, then the front door popped open.

The woman who greeted them in the second-floor doorway was tall, her neck slightly exaggerated. She wore a black dress and had pink Marigold gloves on her hands. Her dark hair was tied up in a bun.

‘I can only apologise for him not being here. Why do you want to talk to him?’

‘We need to ask him a few questions about one of his patients,’ Holly said.

‘Have you contacted the prison?’

‘We have. They said he took annual leave.’

‘Yes, that’s right. I don’t know if he’s actually gone away

somewhere – I doubt it, he hated travelling. He wanted time to move his things out and get resettled. I'm afraid that's all I can tell you – we didn't exactly separate on the best of terms.'

'I'm sorry to hear that,' said Holly. 'You said you had the address where he's staying?'

Sylvia turned and took a pad from the hall stand, ripped off the top sheet of paper and handed it over.

'Thank you,' said Bishop. 'He had a private practice in Westminster, didn't he? Do you know why it closed?'

'It wasn't a viable business. He shared the building with four other therapists but ended up spending more and more time at Broadmoor and never built up the clientele he needed.'

'He was only at Broadmoor part-time though, wasn't he?'

'He was, but he thought the prison system was outdated and took it upon himself to try and help reform it. He was always writing letters and proposals to the board of directors at the prison and interviewing prisoners about conditions and their welfare.'

'Was Sebastian Carstairs one of them?' Holly said.

'Yes. God, we had arguments over that man. Is that the patient you want to talk to him about?'

'It is,' said Bishop.

'Hedley would bring his work home with him – taped sessions with that vile man that he would play in the study and try and make me listen to.'

'And did you?'

'No. He wanted me to write an editorial piece on him – I refused, of course. I found it all rather unsavoury, to be honest.'

'What was the editorial piece about?'

'Prisoner reform. Some of it I understood: conversion therapy, giving the prisoners more freedom and better education.

He wanted me to agree with his view that the prisoners were victims too, but I couldn't. Education, yes, of course, give them that, but everything else? Sorry, I'm a staunch believer in "you do the crime, you do the time", something I brought back from Philadelphia with me.' She rolled her eyes. 'Hedley's rather unhealthy interest in that man was the nail in our marital coffin.'

'What do you mean?'

'He would listen to the recordings they had together for hours when he got home. He'd shut himself in the study and lock himself in. I would be outside the door sometimes and it was as if there were two normal people in there having a conversation about the weather or life in general.' She softened slightly. 'But they weren't normal, were they? One was a serial killer and the other was a man whom I thought I once knew.'

'Do you know if he left any of those recordings here?' Holly said.

'Hedley took everything with him, including some of my USB sticks, which annoyed me. I have interviews with clients on there that my publishers are waiting for.'

'Did Hedley ever mention that he was working on a book deal with Sebastian?'

'Yes, he did actually, and my publishers wouldn't go near anything like that.' She was about to close the door when something occurred to her: 'Oh, when you see him, tell him I want Bessie back.'

'Bessie?'

'Our black Labrador. I've already informed my solicitor to make it a priority.'

Thirty-Five

Hedley Phelps' flat was on the way back to the police station.

It was on the second floor of a large, rather run-down Victorian block with a caged lift and narrow stairs. The building smelled odd; it could have been the carpet or the trash bags that someone had left outside their door at the end of the corridor. It was a stark contrast to Phelps' previous home and Holly wondered why he had chosen this place.

Bishop knocked several times and there was no reply.

He wrote a short note on one of his ID cards and pushed it under the door.

Back in the basement, they ate sandwiches at their desks, sitting with their chairs turned to face the incident board.

'What are you thinking?' Holly said.

'Hedley Phelps is a man in a marriage that isn't working, with a wife who has been having an affair and then The Animal comes along—'

'And offers him a shoulder to cry on and lets him know he cares.'

'As well as the possibility of a book deal that could change his life forever.'

'It feeds his ego.'

'I guess the question is, would Hedley be gullible enough to try and help his patient escape?'

'Not necessarily gullible – more star-struck and wide-eyed,' Holly said. 'It's out there, but not beyond the realms of possibility.'

She was still playing with the thought when the door opened and Max entered. He sat down and wiped his hands over his face and through his hair with a post-cocaine tremor.

'You okay, Max?' Bishop said.

Max didn't say anything, he just kept rubbing his hands over his face.

'Do you want a coffee?' Holly said.

Max nodded, but Bishop gestured her to stay where she was and went to do it himself. He made the coffee and kept it strong, black with three spoonfuls of sugar, and he added some water from the cooler.

'Drink it,' he said as he handed over the mug. 'It's not that hot.'

Max took a sip that emptied half the mug then his hands went back to his face again.

'Have you eaten?' Bishop said.

'No, and I'm out of cigarettes.'

Bishop handed him a pack. Max lit one and took a deep draw. He coughed until his eyes watered, then finished the rest of his coffee and lit the same cigarette again.

'Did you stay here last night?' Bishop said.

'No. I crashed with a friend. Not that you guys haven't made your penthouse suite enticing and dare I say very affordable, but I don't like being underground. Reminds me of a death camp in Afghanistan.'

He took another breath then opened his eyes and stared at Holly.

'I found her,' he said matter-of-factly.

'Cassandra?' she said, and was up on her feet before she knew it.

He coughed again and nodded.

'She works in a pet shop in Hampstead. The reason you couldn't find her tax records and bank accounts is because she's changed her name to Johanna Muller.'

'Johanna Muller?'

'It's hard to lose a German accent so she's adapted and created a whole new backstory for herself as far away from the truth as possible. She says she's an only child who was born in Baden-Württemberg in south-west Germany and studied English and Spanish at the International School of Stuttgart, but decided to become a veterinarian instead. I imagine she reels off this list of fake life experiences to everyone she meets. The alternative is to tell the truth, and I can't imagine that working out for her.'

'How do you know all this?'

'She has a LinkedIn profile and after she left the shop on her lunch break I went in and made discreet enquiries, then followed her home.'

'Are you sure it's her?' Bishop said.

'Only one way to find out. On her way back to work she went into a café and ordered a cappuccino. She drank it outside while on her phone and threw the empty cup in a bin.'

Max reached into his jacket and pulled out a plastic bag.

Inside was a paper cup. Using a tissue, he carefully put it on the desk.

Holly put on a pair of latex gloves and picked it up. There was bright-red lipstick on one side of the rim.

'Well done,' Bishop said.

Thirty-Six

Holly sat at a corner café on Hampstead High Street.

It was always busy here: shoppers, workers, but mainly locals on leisurely lunches. She was at a forty-five-degree angle facing the shops on the opposite street: three restaurants, a travel agent, a boutique clothing store and the pet shop they had been watching for the past forty minutes.

Max was positioned three tables away to her left and was reading a newspaper. Every now and then she glanced over at him, but he ignored her completely. Cassandra was supposed to have finished work at six o'clock. It was twenty-five past and Holly was worried the woman had exited from another part of the building, or perhaps decided to stay later for whatever reason. After a few minutes more, Max casually folded up the newspaper and left cash by his empty cups. As he passed Holly, he gave her a nod and her attention shifted back to the front door of the pet shop.

The woman who had just exited was tall and thickset. She was well dressed in a blue satin shirt, black trousers and jacket, and her hair was dark brown and tightly curled. She wore an orange paisley scarf and Gucci sunglasses.

Bishop and Max had discussed the best strategy to approach Cassandra, and all three had agreed an introduction at her workplace would be disastrous. Holly needed her alone, so she followed the woman along Heath Street until she took a left on West Heath Road and entered Hampstead Heath, using the heath as a cut-through to Mansion Gardens, where Max said Cassandra lived. It was the perfect location to interact. The paths were wide, there were picknickers on the grass and dozens of other walkers. Holly closed the distance.

'Johanna?' Holly said.

The woman carried on walking.

'Johanna Muller?' slightly louder.

The woman stopped and turned. Her eyes were hidden by the Gucci shades but she looked surprised.

'Yes?'

'I thought it was you but wasn't sure. I came into the pet shop a few weeks ago, asking about a chihuahua.'

Holly had closed the distance.

'Are you looking for one?'

'Yes, we spoke briefly.'

'We did? I don't remember, I'm sorry. What was your name?'

'Holly. Holly Wakefield.'

Holly handed over one of her cards. The woman glanced at it, half-smiled and seemed to give up on her memory.

'I've finished work for the day and I'm about to go home – perhaps we could talk tomorrow?'

'I'd rather talk now, actually.'

'Can't it wait?'

'No, it's . . .' as delicately as she could, Holly told her, 'it's because I know you're not Johanna Muller.'

The woman looked genuinely confused and gave a dismissive wave with her hand.

'I'm sorry?'

'I know who you really are.'

'My name is Johanna.'

'No,' said Holly. 'Your real name is Cassandra Carstairs.'

'Don't be ridiculous. I am who I say I am.'

'You were born in Lüneburg, Germany, twenty-fifth February 1962 and you're fifty-seven years old. You have a brother, too. Sebastian.'

The woman was tall but she seemed to get taller as she straightened.

'Why are you saying this? Who are you?'

'I know who you are,' Holly said. 'Please, I just want to talk to you.'

'Well I don't want to talk to you! I'll call the police.'

She turned and walked. Holly followed.

'Cassandra—'

'That is not my name.'

'Your brother killed my parents.'

'He did what?'

She stopped, shook her head and carried on:

'I have no brother. I was an only child and was born in Baden-Württemberg in south-west Germany—'

'—And you went to ISS, the International School of Stuttgart and studied languages,' Holly said. 'You thought about becoming a translator at the UN when you were eighteen, but decided to become a veterinarian instead. I read your LinkedIn profile. I know you have created a fake past for yourself and, trust me, I understand why. Please stop, Cassandra.'

'Stop calling me that! My name is Johanna Muller. What else

would you like to know about me? I have lived in Hampstead for the last six years with many happy memories of my husband who sadly died on seventeenth April 2017.'

'Truth or a lie? I don't know, but I'll let Max know.'

'Max who?'

'The man who followed you in the park today after your lunch break. You wouldn't have seen him, he's very good at what he does. On the way back from your home you went to Café Rouge on the High Street. You ordered a small cappuccino and after you had left, Max removed your cup from the bin and took it with him.' She paused. 'Your DNA and fingerprints are on file with the police.'

The woman stopped walking and her shoulders sagged. Her voice cracked when she spoke.

'Then the cat is out of the bag,' she said, and took a resigned breath. 'I am who I am and it doesn't matter any more. I'm sorry, but I don't— I've said this a million times and no matter how many more times I say it, it will never make it right. I'm sorry, Holly Wakefield, that he took your parents away from you. I truly am. My brother wasn't right in the head, but he too is dead now. So let us just say we are both done. That is my confession, and if that was what you were after, so be it. Now please excuse me.'

'Your brother isn't dead.'

Cassandra stopped in her tracks.

'He's still alive. And he's killing again.'

The woman took her Gucci shades off and her crystal-blue eyes flashed angrily.

'*Lieber Gott!* You are another one of the crazy ones then?'

'I'm not crazy.'

'Yes, you are. This is not a joke? Is there a hidden camera

somewhere? You think you can make money from me? Did he really murder your parents or are you just another journalist? Another ghoul? I know your type, and I have dealt with your kind for over twenty years, so go ahead, print your stupid fantasy and stories. You cannot hurt me any more than I have already been hurt.'

'My intention is not to hurt you.'

'In fact, I'll give you a story. Everybody's life has been ruined and I will not— I refuse to feel guilty any more about what he did. Now, you will leave me alone please and you will go on your way.'

She walked. Holly followed.

'He's alive, Cassandra!'

Cassandra didn't stop this time. If anything, she increased her pace.

'*Blöde kuh!* You say he's alive?' She suddenly turned. 'HE IS DEAD!' she screamed. 'My brother was cremated at Hammersmith crematorium. I saw it with my own eyes!'

'So did I!'

Cassandra took a faltering step.

'You were there?'

'I spoke to you afterwards, by the fountain.'

'Now I remember you.' Her eyes glazed slightly. 'Is it just you and Max who were looking for me, or are there others?'

'I just want to talk.'

'You are insane.' She pointed at Holly and shouted so people close by would hear: 'Insane woman in the park! Insane woman following me!' And then her voice dropped to a whisper.

'Leave me alone. Enough is enough.'

Thirty-Seven

When Cassandra Carstairs got back to her flat she was shaking.

In the bathroom she took two Minoxidil pills for her blood pressure and in the kitchen she drank a cold glass of water and splashed the remains on her face, running her fingers through her hair, pulling at knots and ending up hurting her scalp.

Her gut wrenched.

Meeting the strange woman was the last thing she had expected today, and the conversation had rocked her. Throughout her brother's incarceration people had always tried to track her down and the number of journalists she had sworn at, slapped and kicked was more than she cared to remember. Would they never stop? Cassandra went to the bay window and pulled the curtain to one side, but the woman was nowhere to be seen and Cassandra let the curtain fall back into place.

Her home was a Victorian terrace with small rooms and big shadows. There were no photos of Sebastian on display, but on a Biedermeier walnut sewing table by the window was a faded picture of her mother and father when they had been young. He with a tan suit and a wide knitted orange tie and she wearing an A-line blue dress, with gloriously blonde hair and blue eyes. They looked to have been in their mid-twenties.

She opened the hidden drawer on the sewing table and lifted out a scrapbook, wiping a hand over the cover of embossed flowers that circled a large red heart. Inside was a collection of newspaper and magazine articles chronicling her brother's murders. It was something she had taken great care with for the sake of the victims and she had written *Es tut mir Leid* (I'm sorry) *Er weiß nicht was er tut* (He knows not what he does) on every single page.

So who was this Holly Wakefield?

Had her parents been killed by Sebastian or was that just make-believe? She took out the card the woman had given her. Just a name and a phone number and nothing on the reverse. She flicked through the collage of newspaper cuttings, looking for the victims with surviving children. The woman would have been thirty, thirty-five, so she went through all the murders looking for the name Wakefield. There were no victims with that last name so the woman in the park had been lying. Unless – and Cassandra hesitated – unless the woman had changed her name, like she had.

She went through the pages again, looking for suitable next of kin and stopped on Charles and Patricia Ridley, victims number seventeen and eighteen. They had left behind a nine-year-old girl called Jessica, and for whatever reason, Cassandra knew that was the woman she had just met.

Jessica.

So she *had* changed her name.

She read a few of the articles: brought up on a farm in Hampshire, her parents had been killed in the kitchen and the young girl had discovered their bodies. She turned another page – a startling colour photo she had forgotten about – showing the young girl in a corridor at the courthouse lying on top of her brother with a knife in her hand. *Ten-year-old daughter of victims tries to kill The Animal* read the headline.

Lieber Gott! This had to be her. The madwoman in the park was real and she had tried to kill Sebastian when she was a child! She had held onto that anger and thirst for revenge and now she walked the streets looking for the man who killed her parents, even though she'd attended his funeral and knew he was dead. Did she want revenge on Cassandra now? Would she try and kill her as well?

She googled *Holly Wakefield* on her computer: she was a criminal psychologist who worked at a place called Wetherington Hospital in central London. She also lectured at King's College and it said she had helped the police in several high-profile murder cases during the past few years. How fascinating. And now she thought Sebastian was still alive. It was madness, no matter what.

She ripped up Holly's business card and threw it in the bin. Her hands trembled when she closed the scrapbook and put it away.

She had been at her brother's funeral three months ago. She hadn't shed a tear, but she had done her duty as the sole surviving member of the family, and after that she'd thought it would finally be over, but it seemed there would always be strange people fascinated with him, and therefore by default fascinated with her.

There was a chattering sound and birdsong from the cage in the corner of the room.

She should check on Jonas and Finn. They would be getting

anxious. She lifted the blanket and the two bright yellow canaries fluttered from perch to perch. They could sense her unease as they pecked at the cuttlefish bones stuck between the bars. Their unblinking faces reminded her of her brother and how things had been back in Germany.

When she was a baby, if she fell over and cried, Sebastian would pick her up and kiss her better, and if he banged his head, she would kiss him and call him her *little soldier* and hold him tight until the pain went away. Through school he had become more distant, but he always had time for her, and when he had gone into the army, she missed him terribly. She had survived, avoiding her father's hands as much as she could by night and focusing on her studies by day, but when her mother died her life became unbearable. Her father had expected Cassandra to step into his wife's shoes, and clean for him and bake for him and sleep with him, and rub the cream into his cracked hands when he came home from work, and she wondered after several weeks of this routine if this was now her new life.

She thought bad thoughts and talked to herself about death all the time and found herself drawn to the bottles of alcohol in the living room cabinet. She contemplated suicide so many times and finally wrote to her brother begging for his help. He had immediately returned and taken her away from their father. In doing so, she knew he had saved her life. And during those first few weeks when they had relocated to Lorrach near the French and Swiss borders, she had grown to absolutely adore Sebastian all over again.

Even though she was two and a half years his junior, she had played big sister when Sebastian went to work on his building projects. She cooked meals for them both and cleaned the home and continued to study until she had passed her veterinary courses. When Sebastian had relocated to England, she had kept the house and started work in south Lorrach at a family-run clinic for pets. She missed her brother and when he had asked if she wanted to come to England, she had jumped at the chance. It took her a further two years to qualify for her British veterinarian qualifications equivalent, but after that it was relatively easy to get her dream job in a small animal hospital on the King's Road in central London. She had done everything legally, got her papers, her visa, and she was well-liked and respected and was glad to finally leave the memories of Germany and her parents behind.

The first hint that something was not right with Sebastian was when he came home late at night on 13 February 1986. She found out later this was the day Raychel Raynes had been killed. Sebastian had been gone all day and when he finally arrived his eyes were red-veined and expressionless as if he had been sucked dry of emotion.

'What's happened to you, Sebastian?'

'You don't need to know.'

'You look strange.'

'I am okay, but someone else is not.'

'Who? What do you mean by that?'

'You don't need to know.'

She thought perhaps he had got into a fight with a client at work or upset his girlfriend, but instead of explaining further he held out his big hands and offered her a round cake in a brown paper bag. She smiled when she saw what it was. The cake was called a Berliner, and was the doughnut's German cousin, a pillowy soft sweet dough that melted in your mouth. When they were children they would save their pocket money and once a week would walk into town to the bakery and buy one Berliner each and sit on the wall opposite the bakery and eat them. The icing sugar would be sticky on their hands and their lips almost melted with the hot apple inside.

'Where did you buy this?' she said.

'There's a new German bakery about a mile away. I thought you might like it.'

'I do. Thank you.'

It wasn't morning crisp when she took that first bite, but the smell was the same as she remembered and so was the taste. He didn't eat any, he just watched her, and she barely enjoyed it as she replayed the words he had just spoken in her head.

'Are you depressed, Seb? Do you need to talk to someone?'

'It won't help. Now stop asking me questions,' he said. 'Is there food?'

'There will be if you give me ten minutes.'

She set aside her Berliner and started to cook strips of steak with Jager sauce, still trying to get an answer from him:

'Come on, Sebastian, no secrets, we're not children any more.'

'Even more reason for you not to know.'

She shook the memory away and fed Jonas and Finn some fresh bird seed.

Then she opened the fridge in the kitchen and prepared the drink that she made herself every day. She needed her vitamins and iron because of her low blood pressure, so she cut up tomatoes, celery and kale, and put them in a blender and added Cayenne pepper, lemon and tomato juice. Jonas and Finn flapped and cawed when she put the blender on as they hated loud noises, but she let it go for a full minute. She took a sip that turned into a swig and felt the red pepper and lemon sting the back of her throat.

What should she do about Holly Wakefield?

There were people still out there intent on destroying her life by bringing up the past and if this woman had found her, then others would soon follow.

She loved her job, her friends and where she lived, and for the first time in many years felt as though she had found peace, but now she knew it was time to get away from London and from the people who would find her.

She had bought a property in Bath last year and had spent the last six months obtaining the necessary planning permits and architectural plans for the crumbling eighteenth-century cottage. The workers had finished rewiring the electrics and fitting the plumbing last month so the cottage would be habitable in a few weeks. She could take a short-term let in the town centre while the renovation was being finished. She would make her apologies at work. She had to leave immediately because of a family emergency, a sudden inheritance? Whatever she told them, they would understand.

Damn you, Sebastian.

There was a full-length mirror behind the door and she stared at her reflection and whispered:

'If they can't see me, they can't find me. If they can't see me they can't find me . . .'

She picked up the photo of her parents and threw it at the mirror.

The mirror smashed and Cassandra stared at herself in the shattered glass. Her reflection stared back at her, angry and old. She was someone's little girl, broken and torn apart, and when she closed her eyes the tears finally came.

Thirty-Eight

'Cassandra Carstairs thinks I'm a crazy person,' Holly said.

'I think you're a crazy person,' said Max.

'Thank you.'

The three of them sat in the basement office. Max looked as if he had had a shower and was eating a bag of cheese and onion crisps.

'For what it's worth,' Holly said, 'I don't think she knows if her brother is alive, and short of seeing him right in front of her, I don't think she'd ever believe it.'

'Maybe she's been through enough,' Max said. 'You want me to look for him now?'

'You won't find him on LinkedIn,' Holly said.

'What about when they were kids – how close were they?'

'Very close. They suffered at the hands of the same abuser.'

'And what happened when her brother was caught? Did she ever visit him in prison?'

'Three times in the first three months, then nothing for seven years.'

'And then she started seeing him again?'

'Sporadically, yes,' Holly nodded.

'So after seven years, she forgave him enough to go and see him or try and understand what he had done. I'm just saying – if it were me and I was this killer-guy who my little sister used to look up to when we were kids and used to visit me in prison and I got out then I'd want to check in on her and see what she was doing. Is she married, does she have kids, where's she working, does she need anything?'

'So he could be watching her?'

'Possibly.'

'Christ!' Holly felt suddenly sick. 'So he could have seen us today?'

'Sure, if your phantom man is alive,' and he smiled when he said it.

Max was treating this like a game and the noise of him eating the crisps was annoying her. Bishop was still in his seat, staring at nothing in particular. She took a breath and realised how tired she was. Annie Wilkes, Hedley Phelps, Cassandra – there were so many moving pieces it was giving her a headache.

'We should go, Holly,' said Bishop.

She got up quickly. She didn't care where, she just wanted to get out.

'Can I come?' said Max.

'No,' said Bishop. 'We have to meet with my boss and you're not supposed to be here, remember?'

In the corridor walking to the stairs:

'You think Max is right?' Holly said. 'About The Animal watching his sister?'

'I hope not,' said Bishop, 'I really do.'

Thirty-Nine

Holly took off her jacket and hung it on the back of one of the mahogany chairs.

They were in Chief Franks' dining room and if he was bothered by her actions, he didn't show it. He appeared to be in a conciliatory mood and poured them tea as he spoke:

'I had a specialist compare the handwriting sample from the Newsome murder scene to that found in the bathroom of The Animal's eleventh victim, Tibor—'

'Slovenski,' Holly said.

'Similar but inconclusive, I'm afraid,' he said. 'What else do you have?'

'I contacted the security detail who escorted The Animal to and from Broadmoor to the Phoenix Hospital,' Bishop said. 'They were efficient in his handling and there seemed to be no way he could have escaped while in their custody. Gary Fitzroy, the oncologist who administered his chemotherapy, saw nothing out of the ordinary. We've studied the hospital and prison CCTV. The Animal had visitors, and we've spoken to nearly all of them – apart from a priest who is on sabbatical in Greece, but we're hoping to talk to him in the next few days. We also made contact with Cassandra Carstairs.'

'You found her?'

'We did, sir.'

'And?'

'I spoke to her,' Holly said, 'but she seemed shocked at the thought that her brother might still be alive.'

'Do you believe her?'

'I do.'

Chief Franks didn't seem surprised. He merely nodded, then said:

'Follow me.'

They passed through the kitchen and into a small study where Franks introduced them to Sergeant Rice, one of the after-hours technicians from police headquarters IT division.

Rice was wearing headphones and seated at the dining room table by a stack of professional sound equipment. After the introductions, Rice said:

'Three minutes and twenty-two seconds of the recording had been deliberately distorted, as if whoever did it tried to wipe it clean, but even digital recordings leave a trace. It was a bit of a mess and I couldn't make out a thing when I started, but I took the file and compressed it – it was twelve-bits, twenty-four hertz – changed it into RX, increased it by about five hundred hertz, cleared out the low frequencies . . . and even then we can only get a portion of what was originally on there, but we got several hits. A few phrases linked together, spoken by three different voices, one female and two male, and then two sentences of a conversation between the two males. You guys didn't tell me who was on this and I don't want to know, but whoever is speaking sounds seriously creepy.'

He pressed play. A second's pause and then:

'*Killing is like being a mother and a father. I'm giving birth to something new.*'

'That's him,' Holly said. 'That wasn't audible at all last time.'

There were a few seconds of static and then the woman's loud and cheery voice cut in:

'*I have cookies, just come out of the oven! You want one?*'

'The female voice, we don't know who she is,' said Bishop.

'It could be Hedley's wife, Sylvia, or one of the clients she interviewed. She's a journalist and they would use the same USB sticks when they recorded conversations. Maybe the recordings got mixed together somehow?'

'It's possible,' Rice said. 'This particular recording of the female voice appears to be a lot older than the other ones,' Rice said. 'It's still digital, but the quality is lower. After the cookie woman there was a five-minute lapse and I couldn't salvage anything until phrase two, which is here.'

More static, almost a whine then:

'. . . *Forgive me, please.*'

The voice was low and guttural. Holly knew it was The Animal immediately and she nodded at Bishop, whose face was lost in concentration.

'That's male voice number two,' Rice said. 'Phrase three comes approximately twenty seconds later.'

'. . . *this world with nothing* . . .'

The machine stopped and Holly said: 'What is that? Play it again.'

'. . . *Forgive me please* . . . *this world with nothing* . . .'

'That rings a bell,' she said, thinking for a second: 'It will come to me.'

'And then approximately forty seconds later we have a bit of dialogue between the two males.'

Static again and The Animal spoke:

'*Thank you, Hedley. I couldn't have done it without you.*'

'*My pleasure, Sebastian.*' A pause. '*Do you think she'll read it?*'

And then it ended.

'Is that it?' Bishop said.

'That's it, I'm afraid,' Rice said.

'Replay the last section.'

'*Thank you, Hedley. I couldn't have done it without you.*'

'*My pleasure, Sebastian.*' The pause. '*Do you think she'll read it?*'

The recording stopped.

'What couldn't he have done without him?' Bishop said. 'What was Hedley helping him with?'

'Some sort of therapy?' suggested Franks.

Holly stayed quiet, deep in thought.

'Thank you,' Chief Franks said to Sergeant Rice. The man got up and packed his equipment in a matter of seconds.

'Let me know if you need anything else,' he said before he left and closed the door.

Franks handed Bishop the USB stick.

'Let us retire to the library.'

They followed the chief and once inside the book-lined room they sat by the fireplace.

'Update me on the Newsome case,' Bishop said. 'Has Thompson found this Thomas Kincaid yet?'

'No, he appears to have gone underground. And the girl who lived next door to the Newsomes who said she saw a car was too young to be of any help. According to her it could have been a four-door car or a two-door van, black, green or red. I have a copy of today's report for you.'

He passed it over and Bishop flipped through the pages.

Holly was aware they were still talking, but had switched off from the conversation. The recording she had just listened to was bothering her and she played it back in her head.

'*Thank you, Hedley. I couldn't have done it without you.*'

'*My pleasure, Sebastian. Do you think she'll read it?*'

Who was the *she* that would read it? Did they mean *her*? And then her memory saved her.

'It's the letter,' she said suddenly.

The two men turned to her. Bishop said:

'What is?'

'The letter on the tape we just heard The Animal and Hedley Phelps talking about. The lines "*Forgive me please*" and "*this world with nothing*" – they're part of a sentence from the letter. "***Forgive me please**, I ask of you, for in God's eyes am I not your brother too? Simply a lost soul? I will leave you and **this world with nothing** but love.*"'

'What letter?' Franks said.

Holly was on her feet.

'The one The Animal sent to me three months ago. Christ, Bishop – Hedley Phelps helped him write it.'

Forty

Bishop knocked loudly on Hedley Phelps' door.

'Hedley Phelps? It's the police. Could you open the door, please?'

Holly noticed that the two trash bags by the far door had been removed but the hall still smelled a little strange. Bishop knocked again:

'Mr Phelps?'

A door opened along the corridor and a woman stepped out carrying a baby in one arm.

'I don't think he's in,' she said.

'I'm DI Bishop,' he showed her his warrant card, 'and this is Holly Wakefield. We're trying to get hold of Mr Phelps.'

'Is he in trouble?' she said.

'No, we wanted to talk to him, that's all. Nothing to worry about.'

'I heard him leave this morning and I don't think he's been back since.'

'Did he say where he was going?'

'To work.'

'So you talked to him?'

'Uh-huh, not for long. I think he's going through a divorce, he's just moved in.'

'Is there a landlord here with a spare key? Do you know who he rents the property from?'

'He probably rents from the same people as me.'

She gave him the number: it was a local company. Bishop made the call, and they had a representative there within twenty minutes. The landlord's name was Terence Sykes. He had a set of keys in his hand but wasn't reaching for the lock. He knocked on the door and called out 'Mr Phelps' for a full minute before he finally shook his head and turned to Bishop:

'I don't like the idea of you going into someone's flat without their permission.'

'We just want to make sure he's okay,' Bishop said. 'When did he take over the tenancy of this place?'

'Three weeks ago. He came into the office, had a look at a couple of properties but decided on this one. He wanted it for one year, gave us a cash deposit and paid first and last month's rent as well.'

'You showed him around?'

'Yes. Can you tell me why you're interested in him?'

'He's helping us with our enquiries.'

'Christ, I watch the news on TV, that means he's guilty of something. Shit, we had a crack dealer on the third floor of this building that turned into a bloody nightmare. We couldn't even evict him.'

'I don't think you'll have that sort of problem here.'

'Good.'

'What's the layout like? How many rooms are there?'

'Um – you walk into the living room, the open-plan kitchen

will be to your right and there are two doors in the opposite wall. The first is the bathroom and the one on the far left is the bedroom.'

'No attic?'

'No, that's it.'

The landlord looked nervous now as he put the key in the lock and turned it.

'I'll go first,' Bishop said. 'Holly?'

She tucked in close behind him as he opened the door.

Forty-One

The moment Holly stepped over the threshold she put a hand to her mouth.

There was a fetid smell. The air was thick and heavy, almost cloying, and it made her cough. Then she saw the coffee table and the sideboard were covered with hundreds of ash trails, where dozens of incense sticks had been allowed to burn. As she closed the door, leaving the landlord outside, she had one last look at him. His eyes were wide and there was an expression of puzzlement on his face; she wondered if he could smell what she did.

She and Bishop snapped on latex gloves.

The kitchen was nothing more than a tiny alcove with a fridge, an oven and pots and pans, all of them neatly stacked and clean. The cupboards and shelves were bare, with no food and no drinks. Bishop opened the fridge, which was empty. It was as if nobody had lived here.

A quick push of the first door revealed the clean unused bathroom. Bishop had his hand on the doorknob of the bedroom door when they heard the landlord's voice:

'What's going on in there?'

'Stay outside please, Mr Sykes,' Bishop said. He looked at Holly and she nodded her head.

Bishop pushed open the door and Holly nearly gagged, the smell was so bad. That was why the incense was there, to cover up the reek of decomposition.

She wondered how Bishop did it, as he walked calmly ahead of her into the dark room, hands raised as if he were about to throw a punch. Holly lifted her elbow to her face and covered her nose with her sleeve.

When Bishop switched on the light, the first thing she saw was the dark purple writing on the opposite wall.

Do you remember their smiles, Holly?
What would you give to see them one more time?

And she suddenly felt the sweat on her upper back and rubbed her eyes as she saw a photo of herself pinned to the wall above the message. She was too far away to see it clearly, but she knew it was recent. She was aware Bishop was talking to her, but she couldn't respond, she was concentrating too hard on trying not to lose it.

'Holly?'

She looked at him and felt her lips tremble as she spoke:

'It's him, Bishop. *It's him.*'

'Eyes down,' he said.

She suddenly realised how far she had walked into the room and what she was about to step on. There should have been a bed in the centre, but it had been pushed to one side, and in its place was a body.

Hedley Phelps.

She stared expressionless at the fat naked man, his wrists and ankles cruelly bound with wire which cut into his skin. There was a perfectly circular hole in the centre of his forehead and his dead eyes stared back at her like punched-out, blackened windows. On the brown carpet beneath him was a great bloodstain shaped like a popped balloon.

And lying by his side, with one paw gently resting on Hedley's left leg, was a very dead black Labrador.

Forty-Two

The coroner was crouched by the two corpses, but stood up when Bishop approached:

'Do you know who he was?' Angela Swan said.

'His name was Hedley Phelps, he was a psychiatrist. How fast can you get to this, Angela?'

'I have a few bodies backed up, but let me get back to you. And Mr Phelps is the owner of this unfortunate dog?'

'Her name is Bessie.' Bishop shrugged and took a breath. 'I'd better go and tell his wife.'

Holly watched him leave and her gaze went back to the bodies. They had been placed in the centre of the room neatly, almost lovingly, the dog like a knight's familiar.

'The man was tortured before he was put out of his misery,' said Angela. 'Cut marks on his back and buttocks, thin criss-crosses probably made with a razor. Deep enough to cut through the subcutaneous fat – and judging by the amount of blood, he hit a few arteries as well. The killer cut him and let him drain as if he wanted to get as much blood out of him as he could. The victim was definitely conscious throughout.

There's evidence of tape residue around his mouth, so he was gagged during his confinement. He struggled a lot, nearly cut through one of his wrists with the wire that was binding him, in an effort to escape.'

'What killed him?'

'Blunt force trauma to the head. The circular hole in his forehead is consistent with the shape of a ball-peen hammer, but it's very deep, approximately four inches, and almost too neat. I'll get back to you on that once I've examined him under the lights.'

'And the dog?'

'Killed with the same weapon. Death would have been instantaneous for both.' A pause. 'I have to ask,' Angela said. 'The writing on the wall, it's like the other crime scene, and now there's a photo of you.'

Holly nodded.

Angela turned to one of the SOCOs:

'Melissa, have you got everything you need?'

'Yes.'

'Then you can take the deceased out, please. Use a child's bag for the dog. And the photo from the wall – bag it and bring it here.'

When Angela had the photo in her hand she gave it a quick glance before she handed it to Holly.

'Be careful,' she said as she left the room.

The photo was a candid half-length shot of Holly staring to the right of the camera. She was wearing a jacket that she wore most days. Her hair was pulled back into a ponytail. It was daytime and behind her was an orange and brown brick wall. She wondered where it had been taken. How close had he been?

Back in the living room there were a half-dozen SOCOs

moving inch by inch across the floor and furniture. She felt like she was in the way but didn't want to leave.

She watched the bodies being carried out through the front door and caught another glimpse of the landlord. His look of puzzlement had changed to abject horror. She was about to go and talk to him when she heard a shout from the bedroom. She went back in and saw one of the forensic team studying the writing on the wall with a magnifying glass.

Up close, Holly could see the letters were made up of tiny dots.

'How did he make the dots?' she said.

'They're not dots,' replied the SOCO. 'They're fingerprints.' He took a sample on acetate and peeled it off delicately. 'It would have taken a lot of time to do this, and it looks like they're all from the same finger.'

'Do you think we'll get a match?'

'I can't believe whoever did this is not in our system.'

He handed the acetate to another SOCO and turned back to the wall and squinted through the magnifying glass again.

'There are more traces of blood above the writing,' he said. 'Barely visible, but they seem to be fingerprints again, or at least partials heading in an upwards direction. Impossible to see in this light.'

Bishop returned, frustrated: 'This building has no CCTV. We might get lucky and catch a glimpse of him on local street cameras, but if he used the rear exit, he'll have got away.'

Holly told him what they had found and he called out to the female SOCO:

'Mel, can I get some luminol, please?'

She handed him a spray.

'Angela Swan?' he shouted.

The coroner reappeared at the door.

'Can I go dark in here?' he said.

'Yes.'

'Use this,' Bishop said, and gave Holly a black-light torch. Then, to no one in particular:

'Someone turn off the lights please, and close the door.'

The bedroom lights went off, the door closed and the room was plunged into darkness. Holly flicked on the black-light torch and shone it on the wall. Bishop aimed the luminol spray and pressed the plunger.

The message in blood surged to life, icy and ghoulish, and then she saw the faint dots of blood higher up on the wall that had been invisible before. Bishop sprayed the luminol again and Holly aimed the black light. The trail of fluorescent fingerprints led to the ceiling.

Bishop called out, 'I need a stepladder in here.'

One was found and Bishop climbed it and sprayed the luminol again. Holly shone the black light and a swirling mass of fingerprints flickered like stars in darkness.

'There's hundreds of them,' he said.

'Thousands,' she said softly. 'That's why he needed all that blood.'

Wherever Bishop sprayed the luminol, Holly's light was soon to follow. The swirling lines of fingerprints led them clockwise across the ceiling and down the far wall, then over a framed print hanging above a chest of drawers, and then past the room's window and across the fabric of the curtains and the back of the door, until they had almost returned to where they had started, and there, the prints forked upwards to the ceiling again and carried on towards the centre of the room. They followed until the pattern stopped abruptly about two feet from the light.

'That's it,' Bishop said. 'There's nothing there.'

'There has to be. The bodies were positioned in the centre of the room, looking up. Spray the ceiling light,' she said.

He did, and under the black light it glowed, completely covered in traces of blood. Bishop tried to twist the shade off but—

'The screws have been glued in,' he said. Then to a SOCO: 'I need an electrician and I want this light taken down.'

It took five minutes to find the fuse box and turn it off and another five to add a dissolving gel to the glue around the ceiling light. Bishop unscrewed the shade. It squeaked on the final twist and he lowered it to Holly, who laid it on the floor. He sprayed the inside with luminol. and when Holly shone the black light she saw a long twisted string with tiny organic branches attached along its length. It glimmered purple under the dust and dead flies. Bishop reached in a tentative hand and removed it. He blew off the dust and rested it in his palm.

It was Sandra Newsome's coral necklace.

Forty-Three

Holly and Bishop stepped out of the apartment block, uniformed officers either side of them.

Some of the press photographers in the street sprang into action, cameras flashed and a rumble came from the crowd.

He took her gently by the arm and they headed away until they reached his car. They both got in, closed the doors and Bishop turned the ignition on. They sat and watched the moving crowd through the windscreen as police pushed people away from the roadblock and mobile phones filmed constantly.

'He took Sandra Newsome's necklace and left it for us, knowing we would find it. It's his signature now as well as his MO. Everything fits, Bishop.'

'Including you?'

She held up the photo of herself they had just found at the crime scene.

'He's leaving me a trail, but I don't know where it's going to end.'

He took the photo from her hands.

'It's very recent,' he said. 'I can't make out the background clearly, but it's not at the police station or your apartment.'

'But when did he take it? This morning? Yesterday? The day before? He's so close.'

They waited in silence and then Bishop said delicately: 'The message on the wall about your parents: *Do you remember their smiles?*'

'Sometimes. And sometimes I forget them and I forget their faces too. Sometimes I need to look at a photograph when I can't picture them, but I never forget the feeling.'

'What feeling?'

'Of being loved. One of the exercises they had me do at crisis counselling when I was twelve, was try and remember how much my parents loved me. We did sums and I calculated that they kissed me goodnight three thousand seven hundred and twenty-two times and I had two thousand and six hundred hugs.'

'That's a lot of hugs.'

'It was never enough,' she said. 'What would I give for one more smile? Nothing? Everything? Maybe that's what he wants? Maybe he wants me to sacrifice something?'

'Like what?'

'What would I give to see their smiles one more time?' Her voice trailed away and her face was wet with tears. 'I get scared because I think he knows exactly who I am and what I think about at night.'

'What do you think about at night?'

The question caught her off guard.

'Too many things,' she said.

She felt his hand find hers in the darkness and he held it tight. His grip was warm and welcoming. It gave her confidence that she would get through this. It made her realise she was not alone.

'You think it is him, right? I'm not crazy, am I, Bishop?'

'No, it's him,' he said. 'I don't know how, but it is. The problem is, we're several steps behind him. He has a mission and it involves you and we don't know what it is. But by definition, if it involves you it involves me as well. And together we can beat him, Holly. Together we can beat him.'

Bishop stared at her for a few more moments then said: 'Let's get you home.'

Holly didn't say a word on the journey back from Hedley Phelps' flat.

Bishop had offered to come inside but she had refused. She wanted to be alone. Even when she got out of the car, all she gave Bishop was the briefest of smiles before she shut the door and entered her apartment block.

She turned at the window – she knew he would wait to make sure she was safely inside – and watched as his car pulled away from the kerb.

In her apartment she left her shoes by the front door and turned on all the lights. She showered and emerged from the bathroom wearing a dressing gown and a towel around her head. She lifted a hand to the butterfly necklace, playing with it unconsciously, then she got dressed in sweatpants and an old sweatshirt of Bishop's that he had given her last year.

She pulled down some of the files on The Animal that were still hanging from the wall and read them as she walked toward the sofa. Passing the TV, she flicked it on without breaking stride. It was the ten o'clock news and there were flashing blue lights by the apartment block she and Bishop had just come from and a reporter talking down the lens. She glanced up from the file at the reporter, turned up the sound for a few seconds and studied him briefly, then muted it and went back to the files. She finally dropped everything on the floor and picked up DCI Warren's memoir. She squinted at the text and shook her head as she read aloud:

'"It was as if I could see my victims before they existed," The Animal had stated when looking back at his murderous years in an interview in 2004. "I could somehow see them in my head before I met them. I felt I had known all of my victims without ever meeting them in real life, and so when I killed them it was like looking into the eyes of a best friend."'

She closed her eyes and all she could see were the letters in blood on the wall:

Do you remember their smiles, Holly?
What would you give to see them one more time?

She stared at words in her mind and pushed the tears away by will alone.

'You can't break me, Sebastian. I don't have a breaking point.'

Bishop was getting very worried about Holly.

He had updated Chief Franks, who shared his concerns about the ongoing investigation.

'The Animal's psychiatrist from Broadmoor is dead, sir,' Bishop said. 'No matter how it gets painted, it doesn't make a pretty picture. We can't pretend we're not investigating him any more.'

'We must tread carefully, DI Bishop. Everything we have so

far is circumstantial. The necklace has been confirmed to have belonged to Sandra Newsome?'

'Yes, sir, and the fact that there was another message to Holly on the wall and a photo this time – everybody on the task force will ask why she isn't working the case.' A beat. 'Sir?'

The silence lengthened and he wondered if the chief was still there.

'Hand the Hedley Phelps murder case over to DI Thompson. It's his now,' Chief Franks said.

'That's not going to work, sir.' He took a breath – reluctant: 'Thompson will ask me what the hell I was doing there in the first place.'

'And you tell him the truth. You were investigating a cold case file and one of the witnesses happened to be Hedley Phelps.'

'Sir—'

'Don't be so blinkered, DI Bishop. Sebastian Carstairs wasn't the only murderer Hedley Phelps dealt with. He had a lot of other patients at Broadmoor, some of whom need to be investigated. We'll talk tomorrow.'

The chief hung up. Bishop opened a bottle of his regimental port, a 2012 Oporto, and slumped onto the living room sofa. He was hungry and yet he wasn't. He wanted to sleep but he knew he couldn't.

He left a message with DI Thompson, then he called Max. After he had updated him, he asked:

'Are you staying at the station tonight?'

'The Bates Motel? Yeah.'

Bishop wasn't sure if he heard another voice in the background. A woman's voice.

'You okay?'

'I'm fine – I'm with someone. Text me if you need me.'
'Will do,' and he ended the call.

What would you give to see them one more time?

He thought of Sarah, the fiancée he had lost in Afghanistan in 2009. They had been engaged and she had been pregnant when the IED had taken her. He had accepted there was no right or wrong way to grieve, but he knew his memory of her somehow defined him. What would he give for one last smile from Sarah?

He sat for a while, then opened the book he had ordered, and started to read *Das Parfum* by Patrick Süskind – the book Cassandra Carstairs had been reading when she had visited her brother. He was on page three when the phone rang.

It was Angela Swan.

'I'm glad you're still up, DI Bishop. I've just started the autopsy of Hedley Phelps – you're more than welcome to come down.'

Forty-Four

Holly was still reading the reports when the phone disturbed her.

She fumbled for it and the papers on her lap scattered on the floor.

'Hello?'

'You want to come down to the morgue?' Bishop said.

'You're such a charmer.'

She thought about him holding her hand in the car again and it made her blush.

'It's late, but is this an official date?' she said.

'Yep. Everything's on ice – just bring yourself.'

She pulled herself upright and ran a hand through her bed-head.

'Give me five minutes.'

'You've got two, I'm already outside.'

She got out of bed, grabbed a jacket and trainers and ran-walked out of the apartment.

The morgue at 25 Bagley's Lane was a sombre place during the day, but at this time of night it gave Holly the shivers.

She stood next to Bishop in the cold suite with Hedley Phelps' large body on a gurney covered with a dark green sheet. Angela had gone to collect something and asked them both to wait. The silence lengthened and the smell of the preserving and sanitising agents seemed stronger than usual.

'This place feels like the opening scene to a horror movie,' Holly said.

'What happened to Holly-kick-sass?'

'I'm trying to not think about zombies, okay?'

He suddenly pointed at the gurney:

'Did you see that? I think the sheet just moved.'

'Shut up – don't say things like that—'

She was about to give Bishop her best withering look when the door swung open and she got a fresh round of goosebumps.

Angela appeared in her scrubs and mask. She was carrying a bizarre-shaped drill that she put on a white cloth next to Hedley's body.

'What is that?' Holly said.

'An example of a captive bolt pistol, also known as a cattle gun,' the coroner said. 'Usually used for stunning animals before slaughter, but in this case I believe something very like this inflicted the fatal wounds to both the victim and his dog.'

'Where did you get it?' Bishop said.

'This one was from storage, but you can buy them almost anywhere: eBay, Amazon, old farm stock – they're not exactly hard to come by.'

'Have you seen this type of injury before?'

'Only in textbooks. It's very unusual. Shall we begin?'

Angela pulled the sheet down. Hedley's large body was white and shiny like wet rubber and Holly could see the purple mess inside the hole in his head.

'The injury that killed him is 5.25 millimetres in diameter and matches the exact diameter of the steel bolt in the example of the cattle gun removed from evidence locker 2AB-667-UPO. Note the almost perfectly round depressive fracture in the centre of the victim's forehead, approximately two and a half centimeters above the brow line. This resulted in the immediate destruction of the brain tissue in the frontal lobe in a fatal subarachnoid haemorrhage. Death would have been almost instantaneous,' Angela said, and passed over a CT-Image of Hedley Phelps' skull. Holly held it up to the light.

The skull outline was white, the brain grey with a seven-centimeter-long black line where the parenchyma of the brain and the nervous tissue had been destroyed.

'Anything else?' Bishop said.

'The tape over his mouth is your standard electrical tape available from any hardware store and the material used to bind his wrists was galvanised wire rope, 4 millimetres thick, again, available to purchase from every hardware store and online. Bishop, could you give me a hand? There are gloves, if you want them.'

Bishop gloved up and helped Andrea shift the victim's right leg. Together they twisted the torso to one side. Although clean, the skin on Hedley's buttocks and lower back looked puckered and raw and there were patches of yellow pus that had seeped onto the gurney below.

'The high vascularisation of the areas of torture and the fact that something like a straight-bladed razor was used repeatedly in the same wounds made it a lot more difficult for the cuts to clot,' Angela observed. 'But several scabs were formed that show an increase in redness and swelling, which indicates that an infection had begun within the initial forty-eight hours of torture.'

'So the torture began over two days ago?' Holly said.

'Yes.'

'That's impossible,' she said.

She turned to Bishop, but he already knew what she was thinking.

'The neighbour, Anita, said she saw Hedley Phelps leave his flat this morning. If it wasn't Hedley Phelps she saw, who the hell was it?'

They walked fast down the front steps and into the morgue car park as a taxi swept past the main entrance into the night.

'Wait,' Bishop said. Holly suddenly saw his body tense. He was looking around, staring at the building, the treeline and the road.

'What?'

'Do you have the photo? The photo of you from the crime scene?'

She handed it over.

He examined it, brow furrowed. 'It was here.'

'What?'

'The photo of you was taken here, at the morgue. Look, behind us, the orange bricks. It has to be.'

He held it up and she saw he was right.

'Which means . . .'

'The Animal was somewhere over there when he took it,' he said. 'Right by the entrance.'

'Christ. When was the last time we were here?'

'The Newsome autopsy on Tuesday morning. There's been an embargo on the case, we haven't even released the names of the victims to the press, so how would he have known we would be here?'

She could feel a sense of cold growing inside of her.

'He's been following me,' she said, and there was an urgency in her voice. 'We have to talk to Hedley Phelps' neighbour. We have to see if she can ID him.'

Forty-Five

They were sitting in Bishop's car outside Hedley Phelps' apartment block.

Holly could see Bishop was still cautious, but she was raring to go.

'Whoever killed Hedley Phelps was in that apartment this morning,' she said. 'We need a positive ID from the neighbour. If she identifies The Animal, they'll have to listen to us.'

'We can't rely on a single eyewitness, Holly, you know that.'

'So what do we do? Just sit here getting cold?'

'No.' He reflected for a while, then checked his watch. 'We go inside.'

They got out of his car and headed to the apartment block. There was an officer stationed inside the lobby and Bishop pressed his warrant card up to the glass. The officer buzzed them in.

'The room's been sealed off until SOCO come back tomorrow,' the officer said.

'We won't be going in,' Bishop said, and they took the lift up to the second floor.

Hedley's flat was cordoned off with crime scene tape and

Holly walked past, straight to the neighbour's door. She heard a baby cry inside the apartment, shot Bishop a look and knocked on the door.

No reply.

And Holly had a terrible thought. What if The Animal had come back and taken care of the neighbour as well? She would be a witness after all, the one person who could identify him. Perhaps they were too late? She was about to knock again when Anita opened the door.

'Yes? I've already given you guys a statement.' She looked exhausted and the baby was still wailing in the background.

'I know, and I'm sorry to disturb you,' Holly said.

'I was awake, in case you couldn't tell.'

'I only have one question. Actually, I just need you to look at a photograph. Is that okay?'

Anita nodded.

Holly showed her a photo of Hedley Phelps on her phone.

'Do you recognise this man?' she said.

Anita shook her head:

'No. Who is it?'

'This wasn't the man you spoke to this morning? The man you saw leave the flat?'

'No, definitely not.'

Holly loaded up another photo. She showed it to Bishop first and he nodded, then she showed it to Anita. It was a photo of The Animal from one of the police files.

'Was this the man you spoke to?'

Anita stared at the image for some time.

'I don't know. Possibly. It's hard to be sure – he was wearing a trilby when I spoke to him and he stayed half-hidden behind his door.'

'Have a good look,' said Holly.

'I mean, I guess it could be him?'

'Would you be willing to put that in a statement?'

'Why? Who is he? Is he the killer?'

'A person of interest,' Bishop said.

'Don't bullshit me.'

'Possibly the killer.'

'Then no,' Anita said. 'I'm not making a statement. I'm not putting my child's life in danger. If he's the killer, then I didn't see a damn thing.'

Forty-Six

Holly, Bishop and Max sat at a round table with a full pitcher of beer.

They were at a lock-in at a bar called Pandora's Box in Ladbroke Grove, west London, one of Max's favourites. It was tacky and fun, the walls covered with trophies, posters and interesting knick-knacks from around the world and there was a Harley Davidson bolted to the middle of the floor. They were the only three customers inside and the jukebox still played for them. The two Greek owners brought them cold sausage and lumps of broken chocolate at midnight and sat behind the bar smoking dope.

Holly, Bishop and Max had talked about the case for the first hour, then Bishop and Max had reminisced about Afghanistan, but now Max steered the conversation back to Holly.

'Come on, girl, tell me more about you,' he said.

'What do you want to know?'

'Your real name is Jessica – who chose Holly?'

'Victim relocation. I had a couple of other choices. If I remember correctly, Lorna was one.'

'Lorna? Fuck's sake – my ex is called Lorna.'

'Then there was Isabelle.'

'Another ex,' said Max.

'Catherine.'

'Been there.'

'Is one of your exes called Holly?' Bishop said.

'No.'

'Thank God for that.'

Max and Holly laughed and clinked their glasses.

'What about The Animal?' he said. 'How did he get that nickname?'

'From the press.'

'Yeah, but why The Animal?'

Holly sighed. Both men stared at her expectantly.

'He was called The Animal after victim number five's body was found,' she said. 'His name was Tip Cullen. He was a sixty-one-year-old retired army officer who lived in Sennen Cove in Cornwall.'

'He was ex-forces?' Max said.

'I'm afraid so. He was found dead on his living room floor on the morning of seventh September 1987. His stomach and chest were cut up, but these knife wounds were a bit different.'

'How?'

'In his retirement Tip was a taxidermist and his house was full of stuffed and mounted animals: pheasant, badgers, hawks, foxes and a crow. When the police found his body, the animals had been taken off the shelves and placed around him in a circle. His blood was spattered on their fur and feathers and dripped from their mouths and beaks as if they had somehow all attacked him. The coroner concluded the lacerations in Tip's stomach and chest had been made with a knife that was never recovered, but on first glance they looked as though they could have been inflicted by any one of the animal's claws. The crow was nailed to Mr Cullin's skull and made to look as if it had plucked out one of his eyes.'

'Jesus.'

'The details of the crime scene were kept from the press, but locals had already seen what had happened through the downstairs windows before the police arrived and the stories circulated and pretty soon the press got hold of them and the name The Animal was born.'

Max was staring at her wildly, his eyes suddenly bloodshot.

'He always took a piece of jewellery, right? What did he take from my man, Tip?' he said.

'An onyx intaglio yellow gold ring carved with his company's insignia. It had been presented to him on his retirement from the Marines. The ring had been cut from his finger.'

'We've got to make this fucker dead,' Max said.

'We're not allowed to kill The Animal,' said Bishop.

'Yes, we can,' Max said. 'He killed one of our own, Bill!'

'Finish your beer and I'll get you another.'

Max got up and said:

'To be continued when I return.'

He headed to the toilets, somehow walking straighter than he had when he had come in.

Holly turned to Bishop:

'You honestly think this is going to end like that?' she said.

'It's going to end, I know that for sure.'

They clinked glasses again. Holly was five beers in and feeling fuzzy.

'You're the wisest man I know, DI Bishop.'

'But Sebastian Carstairs is the smartest, right?'

She didn't acknowledge but looked Bishop in the eye.

'I can't think straight. I need to go home.'

'I'll drop you off, we have a busy day tomorrow.'

Their chairs scraped back as they got up.

'What about Max?'

Bishop shouted at the two Greeks hidden behind the haze of dope:

'Dmitri, take care of Max, yeah?'

No reply but Holly saw a hand give the thumbs up.

They caught a black cab and got dropped off by her apartment. It was cold, but there was a hint of dawn up ahead. They watched the taxi leave and stood by the front steps. It was so quiet they could have been the only people awake, and she found herself staring at him and he stared back and smiled.

'You know I like you, right?' he said.

'I like you too, Bishop.' She smiled back at him, feeling like a giddy schoolgirl. Was this it? Was now the time to tell him?

His fingers brushed against hers and suddenly they were holding hands again. It was so natural and she felt something stir inside her.

Before she knew it, they had kissed.

It answered all her questions and she said:

'Bishop . . .'

They kissed again and when they finished they were staring at each other. She knew where it was going and she didn't mind, but she had to warn him:

'There's something you need to know about me.'

'What?'

'Something that I don't ever talk about.'

'Tell me,' he said.

Every ounce of her wanted to tell him, but she knew she couldn't lose herself tonight and pulled away slightly.

'Not now. Later. When this case is over.'

'Okay,' he nodded. 'When it's over we'll have all the time in the world.'

She hoped he was right.

One more kiss that lasted a minute, then they separated and went their separate ways.

Forty-Seven

The Animal had discovered the hotel several weeks ago.

It was dirty and unstaffed, the sort of place where you pay by credit card at a small booth on the way in and your room key-card is spat out at you like a cash machine spits money. The size and colour of the room reminded him of his prison cell at Broadmoor. Both were small and institutionally grey, but at least here there would be no screaming or banging on the walls.

He checked the hallway to make sure there was no one there, quickly angled the trilby on his head, and exited the room. The door automatically locked behind him. He was on the fourth floor, but ignored the lift and took the stairs. He met no one coming up and was onto Hammersmith High Street in less than thirty seconds. The police station where DI Bishop and Holly were working from was less than a quarter of a mile away. He glanced in that direction then turned his back.

It was short walk to Kings Mall and he entered a craft store where he bought modelling plaster of Paris and cotton wool. Next stop was a chemist where he purchased two rolls of bandages, a pair of scissors and some dark brown hair dye. A final visit to Tesco and he left with a container of pre-mixed sugar and cinnamon cookie-dough, a baking tray and an Emma Bridgewater plate with red and pink hearts on it.

On his return to the hotel room he put the Tesco bag with the cookie dough, baking tray and plate on the bed and the plaster of Paris, bandages and scissors in the bathroom. He undressed to his underwear, applied the hair dye carefully, then set up a bowl of water and mixed the plaster of Paris. He laid down a sheet of clear plastic on the floor, sat on the end of the bed and covered his left ankle down to the toes and half-way up the shin with the cotton wool. He taped it tightly then proceeded to dip the strips of bandage into the warm plaster of Paris and wrap them around his ankle. It took him twenty minutes and he was careful not to make too much of a mess. He wrapped the spills and the drips in the clear sheet of plastic, then put it into the black bin liner along with the unused bandage and the bowl with the remains of the plaster of Paris. When he was done, he hopped into the hall and dropped it into the garbage chute.

He rinsed the dye from his hair in the bathroom sink and sat on the end of the bed and waited for the plaster to dry, pressing it gently with his fingers every now and then until there was very little give. When the plaster was set to his satisfaction, he tested it by walking from one side of the small room to the other, leaning first a little, then all of his weight on it. His limp was distinctive and uncomfortable and the top of the plaster grated painfully across the back of his calf. He pushed a sock into the gap, which relieved some of the irritation, and then began to clean up everything he had either touched or used and placed it all inside another black bin bag. He took a pair of crutches from the cupboard and navigated his way to the garbage chute again and disposed of the second bin bag.

In the room he dressed in a T-shirt and denim jacket, and a pair of shorts so he could show off his plaster cast. Then he gave himself a side-parting with his new dark brown hair. He packed Wagner, his tin toy soldier, the Emma Bridgewater plate, cookie dough and baking tray into his black sports bag and slung it over his shoulder. He had booked the hotel for another week but wouldn't be coming back. He left as he had arrived – without seeing anybody and without anybody seeing him.

Forty-Eight

After the kiss, Holly had got home and set her alarm for seven thirty, but she'd woken at six thirty with a blistering headache.

Black coffee had helped, as had meditation, oatcakes, bananas and tea, she had called Dr Bernstein at the Wetherington and made an appointment to see him.

Now, she sat in his office, showered, with slightly damp hair that had been scraped back into a ponytail. She wondered if she smelled of alcohol. Bernstein was behind his desk and cleaning his glasses. She had already told him what she wanted to talk about.

'And you are allowed to discuss the police case with people like myself who aren't involved?'

'If the case affects me directly, yes. Besides, I trust you implicitly.'

'Go on then.'

'The killer has been leaving me clues,' Holly said.

'Leaving *you* clues or the police?'

'Me. He's writing on the walls in the victim's blood.'

'And what is he writing?'

'He's asking me if I remember my parents' smiles. He wants to know what I would give to see them one more time.'

'You're talking about The Animal?'

'Yes. We think it's him and he's killing again.'

He finished cleaning his glasses and rested them on his nose. He stared at her for a long time. She stared back and said:

'I know exactly what you're thinking: I'm suffering from a psychosis of some sort, I'm having a breakdown and the man who is dead is talking to me and I think he's come back to life somehow and is now taunting me.'

'Self-diagnosis is a dangerous game, but you're not far off. So let us just balance the fantasy with reality for the ease of this conversation, and assume what you just said is true and that The Animal is alive and he is real. Are you sure it's him?'

'Everything points to him, and I can sense him.'

'I can sense a lot of things, but most of them never happen. Have you and DI Bishop eliminated everybody else from your enquiries?'

'It appears as though we have. There is one suspect who the police believe it might be – his name is Thomas Kincaid, but he's a paedophile, not a killer.'

'Have you studied his psychosis?'

'I have and it's not him. A paedophile doesn't suddenly become a serial killer of middle-aged men and women. A paedophile has specific sexual urges or lusts. We're not dealing with a lust killer, the bodies aren't sexually manipulated in any way, shape or form. This killer relishes his power and control over the victims. I did doubt myself for a while, but now I am positive it's The Animal – and so is DI Bishop.'

Bernstein nodded slowly and took his time:

'So have you answered the questions that he asked you? What would you give to see your parents smile one more time?'

'I have.'

'Because he is asking hypothetical questions it means there are no right or wrong answers. You understand that? He knows that as well, he is simply trying to make contact with your emotions.'

'Why?'

'Because he let you live? Because you are an empathetic human? You feel what others feel and that's what makes you such a good therapist. But he is a narcissistic psychopath, so in his eyes you are weak. Weak and vulnerable. So why does he want you to feel? Or rather what does he want you to feel? What did The Animal do to you when he killed your parents?'

'He took away the ones I loved.'

'He took away everything: security, intimacy, the future. In the circumstances, it's reasonable to assume you would have developed a fear of intimacy, a fear of losing everything you once had. So he wants to scare you. Is he succeeding?'

'Yes.'

'Then he is winning. But it's more than that,' Bernstein said. 'He is controlling this whole situation – and most importantly he seems to be controlling you, Holly, and that's a very dangerous thing. You have an entity that you cannot prove exists and yet he dictates how you feel, how you react and what you are foreseeing. In essence, he is in total control of you.'

'I wouldn't say total.'

'Really? Yet here you are.'

'So he wants me to suffer.'

'Yes.'

'Haven't I suffered enough?'

'In his eyes – no! In his world you haven't even scratched the surface. To him this is the game, because his ego demands it. He wants total control of you, but to what end? How far will you go? And the ultimate question he is asking is: what will you sacrifice?'

'I don't know.'

She took her time, digesting their conversation, then Bernstein said:

'You should talk to Lee today.'

'I don't want to.'

'Perhaps you should try?'

She bit her lip and said in a low voice:

'I need to tell DI Bishop about Lee. Things are progressing in our relationship and I think he has the right to know, but I can't decide how to bring it up. I feel so guilty that I haven't already been honest with him.'

'Sometimes we can't get past our guilt because we haven't been completely honest with ourselves. You had no choice in what happened to you, Holly, but unless you tell DI Bishop and stop being afraid, you will always be your own jailer.'

She knew he was right and told him as much.

'If something should happen to me,' she said quietly, 'I want you to tell Bishop the truth.'

'What would happen to you?'

'I don't know, I'm just saying. Getting my affairs in order.'

She could tell he didn't like the way she was talking.

'You want me to discuss your medical history with him?' he said.

'Yes, I give you permission.'

'I'll need that in writing, Holly.'

‘That’s fine.’

He stared at her, not unkindly.

‘Then if the situation arises, I will tell him the truth. I find in the long term that always works best.’

Forty-Nine

'Lee? Are you here?'

Her brother's eyes flipped open and he put a hand over his mouth as he yawned.

Holly stayed on the end of his bed as he pulled himself upright and rested himself against the grey concrete wall of his cell.

'You've been drinking,' he said. 'Where did you go last night?'

'Pandora's Box, a little dive in west London.'

'Sounds great – sucking it up with all the evils of the world.'

'Actually it was just the three of us – we had a lock-in.'

'You, Bishop and who?'

'Max, I've told you about him.'

'Ex-regimental friend of Bishop's?'

'That's the one.'

'I like Max.'

'You've never met him.'

'I've never met Bishop either.'

'No, but I think you'd like him.'

'From what you've told me about him, what's not to like?'

She reached out and took his hand. It was cold.

'I'm going to tell him about you.'

His eyes went wide, but he didn't pull away.

'It's been a long time coming. How do you think he'll react?'

She couldn't stop herself and suddenly burst into tears.

'Oh God, Lee. I feel terrible.'

'About what?'

'About everything. I haven't been honest with him.'

'Has he been honest with you?'

'Yes. He lost a woman he loved in Afghanistan, she was blown up by an IED. He's sensitive and caring and makes me laugh.'

'He sounds like me.'

She laughed at that, but suddenly found herself crying again.

'He's going to hate me,' she said.

'No he won't. If he hates you then he doesn't deserve you, Holly. Tell him about me. Perhaps that is the greatest barometer of truth. Maybe one day I'll even see him.'

'That would be too weird.'

He looked pale in the lights of the cell. There was a softness about him today she had never seen before.

'I still think you're going to leave me,' he said.

'I can't, you idiot, but I probably won't see you as much.'

'I can live with that, provided you're happy.'

'I want to be happy, Lee. I think I've finally worked out that I deserve to be.'

'You do, and I will always be here for you, no matter what.'

'I know.'

He suddenly got out of the bed and gave her a hug.

'Get out of here,' he said, and kissed her on the cheek.

She turned at the door.

'I love you,' she said.

He didn't answer, but he didn't need to.

Fifty

Holly and Bishop shared a simple hug and a smile when they met later that morning.

The kiss last night had moved their relationship to a new level and Holly felt different sitting in the car with him. The bugbear was still clinging to her back, but now she just had to decide when she would tell him. She was proud of herself though; she had taken the plunge and couldn't back out now. It felt more intimate without having to say anything, although she did bring it up:

'So . . . about last night.'

'Yes?'

'I'm glad it happened.'

'Me too.'

They enjoyed the silence as he drove to Chief Franks' house. She wanted to hold his hand again.

'Anything else you want to share with me?' she said.

He gave her a quick smile:

'Your top is on inside out.'

*

Their good mood was obliterated the moment the chief took them into the living room.

'I need you to stop everything you're doing,' he said gravely. 'The fingerprints on the walls at Hedley Phelps' house have come back from the lab and they're a match to Thomas Kincaid. Your investigation is now officially over. We have our killer, and I appreciate everything you have done, but it would seem we have been chasing up a blind alley all along.'

Holly felt her heart in her throat. She thought she had misheard when Bishop asked:

'Is Kincaid in custody?'

'No, but we're closing the net and working on a tip-off, so should arrest him within the hour.'

'But we're gathering evidence now,' Holly said. 'We have an eyewitness. The neighbour who saw—'

'We have already re-interviewed her this morning,' Franks said. 'We showed her a photo of Thomas Kincaid and she said it could have been him that she saw leaving Phelps' flat Wednesday morning.'

'She said that about The Animal too.'

'But Kincaid is alive, Miss Wakefield, that is the difference.'

'The eyewitness is scared,' said Bishop. 'She'd say anything.'

'Which is why we have moved her and her baby out of the flat and arranged twenty-four-hour police protection until this is over.'

'Thomas Kincaid is a paedophile, not a mass murderer,' Holly said. 'And why the hell would he be so interested in me?'

'Perhaps Thomas Kincaid can answer those questions when we interview him,' Franks said.

The next thirty minutes was strained and tense as Holly pushed her point. A step-by-step account of all she and Bishop had done: from the second message on the wall and the photo of herself that was found at the murder scene. And finally The Animal's signature: Sandra Newsome's coral necklace, recovered from the ceiling light.

'It's all circumstantial. Thomas Kincaid's fingerprints at the scene are not.'

'So what do we do?' Bishop said.

'Go back to the station and clear up the basement office. The cold case files can go back to storage and any new data you gathered on The Animal – get rid of it.'

Bishop and Holly were shell-shocked and silent in the basement.

Bishop was up by the incident board. He had taken down a few photos, but his heart wasn't in it. Holly watched him then turned her attention to the never-ending parade of pedestrian feet that passed outside the basement window.

'This is so wrong,' she said. 'The fact that Franks can't see this is ridiculous.'

'He's covering the bases, Holly.'

'But that's not good enough. The Animal is incredibly smart and clever and he has had his share of luck and so have we, but we've also had some bad luck and no real leads, just supposition and weak links. We missed him by a matter of hours at Phelps' apartment – that was the closest we got to him. Phelps was the key and we lost that opportunity. Now we have no idea where he is— No, scratch that – we do. He'll be somewhere nearby. Waiting.'

'Waiting for what?'

She shook her head, took out the photo of her that had been left at the Hedley Phelps crime scene and pinned it to the incident board.

'No matter what Franks just said to us, it doesn't explain this,' she said. 'How does he know what I've been doing?'

Bishop shook his head, watching her quietly.

'I don't know.'

'Unless he has me under constant surveillance?'

'That would be impossible for one man,' he said.

'Maybe there are others helping him?'

'Who? Friends, relatives? The Animal always worked alone.'

The butterfly necklace glinted in the sunlight of the photo and she instinctively reached up to her neck and felt it.

'He's always one step ahead,' she said.

And then it hit her.

Fifty-One

The butterfly necklace lay under a microscope.

Holly saw flashes of its blue and green enamel wings on a large computer screen which reflected what the man was seeing under the eyeglass. The man was a friend of Bishop's called Red, and that was all he had been introduced to her as. She had no idea what he did for a living and decided not to ask. Ex-military? Had to be. He was five foot six but wiry with a red beard and mutton chop sideburns. His hands were tiny, his knuckles red and bruised.

She watched something edge into the frame – it looked like a big pair of silver chopsticks, but was actually a tiny pair of tweezers. They tugged at a small flat square of black nestled amongst the silver on the back of the necklace.

'Hold on,' Red said.

He grabbed a can of liquid nitrogen from his workbench and sprayed the necklace. When the white mist cleared, the tweezers pulled at the flat black square again and this time it came loose. Red released the object onto a glass slide which was in turn placed under another microscope and magnified on screen.

'Looks like a Hornet,' Red said.

'A what?'

He turned to Holly. She noticed he was missing an ear as well.

'A Micro or Nano Hornet GPS chip.'

'A tracker?'

'Manufactured in Munich, Germany, by a company called Origin. It's pretty sophisticated, it's got an integrated antenna, along with all the filters, radio frequency shields, and processing capabilities of the full-sized chips. It can locate you within one second of being connected to a satellite and is accurate within two metres. Only weighs about two grams. How long have you been wearing the necklace?'

'Three months – ever since I got it back.'

'What was it? Ex-husband give it to you?'

'No,' Bishop said. 'It's to do with a case we're working on.'

'So he has been following me,' Holly said.

'Not necessarily following,' Red said, 'but he'll know what you've been up to.'

'Jesus Christ. So he's been playing me all this time? Son of a bitch! The only reason he agreed to return the necklace to me in the first place was because he had an ulterior motive. And if he's been tracking me, he's been tracking the case, Bishop. He knows I went to see Annie, he knows we've found Hedley Phelps' body, and he knows I'm here now.'

'And he knows where you live,' said Red.

She had underestimated The Animal. She had been an absolute fool. To Red she said:

'Can you destroy the chip, get rid of it?'

'No problem. I can burn the little puppy.'

He picked it up with the tweezers and flipped on his lighter.

'Medium or well done?'

'Hold it,' Bishop said.

'No,' Holly said. 'I want that thing destroyed.'

Bishop shook his head. 'This could work in our favour.' To Red: 'Can you find out where the tracking signal was sent to?'

'Possibly. Just got to find out which satellite it's using and clone the frequency. You want me to do it?'

Bishop nodded.

Red fitted the Hornet to a USB adapter and fired up his computer. 'The hunter becomes the hunted,' he said.

Fifty-Two

The Animal caught a taxi and got dropped off three blocks from his destination.

He was early and stopped for a coffee and a cigarette at an outside café where he people-watched. He paid and made his way east along Fifth Way, leaning heavily on his crutches, then turned right onto First Way and followed the busy road through the industrial estate towards Wembley Stadium. After another five minutes he arrived at Access Self-Storage and showed his ID. He explained he was expecting a delivery to unit 11 and was allowed through. The units were all in neat adjoining rows, made of sheet metal, some with roller-shutter doors that disappeared into the ceilings when unlocked and others with conventional doors. Unit 11 had a conventional door and was near the centre of the facility.

The Animal unlocked the padlock.

He glanced to either side before he opened the door and immediately locked it when he was inside. He flicked the light on. The space was twenty feet by twenty feet with a concrete floor and lumpy furniture covered by thick blankets. He put his crutches down and pulled the first one away and revealed a jet-black Aga. Underneath the rest of the cloths was a butcher's block, three metal barstools, a knife block with six knives, three pot-plants, a mirror, a fold-up bed with sheets and pillows and a bulky suit-holder that hung from a wall bracket.

At nine twenty he exited the unit and stood outside and enjoyed the sun on his face.

At nine thirty-five, the Country and Garden delivery van drove slowly around the corner and he guided them into the space in front of the lock-up. The driver's name was Tom and his helper was Sven, and they unloaded the solid oak kitchen table and four shabby-chic chairs and put them into the unit. Then they unloaded the dove-white matt paint, paintbrushes, rollers and plastic drop-cloths. They were finished and on their way within fifteen minutes, wishing Sebastian a swift recovery from his broken ankle.

He lit a cigarette.

Jakub from the moving company turned up at ten twenty with two other men and a hydraulic pulley which made short work of lifting the Aga from its space and placing it gently in the back of the van. The table and chairs followed, along with everything else, and when it was secured Sebastian was helped into the cab. His crutches rested between his legs as they made their way towards central London.

Jakub asked about Sebastian's work at the Wellness Charity and Sebastian told him the charity helped sick children and provided holiday homes for parents when they needed to get away after a bereavement. He told them he had always worked for charities and had even been a clown at children's parties for five years after leaving school. Jakub found this immensely funny as he loved clowns. Then he tuned the radio to a local station. The music was sentimental and repetitive. Sebastian didn't enjoy it, but he tapped his fingers and smiled when everybody else smiled.

The journey lasted nearly an hour because the traffic had built up, and they arrived in south London by midday. Their destination was a Georgian house, built in the mid eighteenth century, that had been converted into flats within the last thirty years. They parked on a double-yellow line, one of them helped Sebastian with his crutches and he led them up the steps and unlocked the front door to the lobby. The men propped the door open and Sebastian pressed one of the two lift buttons as the men started to unload the van. When the lift was full, they travelled to the fifth floor and Sebastian took a left and unlocked the door to the apartment.

The hallway inside had already had one coat of paint and he showed the men the two other empty rooms and gave them instructions. The places for the furniture were all marked on the floor and he wanted two coats of the white paint on every wall. He was very insistent that the furniture be placed exactly where he wanted it. The workers didn't ask why the windows had been painted over in black.

Sebastian paid half of the cash up front and promised them the rest when they had finished. As they began to unload the van, Sebastian hobbled into the last bedroom on the left, taking his black bag and the suit carrier with him. He told them not to disturb him as he was working and needed to make some important phone calls. Of course, they said, and they would try to be as quiet as possible. Sebastian closed the bedroom door.

He stared at the man and woman who were still tied to the chairs in the middle of the room. He would have to move them soon but not yet.

He placed the black bag on the floor and hung up the suit carrier, unzipped it and removed what was inside. It was a bottle-green overall, the sort of generic uniform a utility worker might wear. He let it hang on the back of the door and lay on the bed. He had Wagner in his hand and stared at the little tin toy and lost himself in his memories. Sometimes he thought he could see inside Wagner's head, but perhaps it was the other way around?

The workmen finished the second coat of paint within the hour and one of them knocked on the door to tell him they were done. Sebastian hobbled to his feet and opened it a fraction, peering at the white-spattered face.

'The rest of the money is in an envelope on the hall stand,' he said.

'Do you want to come and have a look?'

'No, it's fine,' he smiled and gestured to his leg. 'Remind me never to go skiing again.'

The man smiled back:

'Cheers, mate, take care.'

The man picked up the envelope and was gone. Sebastian listened to the front door shut. Then he made his way to the phone entry system and stared into the camera that showed the street. He saw the van pull away. He stayed there for another ten minutes in complete silence watching the road, then headed back to the bedroom. He removed a pair of surgical scissors from his black bag and started to cut the plaster cast from his ankle. It was free of his body and wrapped in a plastic bin liner within five minutes.

He washed the dark dye from his hair and applied a ginger dye, then took off his shorts and T-shirt and got dressed wearing the bottle-green overall from the suit carrier. He attached a name tag to his left breast pocket. The name tag read *David Deadman* from *Speedy Electric.* He put a layer of fake tan on his face then parted his ginger hair to one side. From one of the hall cupboards he took out two twenty-litre Jerry cans full of petrol. He had a lighter in his pocket. He flipped it once to check the flame and it caught on the first go.

There was a full-length mirror in the hall and as he stared at his reflection he whispered:

'If they can't see me, they can't find me.'

Again and again.

And when he believed it, he picked up the Jerry cans and left the apartment.

Fifty-Three

The woman who left Holly's flat later that morning was a constable from the Metropolitan Police with twelve weeks' experience on the force.

Her name was Stephanie Mullins and she had been chosen because she was the same height as Holly and their body shape was similar. She was wearing Holly's jeans, sweatshirt and her trainers. Her light brown hair was scrunched into a ponytail and she had a baseball cap pulled low over her eyes. At the front of the block of flats, she got into the taxi that was already waiting for her.

The taxi was driven by a sergeant from the Met who specialised in evasive driving and thirty minutes later confirmed no one had followed them to King's Cross station. The woman got out of the taxi and caught the first available train to York.

The trip was a direct line and took one hour and fifty-two minutes. At York station she caught a taxi and went straight to Betty's Café Tea Rooms in St Helen's Square and ordered herself a breakfast of coffee and a muffin courtesy of petty cash from the Met. She people-watched as she ate, gently playing with the silver butterfly necklace that hung casually outside her blouse.

Holly and Bishop waited until they knew Constable Mullins was safely in York before they left Holly's apartment and exited through the rear security doors. Bishop's car was waiting for them by the pavement and they headed into central London.

Red had traced the satellite link to a block of flats just outside Croydon and all the signals from the tracker in Holly's necklace had been and were still being sent to a receiver at this location. According to the local council, the flat was rented to a Mr Robert Burrows. He had been there for four years on disability allowance. Mr Burrows had a few minor infractions for drunk and disorderly behaviour and he had attacked two people with a knife last year.

Bishop called Chief Franks and explained where they were going and why.

'The Animal? I asked you both to drop the case, DI Bishop.'

'I know, sir, but I think this is too important to ignore. Whoever this killer is, he has been tracking Holly, possibly for months, and that's why he has always managed to stay one step ahead of us. He thinks Holly is in York so his guard will be down.'

'And you want back-up?' the chief said.

'Yes, sir. We think Robert Burrows is probably involved and will be armed with at least one knife and may be a flight risk.'

'I'll see what I can do.'

Bishop finished the call.

She watched him pop a piece of Nicorette gum from its foil and start chewing.

Fifty-Four

Abandoned buildings slid past their windows as Bishop drove south out of central London towards Croydon.

He slowed at a dozen high-rise buildings that had been built for residential use in the fifties; low-cost housing that was well past its prime.

'Which one is it?' Holly said.

'East block over there. Robert Burrows lives on the seventh floor.'

He pulled up and parked. Four tower blocks were set in a square and at its centre was a concrete playground with broken swings and dumped mattresses. Some kids were playing football. Others were half-hidden in doorways.

'County lines drug gangs,' Bishop said.

He glanced at her, but Holly wouldn't meet his eye. She needed the moment to herself. This could be it. The Animal could be up there somewhere, less than a few hundred feet away. A quiet moment, then Bishop's phone rang. He listened and said:

'Okay.'

He hung up and rubbed a hand over his forehead.

'Chief Franks can't authorise armed police, but they will send back-up.'

'How long?'

'Fifteen minutes.'

'We can't wait. He may be tracking the necklace, but he could be watching us now as well. If he's up there and sees us coming, he'll get out and we might lose him forever.'

'Whoever is inside might not want to go quietly and will probably be armed.'

'What do we do?'

Bishop got out, opened the boot of the car and pulled out a tactical stab-vest. He strapped it onto Holly then fitted his own.

'It won't cover all of you, but will protect your vital organs.'

They started to walk. Out of the corner of her eye she could see the locals getting interested very quickly.

'They know we're cops,' Bishop said.

Her pace quickened through the playground, past iron railings and an old For Sale sign. The metal door to the complex was ajar and the lock had been ripped out some time ago. She pushed it open to reveal a concrete floor with pools of water. Two broken lifts were straight ahead and there were concrete stairs to the right. They took the stairs. On every other landing she caught a glimpse of the communal balconies and the closed doors of the apartments.

Even though the stab-vest was light, by the time she reached the seventh floor she was out of breath and she could hear Bishop breathing heavily behind her. The landing appeared to be deserted: the doors to the flats were in a row on the right and the balcony on the left gave a view of the seventy-foot drop to the playground below. The door to the first flat had been busted open and the room inside trashed.

The second flat was the same. The next three doors were locked and the sixth door was where they stopped. Flat 729. The windows had old newspapers taped over them and the front door was matt black and had a broken doorbell.

From far away a siren wailed.

Bishop knocked on the door.

'Mr Robert Burrows? Are you at home, sir? It's the police.'

A face peeked out from behind a door about fifty yards away and watched them curiously. Bishop said to the face:

'Does Robert Burrrows live here?'

The face disappeared.

'Stay behind me,' said Bishop, and he kicked down the door.

The jamb splintered and the front door swung open to darkness for a moment before swinging back, half-shut, and Bishop caught the edge with his hand.

'Mr Burrows?'

They both entered and Bishop flipped on the light switch and pushed the door closed behind them. The apartment was gloomy, the corridor narrow, with brown carpet and four doors which were all shut. The place smelled ripe; not dead-body ripe, but Holly took out a handkerchief and covered her nose. The first door on the left was a small bathroom, the one on the right the kitchen, and that was where the smell was coming from. The kitchen was tiny; barely enough room for both of them, and on the gas stove were half-empty pots and pans. Food had been slopped over the countertops and in the sink. Dirty utensils were everywhere, along with empty tin cans and jars. Ants and maggots swarmed over bits of half-eaten sandwich and cold stew.

The bedroom was on the left. There was no mattress on the bed, just a metal frame and springs with a sheet spread across it. The sheet was stained and dotted with rust where the springs showed through. There was an empty chest of drawers and a pair of brown shoes in one corner.

Holly opened the door to the bathroom. In the sink were objects covered in dried blood: a pair of scissors and gauze bandages, a bottle of anaesthetic and a hypodermic needle. She pulled the shower curtain aside.

The bathtub and shower wall were splattered with zig-zags of dried blood. The bath had a few inches of cloudy-red water in it with a few bits of floating gauze and a large hacksaw. Some bubbles popped up from the clogged drain.

She stared at the bath contents grimly and felt Bishop's hand on her shoulder as he motioned for her to follow him into the living room.

It was a square room with a tattered pleather sofa, a TV stand with no TV, and a drinks cabinet that had been emptied. There were cigarette butts and heroin foils everywhere and an old tattered rug had been dragged from the floor and hung on the far wall like a form of decoration. Bishop shifted the sofa and there was a squeal of rats as he kicked them away. They all ran to the rug and disappeared underneath. Holly watched them, curious, and took out a pair of latex gloves and slipped them on. She moved to the rug and pressed against it, expecting the resistance of the wall but there wasn't any.

'Bishop?'

She took the edge of the rug and pulled it to one side, revealing a large hole in the plasterboard some five feet high and two feet wide where it had been knocked through to the adjoining flat. They stepped quietly inside. The rats were nowhere to be seen.

The lights were on in this room. Lamps with dusty shades, a few porn mags on a table and a sofa against one wall was piled high with yellowed, once-white pillows.

They passed through the door and into the next room, where an armchair faced two small televisions, both on but with no sound.

In the bedroom to the right was a wheelchair at the foot of a bed covered by a grey sheet, and peeking out from under the sheet was a motionless hand. Bishop leaned forward and lifted the sheet and an emaciated naked body stared back at them with empty, crusted eyes. The man had been tied to the wheelchair with wire that was now loose around his fleshless limbs. There were rodent bite marks all over the waxy skin.

'Robert Burrows?' Holly said.

On the bed was a wallet. Bishop flipped it open and found the man's bus pass and disabled badge.

'It's him all right,' he said. 'Looks like he's been here for some time as well.'

On the wall above the bed was a clutter of overlapping newspaper articles about the Annie Wilkes murders. Some were faded to the point of transparency and Holly moved from clipping to clipping, studying them, taking her time. She stopped at one and lifted its edge, revealing an article underneath that had been preserved from the effects of the light. She ran her finger across the pale print.

'There's handwriting on this one,' she said.

She rubbed the grime away and brought the pen marks out more clearly: a bunch of initials and numbers. She read it out loud:

'PK-4-400CL-6-AJ/W. What do you think? Some kind of combination?'

'I don't know what it is,' Bishop said.

He led her to the living room. A sofa, no TV and another rug on the wall. He pulled it aside and revealed a hole in the plasterboard similar to the first room. It led through to the next apartment.

Fifty-Five

The pair moved cautiously.

Holly could sense they were getting closer to something and she could feel her heart beating in her chest. The first door on the left led to another bathroom. This one smelled bad and there were a few half-burned incense sticks scattered on the floor. The bath was covered by a filthy wet blanket and underneath she could make out a lumpy mass.

Bishop gave her a look before he slowly pulled back the dripping blanket to reveal the body of a man covered in brackish water. He was bloated and fish-belly pale. His thick bearded face was blue and he looked up at them with helpless under-the-water eyes.

Bishop shone his torch on the face. The light reflected off the oily film on the water's surface.

'Thomas Kincaid,' he said.

Holly turned suddenly. She thought she had heard something. A door opening? A footstep? Bishop turned with her and they held themselves quiet for a minute, until he grabbed his radio and punched a number.

'Thompson,' he whispered. 'We've just found your main suspect dead in a bath.'

'Suicide?' the voice came through tinny and distorted.

'I doubt that very much.'

Bishop gave him the address and hung up.

Holly was tucked in close behind him, one hand on his shoulder, as he led her through to the next room.

It was large and dark and the light switches had been removed. The walls were black, and all the large, curtainless windows were painted over. They used their flashlights, illuminating an eclectic mix of antique tables, desks and modern chairs, a green Chesterfield sofa, a spiderweb-smashed mirror and bookshelves on three walls, crammed with hundreds of books. It smelled of incense and wood polish.

Holly had her eyes on an object set on a circular table and leaned forward to study without touching. It was an antique tin lithograph toy: a grinning monkey on a penny farthing bicycle, one hand on the handlebars, the other holding a top hat. As she shone her torch, a tiny solar panel on the wheel was illuminated by the shaft of light, and the monkey on the bike started to pedal. A gentle squeaking noise as its tin legs went up and down and the monkey raised and lowered its top hat with every spin until it completed a full circle around the table and stopped where it had started. Holly, slightly baffled, turned to Bishop:

'Did you see that?'

She aimed the torch at the solar panel again and the monkey on the bike repeated the move until it stopped pedalling with a gentle creak.

'He's recreated his childhood home,' she said, and waved her torch across the room. 'They're everywhere.'

Amongst the shadows of the furniture, hanging from the ceiling and competing for space on nearly every flat surface were more antique tin lithograph toys: a boy on a sled, a lion tamer, racing cars, fire engines, planes, clowns and lumber-jacks with axes chopping logs. Every time the torchlight hit one of the solar panels the mechanical toys would buzz and start moving, either spinning, clapping, or flying on wires or tracks around the room. It was noisy and the two of them cupped their torches.

Behind the monkey was a desk with two drawers and a candle that had been allowed to burn down until the wax trail cascaded like a waterfall to the floor. Her torch wavered across the desk illuminating a human hand immersed in a jar of liquid.

She had a split second of uncertainty when she didn't know if it was real or not, but it had to be. She opened one of the desk drawers. It was filled with at least forty empty plastic prescription bottles for fluphenazine, all made out to Sebastian Carstairs and signed off by Hedley Phelps from the Broadmoor pharmacy.

'What's fluphenazine?' Bishop said.

'An antipsychotic that treats schizophrenia.'

At the back of the drawer she found a Bible and a rosary. She picked up the rosary and stared at it intensely before putting it back. In the other drawer was a jewellery box with a silver clasp. She opened it and found envelopes stuffed with photos of police cars, ambulances, crime scenes and uniformed officers putting up police tape outside buildings.

In the backgrounds of some of the pictures were Holly and Bishop. Shots of them at the edge of the frame, some half in focus, but others where it was just the two of them or Holly and

Bishop by themselves. Holly crossing the street. In another: Bishop and Holly getting out of Bishop's car. Another: Holly and Bishop eating at a restaurant. Another: Holly at King's Cross station, and then photos of Cassandra: walking alone in the park, entering the pet shop, standing at her front door, and then a photo of Cassandra with Holly on the day they had met in the park.

'Christ,' whispered Bishop as he stared at them. 'He's seen everything.' Concerned, he said: 'Come and look at this.'

He led her to one of the bookshelves and on it was a sophisticated computer system with location finders and tracking devices. The screen map was on and a green light flashed in Betty's Tea Rooms in York.

'He thinks I'm still there, so where is he now?' she said, and her gaze was pulled to the bookshelves above the computer. She glanced at Bishop, perhaps sensing something more here. He nodded and they worked in silence, rummaging through the book titles, scanning sheets of loose paper by torchlight, working methodically, looking at the spines of the books and journals as they worked their way in opposite directions.

Holly recognised a lot of the thick, oversized volumes on serial killers, some of which she had at home, some she didn't, and she pulled one out and turned a few pages. There were handwritten notes in English at the margins, but the book was written in Aramaic or perhaps Greek and she mouthed some of the words to herself, but shook her head, not understanding any of them. She put it back and took down a notebook, a thick home-made journal with an unlabelled cover. Inside, the pages were filled with long handwritten sentences with no punctuation, no regard for spelling or grammar, a type of *freewriting* technique, and then thumbnail sketches and blurry, glued-in small photographs of a young woman seemingly cut from a contact sheet.

Holly recognised the woman immediately: it was twenty-one-year-old Raychel Raynes, The Animal's first victim, and Holly's mouth dropped open in horror: was this was his personal catalogue, the memoir of his crimes?

More pages of writing followed that took up every inch of the page and then photos of Raychel, both alive and dead. Grotesque photos of her pleading face with close shots of her eyes, fingers and mouth. Then a flurry of empty pages until the final page where there were three strips of old 16 mm cine film in plastic sleeves. Holly pulled out the first one, held the strip up and shone her torch behind it. There were eight frames of film, all continuous, but with a sloping edge at either end that indicated they had been cut from the main footage. The first strip had been taken of Raychel while she was alive and showed her jogging on a footpath by some trees, each frame taking her slightly closer to the camera. The next film strip showed Raychel lying where she had been freshly killed, her head covered in red. The last strip of eight was darker than the others and further away, filmed at night without lights, and Raychel lay in the same spot as before.

'He filmed them, Bishop,' she said softly, looking up.

'What?'

She showed him the strips of home movie, then searched along the shelf and pulled down another notebook. It was the same as the first, filled to the brim with faded writing on worn pages where the book had been handled again and again over the years. This one was of victim number ten: Luigi Bonomi, the Italian somalier who had been suffocated in his studio flat on 21 October 1988. There were another three strips of cine film at the back. The first strip was of Luigi alive and sitting at a café drinking coffee, the second, dead in his living room, and the third was a close-up of the gold stud earrings that The Animal had stolen from him.

'Nobody ever knew The Animal filmed his victims,' Holly said. 'He must have them all here—' and her heart went into her mouth. She put the notebook back and pulled out another. This one was for Ernie and Samantha Wellcroft – victims number three and four. There was so much information inside – *I watched them all day. They had a BBQ in the park and it has given me an idea. I've read about flames – the greatest leveller of human bodies. The heat will cause the soft tissues of the body to contract, which causes the skin to tear and the muscles and fat to shrink—*

The journals were spaced out between other volumes and weren't in numerical order or even numbered, so she followed their spines, her torch wavering slightly as she pulled out book after book: Martina Jong, Fred Cracknel, Tibor Slovenski, and then she found one with a photo of her parents on the inside cover.

Her mother and father.

And as she flicked through the pages she saw family photos that had obviously been taken from her home, some she had a vague memory of, others she had never seen before. The writing was so small and her eyes strained to read it – *they seem to live a simple life. I saw them first from the fields with the cows. I had a picnic on the hill by the tree the next day and watched them in the garden for four hours and seventeen minutes. They have a daughter.* Holly turned a page – *If I can move faster than they think they can, where will I end up?* Another page: *the farm is large and when I kill them it will be easier than some although what happens next is up to the police of course and DCI Warren. How will he react?*

She felt giddy as she turned to the back of the book, wanting to look at the film of them, but when she got there she saw that the three strips of 16 mm had been removed. She checked through the book again, but they had definitely been taken.

She was about to tell Bishop when the phone rang.

Fifty-Six

It wasn't a mobile phone that was ringing.

It sounded old school, like a seventies rotary phone, a shrill blast, horribly loud. Holly and Bishop glanced at each other and then all around, trying to find the source of the ringing. They played their torches across the room and as their lights hit the solar panels of the tin toys they started to move: a copper-coloured train blew its whistle on its tracks, a hot-air balloon dipped down from the ceiling on wires that made it spin, and on top of a piano, a clown clapped his metal hands and rocked with laughter.

The phone still rang.

Holly and Bishop turned to each other; she shrugged and shook her head.

Bishop got on his hands and knees and looked under the sofa and the chairs. The rats came out and he swore and battered them away. Holly looked behind a chest of drawers, moved one way and then another to try and pinpoint the sound. The noise seemed so close and then the phone stopped ringing and in the sudden, near-silence they both heard a creaking floorboard.

They turned off their torches and froze.

A footstep.

Followed by another creaking floorboard from a different room, but which one? Then she smelled smoke. Not incense, but smoke from burning wood and petrol, and she thought she heard the gentle crackle of flames. She looked at Bishop – he had heard the sounds too. She didn't want to panic but—

And then there was the sound of a handle turning and a door creaking open. She spun at the noise and a second later saw a reflection of movement in the spiderwebbed mirror. She turned on her torch and aimed it and caught a glimpse of a tall figure in the shadows illuminated by flickering yellow flames. The man was stock-still, gaunt and pale. Their eyes met and in that instant she knew it was *him*.

'Bishop! By the mirror! He's started a fire!'

'Get out!' Bishop roared.

And then the man was gone.

The hidden door closed and she heard a bolt slam across. Even though Bishop flung himself at it, it didn't budge. The flames burned through another hanging rug on the far wall and it collapsed onto the floor and the fire began to spread. In the bright light all the tin lithograph toys suddenly came to life.

While Bishop pounded on the door, Holly ran the way they had come in, jumping over tin figures on the floor that were moving and laughing and clapping as she exited the room. Along the corridor and past the sofa and the two televisions and the rug hanging from the wall, and through the first room with the pleather sofa and the foul-smelling kitchen and out of the front door that Bishop had kicked down less than ten minutes ago. On the balcony she raced left. Smoke was billowing from the doorways.

'Bishop, get out!'

As she slammed open the stairwell door and stood at the top of the stairs, she heard footsteps slapping the concrete steps beneath her.

She leapt down the stairs, taking them three at a time, crashing into the opposite wall, bouncing off and leaping down another flight.

Fifth floor and she peered over the railing into the stairwell's centre. Glimpses of the man's arm and a snatch of his head as he looked up at her. There was no doubt it was him.

Fourth floor.

Third floor.

She stopped on the landing and listened, breathing hard. He was still running below her.

Full speed ahead down the next set of stairs.

'Holly!'

Bishop was somewhere above her. Thank God he had got to safety: 'Which way did he go?' he called.

'He's heading for the exit!'

'I'll go the other way and cut him off!'

Good, she thought as she rounded the set of stairs on the ground floor, and then she saw something out of the corner of her eye coming towards her. Head height. A piece of wood. And she didn't have time to duck and it slammed her full force in the face and the last thing she saw was the pavement coming up to meet her.

Fifty-Seven

Holly came to, her head feeling as if it was spinning out of control. She rolled to one side, clutching her temples, then felt strong arms lift her up and carry her as she tried to walk. She didn't think she had been unconscious for too long, but it had been long enough for The Animal to get away. She wanted to ask Bishop if he had managed to catch him, but the voice told her to shush. The hands lowered her against a wall and she managed to squint open her eyes. She was under the ground-floor stairwell and it was dark. She felt her face and when she pulled her hands away they were covered in blood.

'Is it bad?' she said.

Her head lolled from side to side as she took a breath and stared at her trembling fingers, trying to figure out what had happened. She remembered running down the stairs and something flying towards her and a vicious headache was kicking in.

'We were this close to him,' she said. 'Bishop?'

There was no reply.

And in that instant she knew something was wrong.

She blinked the blood from her eyes and went ice cold when she saw the man emerge from the shadows in front of her. She was shaking and she wanted to scream, but couldn't.

It was The Animal.

He gazed at her without curiosity. A cadaverous face hollowed by hatred.

'Hello, Holly,' he said, and he rolled her name on his tongue like toffee. 'Swallow your fear, it doesn't suit you.'

Holly tried to focus and take in everything about him as evidence if she survived. What was he wearing? It was a green shirt that looked like a boiler suit. There was a name tag – something on the side. She would get out of this. She had to. He hadn't killed her yet, he was just looking at her. And red hair – he moved his head and it had caught the light. He had red hair now.

'Finding me was very clever of you,' he said, 'although I did suspect something was wrong when I saw you had boarded a train to Yorkshire to see Annie Wilkes again. What do you think of our mutual friend?'

Holly's throat was dry. She managed to say:

'There's nothing wrong with her, is there?'

'I wouldn't say that. But she didn't kill her brother and sister-in-law. That was me.'

He smiled gently, but his eyes flitted from side to side, seeing things she couldn't.

'It's not the killing itself, Holly, it's the planning. Learning to untangle your moral roots when you want to kill eighteen people takes a great deal of discipline. One victim for every letter of my name. After killing Len and Colette my mission was complete and I wanted to stop – I was so tired. But I waited eight days for the police to say it was me. For them to admit I was the killer, and what did they do? They arrested and charged Annie Wilkes. That poor fumbling girl. Imagine my horror when her name and photo was splashed all over the tabloids instead of mine. Len and Colette were my pièce de résistance. It's like you writing your thesis at Bristol University and then a complete stranger putting their name on it and getting a distinction. What would you have done?'

She could smell his breath. It was almost fungal.

'I wanted to be polite, so I wrote a letter to DCI Warren,' he said.

'What letter?'

'My confession. It was handed in as evidence number: PK-4-400CL-6-AJ/W.'

'The numbers on the wall upstairs?'

'Yes.'

'I don't believe you.'

'I have never lied to you, Holly, and I never will. I am a man who has nothing to lose. I'm not like most killers who pretend they're innocent. I want to be found guilty of everything I have done.'

'But you changed your signature at the Len and Colette murder scene,' she said. 'You didn't leave the bracelet from the previous victim, Lucy Le Bas, victim number sixteen.'

'Oh, but I did.'

'The police never found it.'

'Didn't they? I left it in the wood pile by the fireplace, impossible to miss. It was taken, I know it was, and DCI Warren buried it because by then Annie Wilkes had been charged. DCI Warren wouldn't admit that he had made a mistake and arrested the wrong person, so what did that mean?'

'I don't know.'

'Life is about proving your point. The police wouldn't accept my confession? They wouldn't let me claim my final kill? Do you know how angry that made me? So I had to keep going, and that's where you and your parents came in. Two more people had to die.'

The realisation of what that meant slowly sank in. Holly felt faint and sagged backwards. She felt The Animal's hands on her elbows, but she couldn't talk – her thoughts were moving too fast.

'Do you understand now?' he said. 'If DCI Warren had admitted his mistake and dropped the charges against Annie Wilkes and arrested me, then your parents would never have been killed, Holly. They didn't have to die. How different your life would have been.'

'My mother and father . . .'

'Yes.'

'Now, what would you give to see their smile one more time? What would you give?'

'Everything,' she said. Barely a whisper but she knew he had heard. She suddenly lifted her head and shot out her arms, viper-quick, hands reaching for his face to scratch him, get traces of DNA under her fingernails so that when he killed her the coroner would find evidence – but he swatted her arms away and held them.

'If I wanted to kill you under the stairs, I would have done so already,' he said and watched her with calm, almost lazy eyes.

'Why don't you? Why didn't you kill me when I was nine years old?'

'Because I created you, Holly. All of your journey, your life, since that day has been because of me. And now here we are again, and there is one more thing I want you to see.' He pushed a small flat disc into her hands and wrapped her fingers around it.

'So please accept a small token of my extreme affection,' and he pulled her face painfully towards him. 'I'll whisper in your ear – so you'll know what I'm about to tell you is true. I see your face every day, your eyes wake me up and your lips send me to sleep. And I have waited for this moment ever since the day I first saw you. You just have to understand one thing about me, Holly. Just the one. That I love in a very different way to everybody else. I loved your mother and father and they loved me. I saw it in their eyes. They loved me so much when they saw my truth. The things we do for love.' He stroked her cheek tenderly and she shivered at his touch. 'I'll see you again when this is over,' he said.

And then he got up and disappeared into the darkness. And she tried to follow, but her legs wouldn't move, and she was nine years old again at her parents' funeral. And then she thought of DCI Warren, the man who had spoken to her the day her parents had been killed and then she remembered him from the other day – a shell of a man, lost and confused – but she still hated him and then she was back in the stairwell in the dirt and the pain and her skin burned, and her thoughts were foggy, but throughout everything, she kept whatever The Animal had given her clasped tightly in her hand and held it to her chest.

She stayed there, breathing unevenly, letting the enormity of what she had just been told wash over her, staring at the floor, rubbing the blood from her face with her sleeve, until she heard Bishop calling her name and he appeared in the stairwell entrance. She saw the terror in his eyes as he took her firmly by the shoulders. Calming her and calming himself as well.

'It was him,' she said. 'I recognised him, but I didn't want to recognise him. I didn't want to see that face . . .'

'I've got you,' Bishop said softly. 'I've got you.'

Emotion overwhelmed her and her hands balled into fists and clung to him gratefully. She thought he was going to say something, but he didn't or couldn't. He had his eyes closed and they stayed like that until she saw blue police lights strobing close by and heard the sound of a fire engine.

Fifty-Eight

DI Thompson stared at Kincaid's bloated face in the bathtub with a look of despair.

'It's him all right,' he said.

He pushed a gloved hand into the black water and started groping. Bishop watched him recoil as he grasped something and pulled up a thick oily hand. He dropped it with a gentle splash and rummaged again until he found the other arm. He lifted it and revealed the remains of a twisted stump that had been severed at the wrist.

'Looks like we've found the owner of the hand in the jar,' he said.

The SOCO who was photographing the corpse said:

'We'll have to wait for forensic analysis, sir.'

'Of course it's his, for Chrissake!'

Bishop spared the SOCO a glance and walked back into the main room. The burning smell stung his nostrils. Scorched black walls, dead wires and exposed metal beams hung from the ceiling. A small area by the cracked mirror was still smoking, but the fire chief had given the police and SOCO full access and they were searching through the smoking remains with gloved hands and boots.

'We were lucky,' the fire chief said. 'Whoever set this didn't have a chance to use all of the accelerant they had. The fire was started over by that door, but the door acted like a fire shield when it was closed.'

'Thank you,' Bishop said and wiped the soot off the lithograph toy monkey and put it back on the chest of drawers. He hadn't managed to get much more information from Holly before the ambulance had taken her away, but she had confirmed it was The Animal, and that was all he needed to know. He had put in a call to Chief Franks. He could tell his superior officer was still wary, but Bishop insisted the time for keeping this a secret was now over. However it had been done, The Animal was out and needed to be caught. Franks told him there would be a media blackout on the current investigation until he had consulted with Chief Superintendent Bashir and the commissioner. Bishop asked if he could at least tell Thompson who they were actually chasing? After all, with Kincaid dead in a bathtub, Thompson had just lost his number one suspect.

No. Not a word until I get back to you.

'Yes, sir.'

Bishop hung up and watched the SOCOs circling the hand in the jar like wary animals until they put it in a box and removed it from the room.

Nobody could find any light switches, so large spotlights had been brought in, and every now and then there would be a tinny whirr as one of the lithograph toys was set off. With the added light, Bishop had a chance to look at the place with fresh eyes. It was a labyrinth: there were doors in previously hidden alcoves, some normal-sized and some half-sized, that led to other rooms and corridors.

An officer walked past carrying two black plastic bin bags and Bishop called out:

'What have you got there, Sergeant?'

'Lots of magazines on houses and decorating, sir. And this – it's like a home-made hobby-kit or something.' He pulled out a model from one of the black bin liners – pieces drawn onto cardboard then cut out and stuck down with glue onto thin board, like a child's playset. It had been torn in half and destroyed, but Bishop could still see cutouts of furniture, tables, cooking utensils, and a model of an Aga amongst the rest of the trash. 'Looks like he was planning a home renovation, sir. Maybe for this place?'

'I doubt it.'

'And there are these.'

He passed over various catalogues from furniture companies, and Bishop fanned through them. Some articles were highlighted or circled with a black pen.

'Where did you find all this?'

'In the bedroom. There's a door around the corner on the left, it was in a chest of drawers.'

Bishop followed the directions. He could smell incense the closer he got, the same type that had been used to cover the smell of Hedley Phelps' body. He entered the room. In the centre was a single bed that had been freshly made with a thin mattress and a flat pillow. It reminded him of a prison bunk. There was a large wardrobe to the right and a chest of drawers to the left. Taped to the wall above the chest of drawers were a dozen photos of a little girl. He knew it was Holly straight away. Holly with her mother and father, the three of them at a zoo, Holly cooking at home, Holly in the garden. He must have stolen them the day he killed her parents.

He ran his fingers lightly over them and lost himself for a while. Ending on the same photo he had seen at her flat, the one of her wearing a blue party dress and holding a yellow balloon that said 'Happy Birthday Dad'. That smile was like the sun, brimming with life, hope and love, and he thought of her now and how she had looked a few minutes ago at the bottom of the stairwell. He had seen her smile and laugh in the past, but he knew she was sadder than she showed. Always alone in one way, and in that second he hated The Animal more than he thought possible.

The chest of drawers was empty except for a few neatly folded black T-shirts. In the wardrobe there were clothes on hangers: doctor's scrubs, a police officer's uniform with the name Jefferson and serial number 29909, and a suit with a trilby hat that looked like the same sort of clothing Hedley Phelps had worn. There was one empty hanger, a pair of crutches and three more unopened garment bags.

Bishop went back into the main room and felt Thompson like a shadow behind him. He could feel the man's breath on his neck.

'We've got CCTV.'

Bishop turned.

'What?'

'CCTV of the man who attacked Holly. We've got him.'

'Good,' said Bishop. 'Because we need to have a talk.'

Fifty-Nine

Holly was lying in a hospital bed.

The medics had cleaned her up and stitched her on site and given her painkillers. They had then driven her to West Valley Hospital where she had been checked for concussion before undergoing a CT scan of her skull. She would have a couple of black eyes and needed rest, but there was no other damage.

She was trying to think rationally, but it was hard. She had frozen when she had seen The Animal and everything had happened so fast. She hadn't fought him, she hadn't had the chance to try to scratch his eyes out. After he had held her hands, she had just stared at him as if her senses had shut down. She had thought she was better than that. Was it fear that had immobilised her, because she finally realised he was alive? Or was it that everything her instincts had been screaming out to her had finally been justified?

Tears formed in her eyes, but she stopped herself.

He had planned something else for her and she had no idea what it was.

'I created you, Holly,' he had said. *'And there is one more thing I want you to see.'*

The intimacy with which he had spoken to her made her feel sick. She could still smell him: cloying old flowers overlaid with incense, and she retched and drank from a glass of water at the side of her bed.

There was a knock at her door.

Bishop entered the room and she wiped at her bruised face. He looked anxious and held her for a while. He smelled good and it cleared away her thoughts.

'Let me tell you what happened,' she said.

So she filled him in on what The Animal had said to her in the stairwell: what he was wearing and the colour of his hair, why he had kept her alive, what he'd told her about DCI Warren and the letter confessing to the murders of Len and Colette Wilkes, his claim that he had wanted to stop killing but needed eighteen kills. She told him how DCI Warren had ignored his confession, and how her parents didn't have to die.

'He gave us the evidence number, Bishop. We have to find that letter.'

'We will, don't worry. God, Holly, that's horrendous. I can't even begin ...'

'No ... I don't know how to feel at the moment.'

She wanted to talk about it more, about the past, but knew she needed to talk about the present.

'The Animal gave me this.'

She held up a worn copper penny, bigger than the size of a ten-pence piece, with Queen Victoria on one side and Britannia on the other. Bishop examined it then passed it back.

'What's it for?'

She'd been wondering that ever since she'd seen it.

'The date is 1888,' she said, 'but I don't know how significant it is. It was the year the Ripper first struck in London, maybe something to do with that? He said it was a small token of his extreme affection.' She shook her head. 'What do we do now?'

'We find him.'

'How?'

He gave her the ghost of a smile and said:

'CCTV. We've got a shot of him leaving the building.'

She sat upright in bed.

'We have proof? Proof it's him?'

'Everybody knows,' Bishop said. 'Chief Franks and Thompson are setting up the task force. They're waiting for you to get back to the station before they start the briefing.'

'Then what are we doing here?' Her voice sounded strong when she said it out loud. She thought she would have been more scared, but realised now she had left scared behind in the stairwell.

The doctor entered.

'Miss Wakefield, how are you feeling?'

'Better, thank you.'

'Is she free to go?' Bishop said.

'You've got the all-clear. We just need you to sign a release form, but you can get dressed and wait outside. Don't run around too much for the next couple of days. Go and relax.'

'Just what I intend to do,' Holly said.

Sixty

Holly entered the basement of the police station in a bit of a daze.

The painkillers were holding her, but exhaustion was playing catch-up. The dingy room had been cleaned and tidied up. There were twenty more desks and chairs, and twenty more computers and more than thirty officers working flat-out re-arranging the incident board with CCTV photos of The Animal leaving the Croydon crime scene. Orders and answers were shouted across desks. News reports and possible sightings were tacked to the walls and the coffee never stopped.

Chief Franks was at the far end of the room overseeing the task force. He gave Holly and Bishop a quick nod before he cleared his throat. It got everyone's attention and the room quieted.

'The man we are chasing is known as The Animal,' he said. 'Some of you will have heard of him, others not. We had been led to believe he was dead, but as you can see from the CCTV images he is very much alive. Because of the highly sensitive nature of this investigation I want absolute secrecy – a press embargo – and I also want it resolved within twenty-four hours. Holly Wakefield has been helping us and knows more about him than anyone else, so I'll leave the floor open to her.'

She took a breath and faced the task force. The speed at which everything was coming together was dizzying.

'Thank you, Chief Franks,' she said. 'Sebastian Carstairs, AKA The Animal. Some press reports even called him the Invisible Killer. Well, he's not invisible. I had a confrontation with him less than an hour ago and he is there on the CCTV footage for all of us to see. There's not much I can say at the moment, other than he is exceptionally good at killing people and staying hidden. He is also exceptionally clever. He knows we cannot saturate the media with his photograph because he is supposed to be dead and doing so would confuse the public. He will know we are after him, however, which will make him even more dangerous. Everyone has underestimated him, including me, and we now have a fight on our hands and cannot waste a single moment.'

DI Bishop raised a hand to get everyone's attention.

'The Croydon crime scene is a treasure trove packed with details of his methods and movements. We found the original scrapbooks that he kept on his murders, which began in 1986. These are being catalogued as we speak, but I want everybody here to concentrate on the murders that occurred over the past few weeks: Sandra and John Newsome, Robert Burrows, Hedley Phelps and Thomas Kincaid. Forensics have confirmed the hand found in the jar of formaldehyde belonged to Thomas Kincaid. So it would appear The Animal killed him, cut off his hand and used the fingerprints at the Hedley Phelps murder scene to send us in a different direction, which they did. The coroner thinks Kincaid has been dead for at least seven days.'

His eyes scanned the room: 'Who's working on the home decorating magazines that were found in the trash from the Croydon apartments?'

'Over here, sir.'

A waif-like woman sitting at a desk by the water cooler raised a hand:

'Sergeant Wolsey,' she introduced herself.

'Sergeant, items of furniture were circled and marked as well as tins of paint,' Bishop said. 'Have you found out if they were actually ordered, and if they were, where they were delivered to?'

'The order was placed with a company called C&G Furniture based in east London. I've left a message on their answer machine, but they don't open until ten o'clock tomorrow morning.'

'Contact Companies House, find out who owns the company and call them at home now. If they don't pick up – drive over there and knock on the front door. We need answers tonight.'

'Yes, sir.'

'In the wardrobe of The Animal's bedroom, there were clothes on hangers in garment bags,' Bishop said. 'A police officer's uniform, a doctor's scrubs and three more garment bags. Have we got an inventory yet of the clothing from those other bags?'

Bishop looked around the room and spotted an officer who raised a hand:

'Sergeant Travers? What have we got?'

'They're still with forensics, sir.'

'Make it a priority. There was also an empty hanger in that wardrobe which would indicate he may have taken one outfit with him. Did we get any fibres off that?'

'Bottle-green polyester.'

'That's what he was wearing,' Holly said quickly. 'Like a utility outfit. And there was a label on the left breast pocket.' The memories were suddenly coming back. '*Speed Electric* or something like that, and a name – I think it was *Deadman*.'

'Deadman?'

'Yes.'

'Could it have been Speedy Electric?' Travers said.

'Yes, that was it! Speedy Electric! Who are they?'

Travers read off his computer screen:

'A utility company based in Maida Vale, north-west London.'

'Contact them and see if they've had any uniforms stolen recently,' Bishop said.

'Red hair,' Holly added. 'I don't think it shows up well in the CCTV, but he has red hair.' She frowned, thinking hard. 'A police officer, a doctor, Hedley Phelps and now an electrician. So what's he planning?'

'That's the million-dollar question,' Bishop said. 'And that's what everybody here needs to find out.'

The squad went to work. Franks made eye contact with Holly and approached.

'How are you?' he said.

'I've had better days, but I've had worse,' said Holly.

'Everyone owes you an apology. A full investigation will be conducted into DCI Warren's conduct. No stone will be left unturned, you have my word, Holly. Do you need any other assurances?'

'There's no time for that now, sir, we have work to do. Where was The Animal headed when he left the tower block?'

Thompson stepped up:

'We tracked his escape out of the east side car park but the cameras lost him on Angel Street. We have roadblocks up everywhere. There is no way he can escape London.'

'I don't think he intends to,' from Holly.

'Why not?' the chief said. 'Surely he will abandon his mission now he knows we're onto him.'

'I hope you're right, but I don't believe you are,' she said, and glanced at their expectant faces. 'He'll simply take more precautions.'

'Where would he go?'

'To a safe house,' she said. 'A place we least expect, somewhere we don't know anything about. A place where he can stay until it's time for him to reappear.'

Thompson gave her a nod and shouted an order at the officers watching the CCTV. Chief Franks excused himself and all around her officers swarmed. Although the energy of the team was infectious, Holly was on her last legs. Bishop came up to her and put a hand on her shoulder.

'You need to get some rest.'

'I'm fine,' she lied.

'I'll take you home.'

'No, I can drive—'

'You're not going back by yourself. I'll have a car drive you, and I've arranged for two officers to be at your apartment all night. They'll be waiting for you when you get there.'

She didn't want to leave, but Bishop promised to keep her up to date and she felt grateful when she finally got into the undercover car that drove her back to Balham. There were two officers in the foyer and she recognised them both from previous cases. Sergeant Innes had helped on the Pickford case and DI Janet Acton with the Stickman Murders. She was too tired to talk, and both officers entered her apartment with her and checked every room and cupboard. When it was deemed safe, Holly thanked them and after they left she got dressed for bed. She made herself a hot chocolate and stared at all the old evidence she had stuck up on the wall.

Dr Bernstein was right. She lived her life according to rules dictated by The Animal and it wasn't healthy, so she began to take everything down. The crime scenes went back into boxes, the autopsy reports were put in their folders and the books and magazines were cleared off the surfaces and put neatly back on their shelves.

She sensed it would be over soon, but not quite yet, so she kept one photo of The Animal and stuck it up on the wall above the fireplace.

'Where are you hiding?' she whispered to herself.

An hour later she grabbed an ice pack from the fridge and was asleep before her head hit the pillow.

Sixty-One

The Animal had no idea how much of the apartment in Croydon and the evidence inside had been destroyed, but as he left he had heard the fire engines approaching.

It had been a shock to see them both – Bishop and Holly – and when he had left her in the stairwell he had experienced a curious sense of fulfilment.

She asked him why he hadn't killed her all those years before and he wondered if she asked herself that question every day? Did she go to bed thinking about it? About the hollow terror of her loss and the fear of it repeating itself? Yes, she did. He could smell it on her like a crippling perfume.

What he had planned for her was a fate that had begun during his hours of meditation in prison. Over the years in his mind he had built an incredibly detailed picture of her life from her childhood to the present day.

A lot of the fantasy was of no practical use, but here and there he would find a small quirk about her or idea that thrilled him and he would make a note and add it to his mental carousel. He was a very intelligent man, planned meticulously and possessed the ability to store huge amounts of information about people, places and things. Thinking about Holly had been a favourite pastime while in Broadmoor.

He had spent over a quarter of a century on B-Block, a psychiatric cesspit of extreme and unpremeditated violence, and imagining her eyes fluttering as she spoke to him, her hands clasped neatly together on her lap, calmed him and helped him think of their future.

And he knew they had a future.

He spent years trying to find out what had happened to the 'Girl who survived The Animal' as the press liked to call her, researching her from the prison computer, asking for favours from fellow inmates who were going back to the outside world after their release. He had money in various banks he had never allowed Cassandra to find out about, so compared to the rest of the prison population he had unlimited wealth. A few thousand pounds bought a lot of information and after nearly a decade he had managed to find her.

He had followed Holly through her college years and studies at Bristol University to the present day. He couldn't pinpoint exactly when it was, but after he discovered she had started working for the police in 2017, the germ of an idea had begun to grow, and he decided that, no matter what it took, he would escape from prison.

More money flowed from his banks to contacts on the outside. Bribes were made and information gathered, and all of a sudden, research became planning. He spent years lying on his prison bed, blocking out the noises from the mad, the bad and the sad, staring upwards, making faces in the grey plaster ceiling as the details clicked into place. Many ideas were discarded as trivial or utterly pointless, but after months of thought and introspection he knew there could be only one true plan.

The *where* was the easiest to settle. Then came the *when* and lastly the *how*.

The *where* was beautiful, the *when* was tomorrow and the *how* . . . the *how* had been a struggle and he was still suffering from the side effects of the chemo. Night sweats, trembling and stomach cramps were his constant companions, but he wore them like a day suit, and nobody ever suspected what he was going through.

The Animal finished his meditation and went into the other room.

He unwrapped a brown paper bag and took out a fresh Berliner doughnut. The smell of hot apple jam and vanilla icing sugar took him back to his youth in Germany and his thoughts returned to his sister. His anger had been fleeting when he realised she had been talking to Holly, but his paranoia was rampant. What had they talked about? Holly had obviously tried to convince his sister that he was still alive, but deep down he knew Cassandra wouldn't have believed her. Until now. He had done something bad. He had reacted too quickly perhaps, and part of him regretted it. He adored his sister and perhaps he was weak in his compassion, but she was the only human with whom he had ever caught a glimpse of love.

All his life he had been defined as cold, heartless and inhuman – he had read all of the newspaper articles and the psychological synopses, most of which he embraced, so he knew how others saw him and it was never going to be easy for another person to get close to him. And at times he felt the wavering needle of what he called his barometer of sadness: a wish or yearning to be loved that he knew deep down would never be fulfilled unless it was with Cassandra. It had left him with a difficult choice at a young age when he knew he was different from everybody else: adapt and participate in an empty, unreal life where he would always be rejected when people saw him for who he really was, or don't adapt and live a lonely life isolated from the social community and then sever the last thin connection to the outside world and live a life of violence. Once the path had been chosen, there had been no going back. He had always been grateful for his decision.

Cassandra could be loved, in fact he knew she had been loved as he had followed her life as closely as he had Holly's. He was jealous of her, but he could never hate her. They had been through too much together, an unbreakable bond forged by their abusers.

He took the first bite of his Berliner as he leaned back against the wall.

The woman in the chair had been dead for two days, but the man was still alive and making noises through his gag. The Animal punched him. Something snapped and the chair flipped over backwards. The force was such that the man's restraints came free from his wrists and his hands flopped like landed fish before resting on the floor. The Animal crouched next to him and raised one of the man's arms and let it drop to the ground. He did it twice, curious.

Not a rag doll yet.

The man's mouth was moving. He was trying to speak. The Animal gave him some water which made the man cough. He placed his head on the cold floor so he could hear him.

'Why are you doing this . . . ?' the man said.

The Animal pulled the man upright and sat him back on his chair. He stroked his hair and tidied him up a bit. The man started to cry and his hands groped the air like a lost child, so The Animal caught both of his wrists and held them tight.

'There is no why,' The Animal said. 'Look at me.'

'No . . .'

'You wanted me to come out of the shadows. I'm here now. Look at me.'

Sixty-Two

Cassandra had handed in her notice that morning.

There had been a formal protest from her boss, but in the face of her insistence he had nodded calmly and wished her well. He had also arranged for a late-night dinner party at The Ivy in Chelsea, in which the staff of the pet shop paid tribute to her and wished her well on her new adventure. Cassandra had gone with the surprise inheritance story to back up her leaving London on such short notice, and everyone was curious as to what she would spend her new-found wealth on. She had told them about her dreams of travel with a smile and blush, but she was lying to her friends and it made her feel bad. After they had all said their goodbyes, she had caught a taxi home, shopped at the local store and now carried the bags into her kitchen.

A message had been posted through the door from her landlord: The electric meter had been read in her absence – he hoped she hadn't minded? The chap from Speedy Electric was very professional and quick and the landlord assured her he had locked up after the visit.

The tap was dripping cold water into the sink and Cassandra turned it off and started to put her shopping in the fridge.

There was blood on her hands.

She stopped what she was doing, suddenly scared.

How had she cut herself?

She examined her hands, then washed them off at the sink and dried them. No cuts.

The kitchen counter was clean, so she opened the fridge. There were smudges of red on the carton of milk she had just put inside. She pulled it out and wiped it off with the tea towel. Everything else seemed to be all right and suddenly she knew what it was. She had moved her blended drink; the lid must be loose and some of the red liquid had spilled down the side and touched her fingers. She was angry with herself she had got so scared. The sooner she got out of here the better.

She unscrewed the container and took a sip from the drink, but quickly put it down as if she didn't like the taste. It was different, more acidic and bitter. The drinks normally lasted two days, but this one had obviously taken a turn. She was about to throw it down the sink when she noticed something sticking out of the middle of the red. A stalk of some kind. Celery perhaps? She touched it and it was hard, like a thin stick. That shouldn't be in there and she pulled it out. It was about four inches long and very thin and had strands of fine material stuck to either side. What was it and how had it got into her drink? She slowly poured the rest of the contents into her hand over the sink and more pieces of tiny stick came out clumped together with fan-shaped pieces. She examined one of the larger stalks and washed it under a tap and as the red juice seeped away she could see a shape and a colour. The strands of what looked like hair were actually yellow.

It was a part of a feather.

How did a feather get into her blender? Curious and horrified, she washed the rest of the clumpy mess and more yellow feathers appeared, and then she felt something harder like a stone, and studied it close under her eye and it appeared to be the tip of a bird's claw, but it couldn't be.

She must be dreaming.

A nightmare.

And she thought she was going to faint as she turned around and stared at her birdcage with its comforting blanket draped on top. And each step was heavy and her mouth was dry as she lifted the blanket and saw that her canaries were gone and on the bottom of the birdcage was a brown paper bag which she picked up with tears rolling down her cheeks and a scream building in her belly.

The paper bag crinkled as she opened it and the smell of a fresh apple and vanilla Berliner washed over her. Her heart caught in her throat. It couldn't be. That would mean . . . and the thought made her feel faint, but deep down it had to be true and she immediately knew who had killed Jonas and Finn.

She couldn't comprehend and suddenly rushed into the kitchen and vomited in the sink. She wiped her sore lips and opened up the trash. She stuck a hand in and pulled out an old can and ripped up envelopes, but couldn't wait so hefted the bin above her head, eyes glowing as a week's worth of household goods and wasted food slopped onto the floor. She sat in the middle of it, like a child in a toy pen, tossing some bits, discarding others until she found what she was looking for.

The ripped-up business card with the name Holly Wakefield embossed on the front.

Sixty-Three

The call woke Holly.

She had a moment of disorientation then grabbed the phone. Her hair was wet. She had fallen asleep with an ice pack on her head.

'Hello?'

At first she didn't recognise the female voice on the other end, it seemed slightly muffled, but hidden behind the sobbing and the yelling, she heard the German accent clearly.

'Cassandra?'

She couldn't work out how Cassandra had got her number, then remembered she had given the woman her card in the park when she had first approached her.

'You told me he was alive and I laughed at you!' Cassandra was shouting. 'I thought you were insane! But I was wrong! He's alive, Holly! He's alive! He came to my flat.' The sobbing got worse. 'He killed Jonas and Finn.'

'Who?'

'Jonas and Finn.'

*

An hour later, Cassandra arrived at Holly's apartment block.

She was frisked and searched by both Sergeant Innes and DI Janet Acton before she was allowed into the lift. Janet escorted her upstairs and asked her to step back as she knocked on Holly's door. After a few moments Holly opened it and the two women came inside.

Cassandra's face was puffy and red with crying and her thick hair hung down in an unruly mess. She sat down on the sofa, staring at the floor and spitting out words in German.

Holly said it was okay for Janet to go, but the DI insisted on staying.

'I'm not going anywhere, Holly. Bishop would have my badge.'

Holly smiled, grateful, and the DI sat next to Cassandra while Holly fixed them both drinks. Janet was on water, but Cassandra downed a glass of cold white wine as if she were drinking the Kool-Aid. She explained who Jonas and Finn were and her eyes hardened like ice:

'He killed them, Holly. The only things I had in my life that I loved.'

'How do you know it was him?'

Cassandra's eyes were drawn to the one photo that remained on Holly's wall of her brother above the fireplace.

'In the same way you knew he was alive weeks ago and nobody would believe you.' She glanced at Janet. 'But they believe you now, don't they?'

Holly nodded.

'I saw your brother,' Holly said. 'I talked to him. We don't know how he managed to escape yet, but he did.'

'But why would my brother come after me? Why would he kill my canaries?'

Holly leaned over to the coffee table and picked up an envelope. She leafed through some of the photos they had found at the Croydon crime scene. The candid shots of her and Bishop outside the murder scenes. She handed them over. Cassandra flipped from one to the next, not understanding.

'He's been watching us,' Holly said. 'All of us.'

And Cassandra found the photos of herself and Holly in the park talking to each other.

'He thought I was helping you?' the woman said. 'Well, I will help you now, whatever you need. I want him dead!'

Her words were chilling and Holly knew she meant it.

'I'd like to send a car over to your address please, Cassandra,' said DI Acton. 'I'm sure your brother won't be there, but it's a crime scene and we'd like to secure it.'

'Of course.'

Cassandra gave her the address and Janet spoke to dispatch and arranged for a SOCO crew to attend.

'He has ruined my life, Holly. After he was arrested and the press found me I was destroyed. My friends abandoned me, I lost my job, I lost everything. And every time I think it's over – he's somehow there, changing my life again and again. He must hate me so much. I loved him like any sister would love a big brother, but now . . .' she trailed off and cleared her throat: 'How will you catch him?'

Holly squared up to her and frowned.

'I don't know.'

Cassandra started to cry again and Holly comforted her. She gave her a white dressing gown to wear and made her up a hot-water bottle. Cassandra thanked her and after a while the woman lowered her head on the sofa and her breathing became more regular as she closed her eyes.

Holly called Bishop and explained what had happened.

'Is Janet Acton with you?' he said.

'Of course.'

'Do you feel safe?'

'I do, but Cassandra's not in any state to go home. She's asleep on the sofa.'

'I'm doubling the officers at your apartment.'

'Okay.' A beat. 'Is there any news?'

'Nothing yet. We've stepped up surveillance and have started using facial recognition software on all of the CCTV that came out of Croydon.'

'He has always been one step ahead of us, Bishop. Tracking me, watching everyone, knowing exactly what we're doing. What if he slips through the net?'

'We'll get him, Holly. It's just a matter of time.'

Sixty-Four

Bishop hung up the phone and prayed he was right.

Everybody in the incident room was running on empty, including him, and coffee wasn't going to fix it. They needed hope.

Facial recognition software was a game-changer but it was slow and there were tens of thousands of hours of CCTV to get through from both government, local council and private business cameras in the immediate area. There were twenty-two officers watching screens around him, rubbing their bloodshot eyes.

'Anything?' he said to them. He had asked the same question a dozen times already and always got the same response:

'Nothing yet, sir. You'll be the first to know.'

He turned his attention to the collection of evidence found at the Croydon crime scene. It had been labelled and spread over a dozen tables and Bishop gloved up as he sifted through it all. Everything was dusty and dirty: old boxes of different coloured hair dye, forensic latex gloves stained black or brown, ripped clothing, newspapers and parts of a moth-eaten rug.

The design catalogues from C&G Furniture with a solid oak kitchen table and four chairs along with some white paint circled in black felt-tip pen. A hardware catalogue showed sheets of 5 mm steel plate, nuts and bolts, a kitchen catalogue had an Aga circled as well as knives and dozens of copper pans, and there was a catalogue for an antique camera company with corners of some pages folded over as bookmarks. There were evidence bags stuffed with cash receipts, including one from a shop in Clapham Junction called Golden Archery. The receipt was for a Wildgame XB-370 crossbow and a dozen custom fledged carbon bolts. The thought that The Animal was armed with something so dangerous made him shudder.

'Where's Sergeant Wolsey?' he said to the room. 'Has she found out where these items from C&G were sent yet?'

DI Thompson answered from behind his computer:

'Everything was delivered to unit 11 at the Access Self-Storage Facility in Wembley.'

'Do we have cars there?'

'Got there ten minutes ago, but the place had been cleared out. According to the storage company's logbook, the unit was emptied at ten thirty yesterday morning by a company called AA Movers.'

'Where did they deliver to?'

'Don't know yet, we're still trying to get an answer from them.'

Of course they were. It was gone midnight.

Beneath the frosted-glass windows, one officer was putting together the strange cardboard model that had been found in the trash. Bishop went over and helped him pick out the little bits of paper, untangle them and try to make sense of them all. The minutes passed and so did the inevitable cups of coffee.

The pile of stubs in the ashtray grew and the stale smoke was making his eyes water.

After nearly an hour they had begun to re-assemble a miniature model of a table, four chairs, a black Aga, countertop and cupboards. There were photos of copper pots that had been cut from a magazine so he took them and wiped them clean. He got an empty box to double for the side of the kitchen and he and the officer stuck the copper pots up with a few dabs of glue as if they were hanging from a wall. Then they put the paper model of the Aga underneath and the kitchen table a little to the left and pushed the four paper chairs underneath and took a step back and stared at it.

For the next few minutes he shifted the tiny pieces back and forth, moving the table to the other side of the kitchen and putting the chairs next to the countertop, covering and uncovering them with other bits of paper they was still finding.

The pieces appeared to match the kitchen furniture that had been ordered through the catalogues.

'But what am I missing?' Bishop said quietly.

Sixty-Five

'Holly?'

It was DI Janet Acton and there was a note of urgency in her voice.

'What is it?' Holly said.

'Something's going on next door. It's not related to what's happening with us, but I thought I should let you know.'

Holly checked her watch. It was three a.m. She had been sleeping and rubbed her eyes and followed Janet from her bedroom to the living room. Cassandra was already up, standing at the wall by the fireplace.

'Are they still at it?' Janet said.

'No.' Cassandra shook her head.

'What's going on?' Holly looked at them both.

'Who lives next door, Holly?'

It was an elderly couple, Mr and Mrs Lomax, both in their mid-sixties, possibly older.

'His name is Vincent and her name is Maisie. I've spoken to him a few times, but don't really know them,' she said.

'There are some noises and banging coming from there,' Janet said. 'Is that normal?'

'There have been renovations going on for the past few weeks, but not at this sort of hour.'

Suddenly there was a dull thunk, followed by a mewing noise.

'It sounds like a cat,' Cassandra said. 'Do they have a cat?'

'I don't know.'

The sound of sawing came through the wall, loud enough to surprise Holly. It was quiet for a while and then another *thunk*. More voices, louder than before and a male shout that trailed off until it became muffled and suddenly died.

'Hey!' Janet shouted and banged on the wall. 'What's going on in there?'

Silence.

She got on her radio:

'Dispatch, this is Janet Acton. I am in situ with Holly Wakefield. There is a disturbance in the apartment next door to her – number eleven – possible male in distress. I'm going to investigate. Request back-up.'

'Roger that, DI Acton. Please hold.' A beat. 'Confirm the flat is owned by a Mr Vincent Lomax?'

'That's correct.'

'Back-up is on the way.'

Janet hung up and turned to Holly.

'Both of you stay inside and lock the door. I'll be back in a minute.'

She went outside. Holly followed her to the door and flipped the deadbolt. She looked through the peephole and saw Janet talking into her radio as she banged on the Lomaxes' front door. Along the corridor she heard the lift doors open and Sergeant Innes from downstairs joined the DI. She couldn't catch all of their movements and then realised the neighbours' door must have opened as Janet and the officer disappeared from view.

She waited but saw nothing else and heard nothing. She went back to the living room where Cassandra was still on her feet by the fireplace.

'Can you hear them?' Holly said.

'No.'

The two women stared at each other and Holly wiped her hands on her T-shirt. She suddenly realised she was sweating.

Bishop was on his way to Holly's apartment.

He had already been updated by dispatch about the disturbance in the apartment next door to her and knew it wasn't connected to The Animal, but he couldn't get rid of the underlying sense of unease.

Janet Acton and Sergeant Innes were both incredibly competent officers and he knew they would keep Holly safe, but dispatch hadn't heard back from them since they had entered the neighbours' flat and that worried him. They could still be talking or negotiating with the residents, but under normal circumstances one of the officers would usually provide updates every few minutes.

His radio rang.

'Bishop.'

'Sergeant Wolsey for you, sir.'

The call was patched through.

'Go ahead,' he said.

'Sir, I've managed to get hold of AA Movers, the company who picked up everything from the Wembley storage facility.

They arrived at ten thirty and delivered the items to a flat in Balham.'

'Balham? I'm on my way there now. What's the address?'

'Thirty-five Western Lane.'

He looked at the radio sharply:

'Thirty-five Western Lane?'

'Yes, sir.'

He kept his irritation under control.

'That can't be right. Please verify.'

'That's the address we have, sir. The movers were adamant about it because the flat was on the fifth floor and they had to carry an Aga.'

'A what?'

'An Aga.'

He felt so suddenly scared that his hands clenched white on the steering wheel.

'What flat number did they go to?'

'Flat eleven.'

He felt his heart judder.

'My God, he's next door,' he whispered in horror.

'Sir?'

'The Animal! He's already there!'

Sixty-Six

There was a *clunk* from the apartment next door followed by a shout.

Holly and Cassandra had their ears pressed up to the wall by the fireplace. There were sounds of movement and then another *clunk* and then the noise of a door opening. The commotion suddenly seemed to move to the corridor outside the apartments and Holly ran to her front door and checked the peephole. What she saw made her body go cold.

Sergeant Innes was standing against the opposite wall in the hallway, hands twitching, seemingly unable to move—

She ran into the kitchen and pulled out the biggest knife she could find from the knife block. Cassandra watched her with wide eyes.

'What's going on?'

'Stay here,' Holly said. She pulled back the deadbolt on the door and rushed outside and saw what she couldn't see before.

Sergeant Innes was impaled to the wall, a crossbow bolt sticking out of his chest. He was dead or close to, his hands had stopped moving and his eyelids fluttered one last time.

There was a trail of blood on the carpet that led back to the neighbours' apartment door, which was still open. There were no lights inside, only shadows.

From that darkness came a loud *twang* and a scream and Holly knew it was Janet Acton.

'Janet?' She found her courage. 'JANET!'

And now other doors were opening along the corridor and neighbours were peering with alarmed eyes and Holly shouted 'Call the police!' and could hear voices and chains being pulled across locks and someone screamed and this time it wasn't Janet – it was Cassandra.

She had followed Holly from her apartment and was staring at Sergeant Innes's body. The woman was so pale she looked dead. She turned and faced the neighbours' open door and raised a hand like a spectre, her mouth twisting horribly.

'*Es ist mein Bruder*,' Cassandra said. '*Mein Bruder!*'

'Cassandra! Go back to the apartment! Cassandra!'

But the woman was shaking her head with glazed eyes. Then Holly saw movement from within the dark doorway and from the shadows a hand appeared on the ground, bloody fingers clawing at the carpet. She heard a moan, rushed forward and flinched when she felt a body. Warm and wet, and suddenly the hand grabbed hers and held it vice-like—

'Holly . . .'

It was Janet.

Holly dragged the DI out of the blackness of the doorway and into the brightly lit corridor leaving a snail-trail of blood on the carpet. The DI had a crossbow bolt sticking out of her hip and it had gone through to the other side. She had one hand on it, clamping the injury, and the blood had started to coagulate.

'We need to get you help.'

Janet shook her head. Eyes squeezed shut in pain.

'The room . . .' she whispered.

Holly leaned in closer.

'The room? What room?'

Holly stared at the dark entrance of her neighbours' apartment. Then back to Janet.

'Where is he?'

Janet was fading in and out of consciousness. Her hand dropped away from the wound and fresh blood seeped onto the carpet. Movement to Holly's right. It was a neighbour. A woman wearing a fluffy blue dressing gown with bare feet. She looked petrified. They locked eyes.

'Did someone call an ambulance?' Holly said.

'They're on their way.'

'And the police?'

'They're coming too.'

'Good,' said Holly. Bishop would be here any minute. Her phone was in her living room. Did she have time to go back in and get it? She dragged Janet further along the corridor. She couldn't leave her yet and she had to check on Cassandra. Where was Cassandra? She looked along the empty corridor.

'Cassandra!'

The neighbour again –

'Was that the woman with you? The woman with the white dressing gown?'

'Yes.'

'She went inside.'

'Where? My apartment?'

'No, she went in there!'

The woman pointed to the neighbours' apartment.

Shit.

Holly squeezed Janet's hand once more and stood up. She gripped the knife and it felt instantly heavy. There was a ringing in her ears and she thought of Lee and Bishop and then she could think of nothing but the fear swelling inside of her.

Time stood still. Her senses in overload. This was it then, she thought. This was her life in one simple second. One decision.

Cassandra.

She held back her scream and went into the apartment after her.

Sixty-Seven

The moment Holly stepped over the threshold the front door closed behind her and she heard a lock click into place.

She crouched low in the corridor and waited agonising seconds for her eyes to adjust to the darkness and then she saw a faint strip of light coming from under the closed door ahead of her. She edged forward.

There was a click and the light under the door went off.

She froze to the spot.

Another click and the light came on again. Cassandra or The Animal? She wanted to call out but held her breath. Her heart was in her mouth as she glanced one more time along the corridor, then she grabbed the handle and opened the door.

There was a soft light from a bare bulb in the ceiling. The room was small, only ten feet square with one other closed door in the far wall. On a table in the centre was an old 16 mm film projector. There was a chair by the far door and The Animal was sitting in it.

His hands rested on his knees and his face was neutral.

Holly blinked. It was hard to focus in the light, but it was really him. He stared at her for a while and licked his lips before he spoke.

'Shut the door, please.'

She did as asked. She wasn't sure whether her heart was beating any more.

'It's a little more comfortable than under the stairs, isn't it?' The Animal said. 'You can scream and shout in here. The whole flat has been soundproofed so I doubt if anyone will hear you.'

'Where's Cassandra?' Her voice was a cracked whisper.

He looked away and shook his head as if contemplating, then said: 'You said you would give everything to see your parents smile one more time. Do you still say that?'

'Yes.'

'Do you have the token I gave you?'

She nodded, and the fear inside her woke and stirred.

'Then I'll leave you alone, but at the end of this there is a price to pay. Do you understand? You have to follow me through this door. Cassandra is on the other side waiting.'

He got up and left the room.

She felt herself begin to shake as she stumbled over to the film projector. At the back of the machine was a narrow slot which said: 'place token here'.

She took the Victorian penny from her pocket and pushed it against the slot. The penny disappeared with a dull clunk. Nothing happened for a few seconds and then the projector light went on against the wall and the reels began to spin.

Light strobed over her as the projector clattered in the dark, running the piece of film through. 'Ride of the Valkyries' by Wagner played as the screen showed bright images of floating clouds in a clear blue sky. Out of the clouds came beautiful angels, superimposed, their wings flapping jerkily like some early Hollywood movie; no matter where the angels flew, their eyes met hers. And the angels changed into different forms and suddenly the clouds were on fire and the angels were tormented souls, ghastly but somehow still beautiful. She couldn't talk as her eyes focused on the flaming figures and then everything flashed white, and gone was Heaven and Hell, and in its place was a home-made cine film of a party in full swing. Not just any party though; it was her father's birthday.

Holly remembered the home-made video that a friend had made for them. It had been so exciting and she had worn her blue party dress and the food had tasted so good and they were outside in her old garden. There were men in shirts and jackets drinking and storytelling and the women were elegantly dressed, doing movie-vamp poses for the camera and blowing cigarette smoke.

'*I have cookies, just come out of the oven!*'

And it was her mother speaking.

Smiling at the camera, holding up a plate of cookies.

'*You want one?*' she said to Holly.

Brightly dressed, eyelids flashing like blue and green butterflies, lipstick perfect.

And the film cut suddenly to her father holding a piece of untouched birthday cake on a plate. A man talked to him on the edge of the frame and whispered in his ear, but her father ignored him and seemed to stare straight at Holly, lost in thought, with a party hat sloped on one side of his head. She felt as close to him in that moment as if he were still alive. She wanted to reach out to him and realised she had put a hand to her mouth as if she were a child.

Then the images sped up: quick shots of her mother, her

father and the birthday friends, all talking and gesticulating, but with no sound. Images of her in the blue dress holding the yellow balloon and then letting it go. Images so rapid they were impossible to process. Smiling, laughing, beautiful and alive. Her fondest memories that she thought she would never see again. And Holly seemed to deflate, as her expression went from happiness to the realisation of what she had lost all over again. Her family. Her world.

It was like being hit in the chest from the inside and she kneaded her breastbone with the heel of her hand and screamed.

Sixty-Eight

Bishop pulled up outside Holly's apartment block and sprinted from the car.

Blue lights were flashing everywhere. Police tape had already cordoned off the area and a crowd had gathered with the press. He ran up the front steps flashing his warrant card as he passed through the lobby, made it to the stairs and carried on running.

He was breathing hard by the time he reached the fifth floor. There were police and firearms officers everywhere. He started along the corridor and saw Janet Acton getting medical help. She looked pale with a drip in her arm and her eyes were closed and then he saw a black body-bag – Sergeant Innes – he had only spoken to him an hour ago and he wondered if his wife had been informed yet.

A breaching unit was using a battering ram on the front door of the apartment where Mr and Mrs Lomax lived and there was a dull thud every time it connected. After six hits with the ram the man passed it to another member of the team who began the same procedure. The noise was horrendous.

'What's taking so long?' Bishop said.

'The door is reinforced and so are the walls.'

'HOLLY!' he shouted.

'There's been no response from the inside, sir.'

'Phones? Radios?'

'No contact. We can't get a GPS on anything in the apartment, which makes me think there are polarising strips on the other side of the walls blocking the signals.'

'What about Cassandra? Where is she?'

'Who?'

Bishop pushed past the officer and headed into Holly's flat. His eyes scanned all the rooms and he went over to the fireplace and the one photo of The Animal and put his ear to the wall.

'Holly!'

He counted the seconds that seemed like an age.

'Holly!'

He could hear something but he wasn't sure what. It may have been the battering ram from the corridor. He ran back out to the team.

'Use the shotgun,' he shouted.

An officer stepped forward and let loose on the door's hinges with both barrels and Bishop smelled the cordite and could feel the heat of the blast. The locks and hinges were obliterated but the door didn't budge. One of the officers traced a hand around the frame.

'It's a sold steel undercoat that looks as though it's been welded into place,' he said.

So they took sledgehammers to the door and adjoining walls and started smashing them, but underneath the plaster were breeze blocks and more sheets of steel.

'The only way we can get inside is if we set explosives, but they'll be hard to control,' one of the officers said.

'How long until we can do that?' Bishop said.

'Ten minutes, maybe twenty before the specialist team can get here.'

'That's too long.' He took a step back and reassessed. He had to keep it together, but he had never felt so angry and frustrated. 'There must be another way in.'

'Through the windows, sir. We could abseil down from the roof?'

Good idea – but he had a different thought.

'Six of you, tool-up and follow me!' He grabbed one of the sledgehammers and ran into Holly's apartment.

He sized up the living room wall with the fireplace and swung the sledgehammer at the photo of The Animal. Plaster cracked and the photo was obliterated. He swung the sledgehammer again.

'The walls!' he shouted. 'We break through to the other apartment from here!'

Sixty-Nine

Holly gasped for breath, clutching pathetically at her chest.

The film had stopped and there was just the clatter of dead reels and the flickering projector light on the wall. She got up from the chair, her feet like lead as she faced the final door. She heard her mother's voice from the other side.

'*I have cookies, just come out of the oven! You want one?*'

And before Holly could stop herself, she grabbed the handle and opened the door.

It was the smell that hit her first – the sugar and cinnamon of freshly baked cookies.

And suddenly she was nine years old again and in her childhood kitchen.

It was identical. Just as she remembered it.

With the country-style wooden cabinets, the solid oak table and the four white shabby-chic chairs to match and the black Aga to the right and copper pans hanging from the ceiling and a pile of cookies on an Emma Bridgewater plate with red and pink hearts on it. This was the place where she used to spend most of her time and laugh with her parents and steal popcorn from the cupboard and eat doughnuts fresh from the fryer at the weekends.

There were two bodies in the room.

Her mother was lying where she had seen her last – face down on the countertop with a knife sticking out of her back, except it wasn't her mother, it was her neighbour Maisie, and on the floor by her feet was her father who had been decapitated – except it wasn't her father but Maisie's husband, Vincent Lomax. She heard a whimper and saw Cassandra sitting against the Aga, crying and clasping something tight in her hands. Her mouth was open, her breath raspy.

The Animal watched Holly from the other side of the room.

'We're back again, Jessica,' he said softly. 'How does it feel?'

Holly felt the fear. Not a gentle ripple, but an overwhelming sense of absolute terror and she took a trembling step backwards as if the whole place was contaminated. There were blood-red footprints where she had walked into the room and she couldn't work out if they were her own. She slumped against the far wall as her knees gave way and she went crashing to the floor. Her body sagged and she seemed quite small and her arms went limp at her side as she heard the words:

'*I have cookies, just come out of the oven! You want one?*'

'Enough,' Holly said. 'Enough . . .'

And The Animal turned off the tape recorder and slowly walked to her side.

'Do you remember what I said to you the last time I was here in your kitchen when you were nine years old? *I've seen things you haven't.* That's still so true. I wish you could see inside my head. The conversation is sparkling.'

He crouched by her side and moved his right hand up as if to touch her cheek. There was a sharp metallic snap and a thin, eight-inch, stiletto blade shot forward from a metal cuff around his wrist. It stopped an inch from her throat.

'I think I made it perfect for you,' he said. 'Did I forget something?'

'Only one thing,' she whispered. 'You underestimated me when I tried to kill you twenty-five years ago when I was a child. You've made the same mistake now.'

She shifted her right arm and the kitchen knife dropped from inside her sleeve to her palm. There was a flash of silver and she slammed the blade into the flesh between his ribs.

He choked on his surprise and stared at her open-mouthed until he gagged and his eyes curled up under his lids and he pulled himself away. The blade was wrenched from her grip and clattered to the floor. Blood dripped in a steady stream as he propped himself up on the kitchen countertop, breath ragged, and when he turned to her she had never seen such madness.

With a cry of rage he lunged, but came up short and crashed into the table, smashing the plate and scattering cookies everywhere. He rolled and crawled to his feet, swung his fists and slammed the table to one side. Holly got up and backed away as he clutched at his gut, frothing at the mouth.

'Cassandra, get out!'

But the woman was catatonic. Holly's breath was heavy in her own ears and at first she thought it was just her imagination, but she could hear banging and shouting. Then to her left she saw a great slab of plaster fall to the ground and the end of a sledgehammer appeared through the wall.

'Holly!' Bishop's voice.

'Bishop!'

She ran towards his voice, but The Animal tackled her to

the ground. He straddled her and placed a hand around her throat. She grabbed his wrist with both hands, clawing for her life. Punching and elbowing him as her breath gurgled. He pulled back his right arm and Holly heard the snap of the silver stiletto knife again. She grabbed his other wrist and watched the blade waver from side to side as he pushed down harder and harder. She heaved her legs up and twisted her head to one side and felt the cold line of the knife miss her throat and sting against the side of her face. She felt along his chest and dug her fingers into the wound in his side. He clamped his teeth shut and hissed, forcing all of his weight on top of her. He was sweating and it dripped into her eyes. She blinked it away, her grip getting weaker as the stiletto knife inched closer to her eye, her mouth and her neck.

She didn't know what to think and for a moment she lost all hope.

Her life didn't flash before her and she didn't feel any pain as she felt the blade cut into her neck. Instead, she had regrets. She wished she had told Bishop she loved him.

And then, as she was fading, she sensed a blur of movement and heard a roar like thunder as the whole wall from her apartment came tumbling down and Bishop and a firearms team rushed through the dust.

There was a series of gunshots, so loud Holly thought her ears might explode and The Animal jerked to one side. Holly watched, emotions overloaded to the point of being numb as his body sagged and he fell. His head scraped against the wall and clunked when it hit the floor, and suddenly she knew he was gone.

Like a rag doll.

Seventy

Bishop stayed with Holly in the ambulance on the journey to hospital.

He waited alone in reception as surgeons operated on her for over two hours. The knife had missed her carotid artery by three centimetres. She had lost a lot of blood and was still in a critical condition. She had a tube down her throat to help her breathe and was hooked up to a machine that beeped her vitals every few seconds.

Bishop watched her as she slept in a private room. All he wanted to do was lie next to her, but he had to make do with holding her hand. The doctors told him there was nothing more they could do and now it was just a waiting game. He kept getting calls from the station and after fending them off for as long as he could he decided to go back.

He sat at his desk and listened to the recorded sessions between The Animal and Hedley Phelps, trying to keep himself occupied while he waited for the call. The task force moved slowly around him, heavy with shock and sadness. Sergeant Innes had been a good policeman: vigilant, funny and wanting to do some good in the world – another casualty of The Animal, whose sinister legacy would surely outlive them all. How could one person cause so much destruction and misery? Not that Bishop was religious, but Sebastian Carstairs truly seemed to have been the devil incarnate.

Thankfully, Janet Acton's condition was no longer critical. As for Cassandra, paramedics had carried her from the apartment physically untouched, but she had been shaking and wailing and clutching at a tin toy soldier whom she had called Wagner. The police had to prise her fingers apart to take it from her and put it into evidence.

Someone offered Bishop a cup of coffee. It was cold but he drank it and as he looked up he saw Thompson give him a nod from the door and wave him over.

'We got them,' the DI said. 'They were at the airport, about to get on a flight back to Greece.'

The men made their way around to the main police station and took the stairs down to the interview rooms. They stopped outside interview room seven.

'What have they said?' Bishop asked.

'They requested a lawyer.'

'Have they got one?'

'Yep.'

Bishop opened the door.

The two women sat behind a table, both dressed in black.

'Ana and Maria Theopolis,' Bishop said. 'It's good to see you both again.'

He took a seat and stared at them both. The mother had her hands clasped on her lap but he could see she was shaking. Ana looked numb, and their lawyer – Bishop hadn't seen the lawyer before.

'Marcus Bellmont,' he introduced himself. 'My clients have written a statement, if you would care to read it.'

He offered a two-page summary which Bishop took and turned over.

'I'll read it later. I have a statement of my own I'd like to make.' A beat as he aimed at the daughter. 'What the hell were you thinking?'

Ana started to cry and said sorry, but it would never be enough.

An hour later Chief Franks arrived at the station and Bishop explained what had happened and how The Animal had escaped from Broadmoor prison.

'For all his attempts to transform the prison system,' Bishop said, 'Hedley Phelps couldn't transform a mass murderer. It was his own ego that led to his downfall.'

'He honestly thought he had changed The Animal?'

'He did. It's all there in the tapes of the therapy sessions between the two men. Phelps was blinded by The Animal's lies – and part of me doesn't blame him. He was a civilian, he wasn't like us. He watched the news and read books, but he'd never sifted through the remains of a bloody corpse or had to talk to victims' families. A back-seat cop, for want of a better expression.'

'But how did Carstairs do it?'

'One of the costumes we uncovered in the garment bags was a black priest's robe, with a purple stole.'

The chief's brow furrowed.

'A priest's robe?' he said.

'Yes, complete with rosary beads.'

Bishop pressed play on his computer and the CCTV from the hospital played as he explained:

'On the last day of his treatment, The Animal had his chemo at the hospital and the priest, his wife and daughter took him into the chapel for final prayers. There are no cameras in the chapel and the security didn't follow them inside. They came out five minutes later – see here? But now the man walking and dressed as the priest is The Animal. Father Theopolis must have shaved off his beard and come to the hospital wearing a fake one; he traded clothes with Carstairs and gave him the false beard, then got into the wheelchair. The Animal walked out of the front door with Ana and Maria by his side while the poor old priest was carted back to Broadmoor.'

'They swapped places?' Franks said, astonished. 'Why would he do that?'

'Michael Theopolis was dying from stage four pancreas, liver and brain cancer. The body that was cremated was his.'

'Wait a minute—'

'Hedley Phelps introduced him to The Animal, told him the killer was a reformed man and they struck a deal.'

'What sort of deal?'

'Hedley convinced the priest that Carstairs had found God and wanted to make up for his past deeds by spending the rest of his life helping others. In return for a "donation" of fifty thousand pounds, Theopolis agreed to swap places with him on the final day of his treatment at the hospital.'

'The cancer screenings? The blood tests?'

'The slides and the blood with the cancer all belonged to Michael Theopolis. He was getting treatment at Guy's Hospital in Southwark. Hedley Phelps signed them off as The Animal's while they were sitting in the hospital fridge, waiting to be picked up by the courier on the Wednesday afternoon. Phelps thought he was doing the right thing. Prisoner reform – a second chance – and he would be the one who was responsible for the rehabilitation of one of the most notorious killers in history. He already had a book deal in the making.'

'So The Animal went through chemo without cancer just so he could get out? It's crazy.'

'Crazy is as crazy does.'

'And the mother and daughter were in on it?'

'The husband and father they loved was dying. I think they honestly believed in Hedley Phelps' crusade, if you want to call it that – and agreed to help out by escorting their father into the hospital and taking Sebastian Carstairs with them when they left. They've admitted to everything.'

A moment while Franks digested the news, then he shook Bishop's hand.

'Well done, DI Bishop,' he said. Then: 'How's Holly?'

'We're still waiting. Thanks for asking, sir.'

'And what about The Animal?'

Bishop was reluctant to say the words out loud, but—

'Last I heard, he's still in surgery. I'm sure we'll find out soon enough.'

Then his phone rang and it was the hospital.

Seventy-One

Holly was still asleep.

She looked exhausted but peaceful.

Bishop sat and held her hand for a while then went to get himself a coffee. When he got back he watched her through the glass window of her room until someone joined him.

'You must be DI Bishop?' the man said. He was in his sixties, slight of build and impeccably dressed.

'I am, yes.'

'I'm Dr Bernstein from Wetherington Hospital. I work with Holly.'

'Yes, she has mentioned your name.'

'How is she?'

'No change.'

'Shall we get a coffee?'

They sat in the café on the lower ground floor of the hospital. Bishop had his coffee but hadn't touched it.

'So how well do you know Holly, Detective Inspector Bishop?'

'Bill, please.'

'Bill, how well do you know her?'

'I've worked with her on and off for the past two years, but recently we've been spending more time together.'

'She talks about you a lot. She likes you.'

'It's mutual. She's had it very tough the last week or so. The case has brought back a lot of old memories.'

'Has she said anything else to you recently – about herself?'

Bishop thought for a second.

'She told me she wanted to talk to me about something. That there was something about her that I needed to know.'

'Good, she said she would bring it up.'

'But we didn't get to it. We've never had that conversation. Is she okay?'

'Oh, yes. She's under very good care.'

'What do you mean?'

'As well as working with her at Wetherington Hospital, Holly is also my patient.'

'How is that possible?'

'In one sense we're all patients. I have my own therapist.'

'You do?'

'My wife, which actually makes it somewhat cheaper.' He smiled and Bishop smiled with him. 'But with Holly it's slightly different,' Bernstein said. 'She gave me the authority to talk to you about something. She was very specific.'

'Talk about what?'

'At nine years old when her parents were murdered she experienced a huge amount of stress and sometimes when we face stressful situations, we need an outlet, we need something to help us cope.'

'I understand that; I was in the army.'

'So you know about PTSD and mental health?'

'Yes.'

'Has Holly talked to you about one of her patients, Lee?'

'She's mentioned him to me in the past. She says she's very fond of him.'

'She is, but it's complicated. When she was a child she needed a safe place, and the police and the detectives and the foster home could only do so much, so she created one for herself.'

'A safe space?'

'It wasn't a safe space so much as a safe person, someone to talk to. Someone to get things off her chest with, and also someone she knew would always be there for her. She created Lee.'

'Created him?'

'Lee doesn't exist, DI Bishop. Or rather, he does exist, but only in her head.' Bernstein permitted himself a thin smile. 'Holly is schizophrenic.'

'I don't know what that means. She hears voices?'

'It's not that simple. It's a certain type of schizophrenia caused by the traumatic situation she went through. Children who have experienced severe trauma are three times more likely to develop schizophrenia later in life. Holly is one of those statistics. She's also a brilliant psychologist. She can see into the minds of people and has helped many patients over the years. Lee is an outlet. All the sessions she has had with Lee have been recorded and analysed, sometimes with her present afterwards. It's a one-way conversation, obviously, but with insight we can understand the conversation that goes on between them. She's talked to Lee about you.'

'She has?'

'Holly is scared of telling you the truth.'

'Why?'

'Schizophrenia is a psychosis, a long-term mental health

condition. It can be managed, of course, but it's not for every-one. You look a little stunned.'

'This wasn't something I'd expected.'

'She's safe, she's on medication and it's something that she can deal with, but she wanted to let you know if something ever happened to her.'

'You mean if she died?'

'Yes.'

'She won't die. She'll get through this.'

'Holly wanted you to know in case she didn't. She's an incredible woman but you'll never know how fragile she is.'

Bishop thought perhaps he did.

'So what do I do?' he said. 'What do I do now that I know this about her?'

'What do you want to do?'

'I need to talk to her,' he said. 'She needs to know that I know.'

Seventy-Two

For Holly, the last few days had been a blur.

She slept most of the time and had seen white-uniformed nurses leaning over her and adjusting the machines that kept her company at night.

Her throat was horribly sore and she had been advised not to speak for at least another two weeks. The only thing that tasted good was ice cream, and she was taking another mouthful of raspberry ripple when Bishop knocked on the door and entered. He was carrying a cooler and put it on her bed.

'Are you going to give me the silent treatment again?' he smiled.

She smiled back, but it turned into a laugh that hurt her throat. He had visited her every day and she had woken up that morning with him holding her hand. It had been beautiful.

'Just nod or shake your head,' he said. 'How are you feeling?'

She gave him the thumbs-up. Then she patted the bed. He sat. She pointed to the cooler.

'You want to see what's inside?'

She nodded.

He took off the lid and angled it towards her. There were half a dozen pints of ice cream from Chin Chin Laboratorists in Camden, London. Her new favourite. She clapped her hands and smiled.

'You want an update on your apartment?' he said.

She nodded.

'It's still a mess.'

She shrugged, then mimed swinging a sledgehammer. It made him smile.

'The Met are going to pick up the bill,' he said. 'It's the least they can do.'

He took a moment, eyes locked on hers.

'This was a close one,' he said.

She nodded. She could feel herself getting teary-eyed, but didn't wipe them away.

'After this is over,' he said, 'you need to get your full health back before you come and join me on another case, okay?'

She nodded again. She wanted a rest and knew she needed one.

'And we have to talk about things.'

What things?

'Dr Bernstein spoke to me. He told me about you a couple of days ago. About your . . .'

She felt her heart drop. He couldn't even finish the sentence. She hadn't wanted it to be like this! Not while she was in hospital and unable to speak!

Oh God!

Here it comes, she thought. He knew her secret. He knew she was a schizoid. He's gonna run a mile. Don't treat me with kid gloves, Bishop, just let me have it. Both barrels – let's get this show over. I'm schizophrenic and every time I was talking to Lee I was just talking to myself. Sitting alone in a cell at Wetherington Hospital with my imaginary friend . . .

He brushed a strand of hair behind her ear.

'It's okay,' he said.

'Bishop . . .'

She shouldn't have spoken. It was like razor blades.

He held her hand.

'Stop talking,' he said. 'You've got another couple of weeks of being quiet and I'm going to take full advantage of that.'

She stared at him through the tears.

'Truth is, I've grown used to you, Holly. You have to take a few pills and need a bit of quiet time every now and then? I'm okay with that. It doesn't change anything between us. Maybe one day you can talk to me instead of Lee, but that's only when you're ready. I'm pretty much in love with you, Holly Wakefield, and I don't want to waste any more time,' he said. 'I want to be with you. Nod once for yes, twice for no.'

She smiled. So this was it then?

Here he is . . . the man of my dreams.

And her whole body sighed with relief. She had expected the worst. She had thought he might walk away – how many times had she played that scenario through her mind? – but he hadn't. He had stood his ground right next to her and was staring at her with his dark-blue eyes.

And he's still here waiting for me to respond. So quit smiling, Holly, and kick-ass.

She nodded once. Laughed, but it hurt her throat. Then she nodded again because she was so happy, but—

'Was that one nod or two?' Bishop said. 'Do you want to be with me or not?'

I'm not going to cry, okay? But at the same time . . .

I'm probably going to cry, she thought. She smiled and nodded once.

'Good,' he said. 'Will it hurt if I kiss you?'

She pulled him close and kissed him and left everything else behind.

Seventy-Three

Six months later . . .

A flash of a SOCO suit in front of a red background and then the video was switched off and the television screen went black.

There was a deathly silence amongst the people from the formal hearing who had just watched the SOCO and coroner's video of Holly's parents' murder crime scene.

At the centre of the head table was Commissioner Sally Reeman, a middle-aged, grey-faced bureaucrat who never seemed to blink. To her left was Chief Franks, to her right, Superintendent Bashir and on either side were several internal affairs officers, name place-cards in front of them. Papers shuffled and there was the occasional clearing of a throat.

'It is an incredibly disturbing video,' the commissioner said. 'And the ordeal Miss Wakefield has endured ever since then has been quite horrific.'

She stared ruefully at DI Bishop, who sat at a small table in front of her. Bishop's suit was jet black and there was a physical intensity about him today. He was simmering, barely holding it together after watching the tape.

'And Miss Wakefield seems to have played an integral role in the most recent case?'

'Yes, ma'am,' Bishop said. 'We wouldn't have stopped The Animal without her. But perhaps most tragically, because of the evidence that has recently come to our attention, her parents didn't need to die.'

'Quite. Evidence number PK-4-400CL-6-AJ/W,' the commissioner said, and there may have been a hint of a conciliatory tone. One of the internal affairs officers passed her an evidence bag which she took and noted and then he passed her another. The commissioner indicated that Bishop could see it and the officer stood up and walked around the table and handed it to him. Inside the evidence bag was a small silver bracelet. Bishop peered through the plastic and could make out the word *amore* engraved on one side. It was the missing jewellery from victim number sixteen – Lucy Le Bas.

'Where was this found?' he said.

'In DCI Warren's attic. Hidden in a cardboard box.'

Bishop swore under his breath. He looked up when he heard Bashir cough and saw that the superintendent's face had reddened.

'DCI Warren made a grave mistake during the Annie Wilkes case and Sebastian Carstairs investigations,' Commissioner Reeman said, 'that needlessly sent an innocent woman to prison for over twenty-five years and cost the lives of two innocent people. However, due to DCI Warren's deteriorating condition of vascular dementia, the CPS has deemed it unwise to follow up with any criminal prosecution.'

Bishop felt a part of his heart sink.

'I'm sorry?' he said.

'It won't happen, DI Bishop. However, the police and government will be issuing a full and public apology to both Annie Wilkes and Miss Wakefield.'

She opened another file and took off her glasses.

'In light of the rest of the report you filed on the serial killer known as The Animal,' she said, 'I feel there are still gaps that need to be filled in.' She flipped through the papers on her desk and glanced at Bishop with some consternation. 'Some of the accusations you have brought to our attention are still pending investigation and therefore we cannot proceed until we have all the facts. In total, eight people were killed in The Animal's latest killing spree, one of whom was a member of our own police force.'

She took a sip of water.

'Let us begin with the psychiatrist, Hedley Phelps . . .'

Holly watched Bishop emerge from the meeting two hours later. He looked shattered.

'How did it go?' she said.

'You're to be granted a full public apology.'

'And Annie Wilkes?'

'A full pardon.'

'Thank you,' she said.

They held each other for a while then:

'Any news on Cassandra?'

Bishop shook his head.

'After she was released from the hospital she disappeared. There's no trace of her.'

'She'll start her life again. She has done before, she'll be okay.'

'What about you? Are you going to be okay?' he said.

She kissed him.

'I'll be fine.'

Seventy-Four

Holly had heard of Fairlie Prison in Birmingham, but had never been there before.

She bypassed the city and there were no road signs to the prison and the approach road was a sketch of a dusty path. She crossed an old steel bridge, its girders like black slashes across the blue sky and there it was: a single-storey building painted the same colour as the seedless fields around it. Fairlie was the only prison in the UK that housed prisoners underground, and it was deep and dark like a dungeon and had only fifty-eight inmates.

Security was paramount and visitors scarce.

The minimum of words were spoken to her by the warden, and she was allowed entry only on presentation of a special visa from the Home Office and facial recognition. After she was thoroughly searched, two guards escorted her through a maze of corridors to the lift. She guessed they were both armed, although she couldn't see their weapons. One of them raised a wristwatch to a code reader panel in the lift's steel wall, there was a beep, and the lift started to drop. The silence was unnerving. Both guards ignored her and stared stonily ahead.

Sebastian Carstairs had been officially dead for over thirty minutes, but when the paramedics gave him CPR and stopped him going into hypovolaemic shock and injected him with a blood coagulant, his heart started again. At the hospital it was touch and go, but after five hours of surgery he miraculously survived, which surprised everybody in the operating room.

It didn't surprise Holly. Somehow she'd known it would be this way.

The government and prison authorities saw The Animal as a problem. His escape, resurrection and recapture had never made it to the press and the Home Office wanted him kept out of sight and out of mind. Their solution had been to put him into solitary confinement and throw away the key.

While he had been recovering from his surgery, the powers that be began construction of a special cell for him in the bowels of Fairlie Prison. The cell was dubbed the glass cage and was six metres by five metres. Three sides were solid bedrock and the fourth was a huge, bullet-proof acrylic wall through which prison guards could watch their prisoner with surveillance cameras twenty-four hours a day. It had a small slit at the bottom, through which guards could pass the serial killer his meals and any other items he needed. The only furniture was a table and a chair, which were both made of compressed cardboard, and his toilet and sink, which were bolted to the floor. His bed was a concrete slab.

The Animal was locked in the cell for twenty-three hours a day, only being freed for an hour of exercise. He was escorted to the exercise yard by six guards, who never spoke to him and he was never allowed any contact with any other inmates. He had no lawyers because he didn't exist, and if any other inmates ever caught a glimpse of him they never found out his name, only his number: 16011966. After three months, one member of the prison board, a lawyer named Stuart McCarthy, put in a request for the release of prisoner 16011966 to the general prison population, citing that the continuing solitary confinement was inhumane, but the request was immediately denied by the Home Office and, according to the latest reports, The Animal would remain in his glass box for the rest of his life.

The lift door opened and Holly was escorted to another door that opened to corridor number two. She had no idea how far underground she was, but it was cold and she could see condensation on the rock walls. They stopped at the only door in the far wall. It was made of solid steel and weighed six tonnes, and one of the guards looked up to a camera in the ceiling and gave a short nod.

The door slid to one side and the cell was straight in front of her, brightly lit, and she immediately saw her reflection in the see-through acrylic wall. She took a step forward and the six-tonne door closed noiselessly behind her. The acrylic looked at least twelve inches thick and she wondered if he would be able to hear her. Then she noticed small drilled holes near the ceiling and felt a slight breeze: fresh air was being pumped into his room.

The Animal was hunched over in a chair with his back to her. Even though he didn't turn, his shoulders stiffened slightly as if he knew she was there. He was blind in his right eye from a bullet wound and what remained of the lid was a milky white scar. He'd suffered a stroke three weeks ago, and apparently his speech was slurred. She took one more step forward and straightened herself.

'Hello, Sebastian,' she said.

Acknowledgements

Thank you so much for reading *When Evil Wakes*.

The initial two Holly Wakefield books began as a street theatre event in Edinburgh, which prompted a screenplay that finally culminated in a four book adventure. That adventure was destined to stay hidden in a Word file on my Mac until it was read by Luigi Bonomi, my amazing agent at LBA, who was the first person to cast eyes on the idea of Holly Wakefield. His kindness, advice and wisdom have helped me more than he can ever know. And to the rest of the team at LBA, Alison Bonomi and Hannah Schofield, who are always there for me, come sun, snow and pandemic. To Hannah Wann, my wonderful publisher at Little, Brown, thank you once again for your help, guidance and kind words whilst book four took shape, and mostly your patience – this is the last draft, I promise (lol). And thank you to the rest of the team at Little, Brown: Jo Wickham, Brionee Fenlon, Sean Garrehy and Kate Hibbert who once again have been incredible with sales, marketing, publicity, cover designs and The Crime Vault! Thank you to Anne O'Brien, my incredible copy-editor – The Force is strong with you – and you cut through my errors, mis-spellings and misgivings with the ease of Kenobi's light sabre. To Nicky Kennedy, Sam Edenborough, Jenny Robson, Katherine West, Elizabeth Guess and Jack Viney over at ILA – my foreign rights team – thank you since day one. You have been so helpful and enthusiastic and just to show how much I love you all, I get excited when I get an email from you. And to Emma Beswetherick, my first publisher, who got rid of the dog in book one, the cat in book two and the hamster in book three, but in book four we kept the canaries. Thank you. x

And now to the humans who keep me going day to day and make me want to be a better person and let me laugh at them. Kate Plantin, my wonderful friend, thank you for your continued support in my life and knowing you are always there makes that road so much easier. To David Solomon – we have talked and screamed with each other and the Heavens have opened and I'm looking forward to a pint and a laugh with you next week – it's your round. To Zoe Henderson, I still love you after all these years and thank you for being who you are.

And finally, my family. Where would I be without you? To my mother, Patricia, my sister, Melissa, and my niece, we have always known that everything is about love and I hope you and everybody who reads these books will find that thread. And to my father who passed away last week. I know you're still here and thank you for being a good dad. x

Have you read all the thrillers in the Holly Wakefield series?

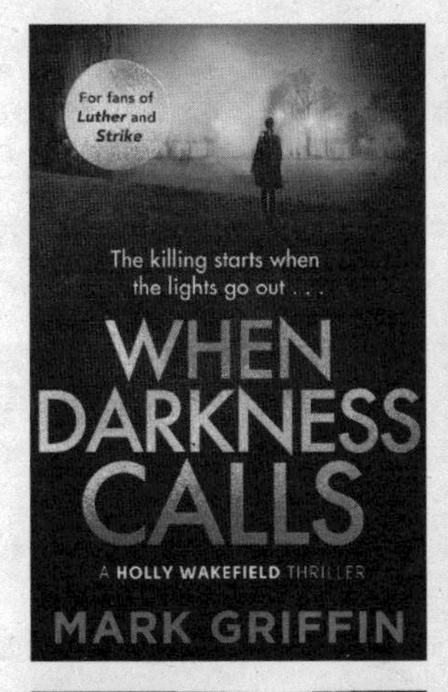

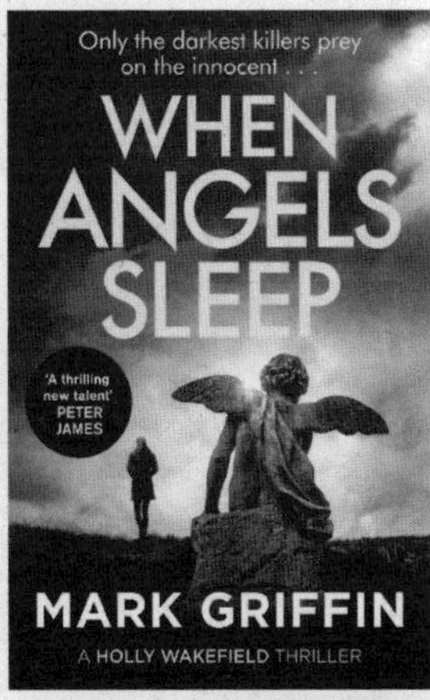

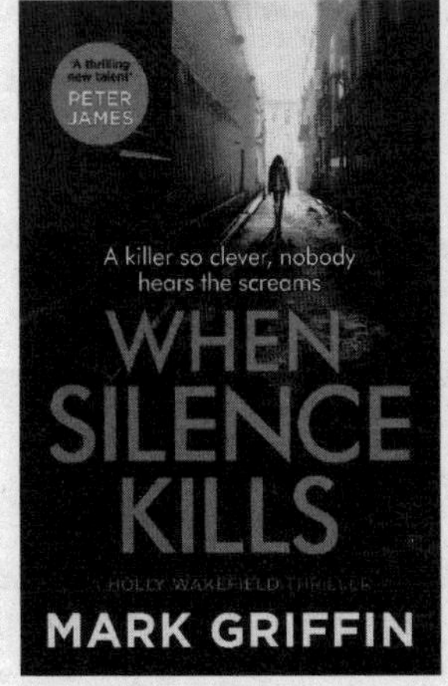

Available in paperback, ebook and audiobook